JIMMY THE STICK

A SUSPENSE NOVEL

JIMMY THE STICK

A SUSPENSE NOVEL

MICHAEL MAYO

A MYSTERIOUSPRESS.COM BOOK

OPEN ROAD

INTEGRATED MEDIA

NEW YORK

For Marcia

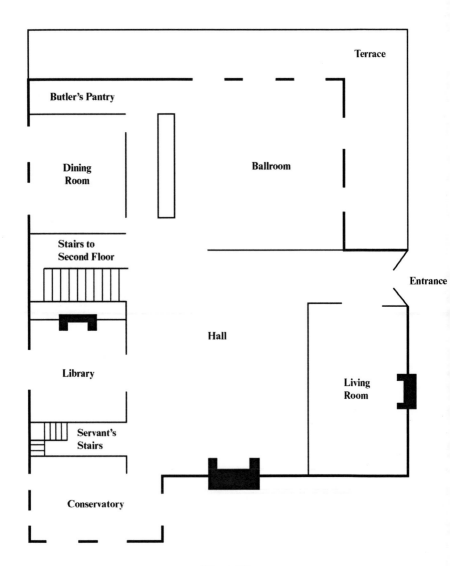

First Floor
Pennyweight House

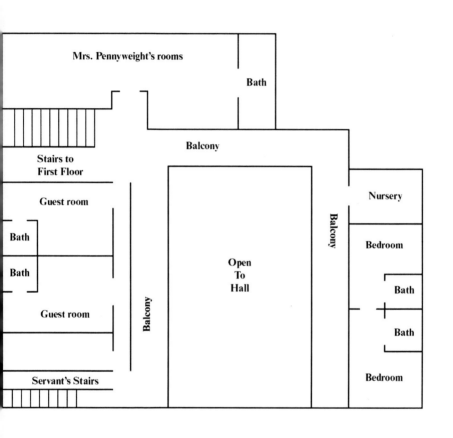

**Second Floor
Pennyweight House**

AUTHOR'S NOTE

This novel is built around events that occurred during the first week after the Lindbergh kidnapping. The details of news reports, police actions, and weather are real. So are the Liberty Bond scam, the meeting between Arnold Rothstein and Meyer Lansky, Charlie Lucania (later Lucky Luciano), the Egg Harbor knockover, Chink Sherman, and the death of Vincent Coll and Vine-Glo. Other real people include Owney Madden, Frank Costello, Charlie "The Bug" Workman, Longy Zwillman, Dutch Schultz, Joe "The Boss" Masseria, and Dixie Davis.

CHAPTER ONE

My name is Jimmy Quinn. I've been a thief, a bootlegger, a bagman, and the proprietor of one of New York's better gin mills. I helped corrupt dozens of cops and politicians, and I was in on the fix of a World Series. It's been a good life.

But there is one part of it that was so screwy I'm not sure I believe it myself, and it happened to me. I don't really know how to tell it either. It started on a Sunday in February, 1932. Actually, it was after midnight, so I guess it was Monday. You see what I mean about not knowing how to tell it.

I was standing naked at the window of my room in the Chelsea Hotel looking down at the traffic on Twenty-Third Street. Connie was still in bed. She was naked, too. The only light came from the little bedside lamp. She was flushed and sweaty with the pillows stacked up behind her back, her hair loose, the sheets kicked away from her legs as she tried to coax me back into the sack. And I was thinking that maybe I was up to a second round. It happened a lot with her, but then I glanced across the street and saw Vincent Coll, bold as brass, stepping out the front door of the Cornish Arms.

Standing next to him was Sammy Spats Spatola. There they

were, the two biggest shitheads I ever knew. I couldn't believe what I was seeing.

These days, not too many people remember "Mad Dog" Coll, but at that particular time, he was about as famous as anybody in New York. He'd been on the run for a month and everybody thought he'd left town. The long and the short of his story was that he'd been in a war with Dutch Schultz over who was going to control the beer business in New York. Lots of guys had been killed in their war, women, too. But everything changed when Coll gunned down a little kid. That's when he picked up the "Mad Dog" moniker. They arrested him and put him on trial but he got off.

He may have walked out of court a free man in the eyes of the law, but not with the rest of us, so he disappeared. Any sane person would have got as far away from New York as fast as he could, but that wasn't Vinnie, I guess, not even with a $50,000 price on his head, courtesy of all the top gang guys in the city. The word was out that if you saw Vinnie Coll, you got in touch with Owney Madden right away. A lot of guys had personal reasons to hate Vinnie, and Owney was at the top of the list. I was right behind him. Nobody gave a good goddamn about Sammy Spats. Not then.

So I told Connie to stay where she was, threw on some clothes, grabbed my stick, and went downstairs as fast as I could. Didn't even take time for my hat or my pistol. At the hotel's phone on the front desk, I tried to get Owney at the Cotton Club, but the line was busy, so I called Big Frenchy DeMange at the other office number.

"Frenchy," says I, "Vinnie Coll just went into the London drugstore on Twenty-Third."

Sounding surprised, he answered, "The hell you say! The prick is on the phone with Owney right now. He's threatening to snatch me again if we don't cough up another thirty G's. The son of a bitch is crazy. But you're sure? It's him. The London Chemists on Twenty-Third."

"Hell yes."

"We got him then. Thanks, Jimmy."

The little drugstore was almost next door to the Chelsea. As I got there, Sammy Spats came hurrying out and almost knocked me down. To this day, I don't know if he saw me, because right about then, a big sedan pulled up to the curb and three men got out. I didn't know any of them. Two stayed with the car. The third, a guy in a big overcoat, pushed through the front door of the pharmacy. I was right behind him.

The phone booths were at the back, past the soda fountain. That late, there weren't more than four or five people in the place. From where I was, I could see everything that happened. Vinnie had jammed himself into the first narrow booth. He was kind of smiling and snarling into the mouthpiece, talking real fast. You couldn't tell if he was happy or angry. But hell, that's the way it usually was with Vinnie. He looked really bad that night—poorly shaved, red hair wild around his red face.

The guy from the car stopped in front of Vinnie's booth and pulled out a Tommy gun from under his overcoat, not rushing anything. A woman nearby yelped in surprise. I could hear other customers hurrying away. The gunman said in this calm, deep voice, "Keep cool now."

Then he pulled the bolt back to cock the piece and Vinnie noticed him and realized what was happening—just like it had happened to all the guys he had killed. But I doubt Vinnie was ever as smooth as the man who got him.

I saw Vinnie's hand come up behind the glass door, and I heard the roar of the gun filling the store, the glass exploding and the muzzle flash giving the bloody scene a white glare.

The guy knew how to use a chopper, I'll give him that. He squeezed off three fast bursts, and every bullet hit Vinnie. Fifteen shots with steel-jacketed .45s. Even that close, you've got to know to control the piece to be that accurate.

I got out of the drugstore right behind the shooter and saw him climb back into the car. Off it went. A couple of police detectives showed up, and a patrolman jumped on the running board of a cab to chase the sedan up Eighth Avenue. They arrived so quick you had to think they'd been tipped off. But I don't know anything about that. All I know is that the guys who shot Vinnie got away clean.

When Owney told the story later he'd say that he kept Vinnie on the line while he traced the call, like he was the goddamn phone company or something. He didn't mention me, and I never asked about the fifty thousand, either.

Not that it really mattered. I went back to the Chelsea and found Connie still in bed with more lights on. She'd heard the shooting and the cops and so she was worried that something might have happened to me. Maybe she was a little scared, too. I took off my clothes again, got back into bed, and explained what happened and who Coll was while she warmed me up. That night, the second round was better than the first.

After Coll got himself killed, things settled down for a couple of weeks. Then, about nine thirty or so on a nasty Tuesday night, a big cop came into my speak.

I was at a table in back with my notepad, the *Daily News*, the *Mirror*, the *Times*, and probably three or four others. I read all the papers in those days. At first I really didn't pay much attention to the guy except to note that he was the twenty-seventh customer of the night. He was a barrel-bellied bastard in a derby and a loud brown plaid suit. About forty, give or take, clean-shaven, a drinker's wide, rosy face. He ordered a King's Ransom, tossed it back, and ordered another. He turned around, hooked a heel on the rail, and aimed his plug at the spittoon. The second scotch went down in two drinks. Something was familiar about him.

That Tuesday was cold and gusty and wet, the kind of night when you might stop by a place for a quick belt to warm the way home but not to stay, not even in a place as inviting as mine was. That kind of night, you wanted to get where you were going and settle in, and so there had been twenty-six paying customers since sundown. When business was slow, I kept count.

My speak was in a brownstone just off Broadway on Twenty-Second Street. We had a polished mahogany bar along one side of the room. Behind it was a big painting of a coy naked young woman stretched out and peeking over her shoulder. Most women giggled and laughed the first time they saw her. Guys tended to be studious. There were six booths on the opposite wall, with tables in the middle and a dance floor that nobody used. The two main things about the joint were good booze and a quiet atmosphere. The gang guys and the cops knew that it was neutral ground, no weapons. Everybody was welcome, but if a discussion became an argument that became a fight, you went outside and around the corner. The neighbors wanted it peaceful and so did I.

Fat Joe Beddoes was working the door and waiting tables. Frenchy Reneau, not to be confused with Frenchy DeMange, was behind the bar. He could mix any drink you might name, but there were some that he simply refused to associate with. His wife, Marie Therese, handled the coatroom and sold cigarettes and served drinks. Connie had been in earlier. When I saw what the night was going to be like, I told her she could take the rest of the evening off. She winked at me and mouthed *"See you later"* and left. Don't I wish it had been so.

As the big cop went to work on his third scotch, I realized where I'd seen him before. He'd been in with a bunch of fellow cops from the Bronx and their girlfriends and wives. They sat at the eight-top table. Had a grand time, laughed a lot. Tipped poorly.

He wasn't laughing that Tuesday. Instead he checked his watch so often I got the idea something was up, something I wasn't going to like. You run a speak, you learn to recognize that kind of thing. He looked over toward my table a couple of times without meeting my eyes. As the man drank, his face flushed and his chest heaved and his breath quickened. The next time he looked over, he pushed back his hat, locked eyes with me, and let his anger show. He pulled out his shield and yelled in a loud cop voice, "Everybody out. The place is padlocked." The regulars, thinking this was a joke, didn't move.

I reached for my cane. What the hell? The guy wasn't a fed. Fat Joe knew the feds on sight and wouldn't let any of them in. I had taken care of the guys who needed to be taken care of. The beat cops, their sergeant, his captain, the boys downtown at City Hall, they'd all gotten their envelopes of cash, hand-delivered by me. It couldn't be a normal raid, then. Had to be something else.

The big cop pushed away from the bar and yelled, "Clear out. Now." He turned to me, his face clouded, eyes wide and crazy, and yelled even louder, "You first."

Knocking over tables and chairs, he bulled his way to the back. He pulled something pale and fist-sized out of his coat pocket and smacked me with it twice. I learned later that it was a sap made from the foot of a silk stocking filled with sand. He kept it in a knotted white sock. Hurt like hell, and he could slug you a lot harder with that thing than he could with a regular spring steel sap. Hit a guy that hard with a steel sap and you'll kill him, punch a hole in his skull. This way he got me across each temple. Two more blows to the back of the head laid me facedown into the newspapers. My cane clattered to the floor and he went to work on my ribs and kidneys. He wanted to hurt me bad and he didn't want it to show. The place cleared out pretty quick after that.

Frenchy reached for the hog leg under the bar but thought better of it, and stepped back without touching it. You don't shoot cops, not even crazy cops.

By the time the guy was finished, I was barely conscious and everything looked foggy. My good leg was weak, and the bad one had become useless. He grabbed me by the belt, hauled me out the door and up the steps to the street, and threw me into the backseat of his car. He tried to book me at the Forty-Seventh Street station, and even though I was still half screwy from the beating, I knew we were in the wrong precinct. So did the desk sergeant. He frequented my place, but he wasn't going to argue with the angry detective. While the big guy wrote up the arrest report, they took me to the back for finger-prints and pictures. The mug shot showed black hair, dark eyes, a thin crooked nose, and a necktie skewed to one side. I saw it later. Like most mug shots, it made me look sullen and stupid. I was neither, but a good beating can do that to a guy. They took their time, and when we were finished, the big detective had disappeared without another word to anyone. The cops who knew me were apologetic.

The desk sergeant held the messy arrest report between a finger and a thumb like he didn't want to touch the paper, and said it was too late to do anything about it. "I called the guys at Thirtieth Street, where you shoulda been brought if this was a serious beef, which I don't think it is. They don't know nothing either. Thing to do," he said, "is just wait here, if that's OK with you, Jimmy. I guess we gotta hold you for a while. Anybody you want to call?"

"Nah, Frenchy'll call my mouthpiece, Jacobson. He'll call the station house and work it out. I'll wait for them. Who the hell was that guy?"

"Never seen him before and I can't even read his goddamn name. Did things get out of hand at your place tonight?"

"No. One minute it's a quiet Tuesday night, the next that big son of a bitch is flashing a badge and cracking my head." Fatigue rolled over me and I couldn't think.

The sergeant shook his head. "Go figure. Look, you want a holding cell or the interrogation room? Personally, I use the interrogation room to catch my winks. It's got a bench you can sleep on and nobody'll bother you there. You want something to eat?"

The windowless room also had a wooden table, an ashtray, a goose-necked lamp, and three straight-backed chairs. The desk sergeant brought me a dry baloney sandwich and a cup of coffee. He said not to worry, they were taking care of things. I thanked him for the coffee and the sandwich and worried. None of it made any damn sense at all. But the room was warm and dark and it didn't smell too bad. So I folded my suit coat into a pillow and paid no attention to the muted buzz of activity out in the hall. As I sank into sleep, I saw the ghost of Mother Moon floating up in a sweet coil of opium fumes, and heard her sharp witch's laugh of a voice saying, "It's a crazy world, Jimmy my boy, and there's nothing to be done for it."

Hours later another cop, a younger guy I didn't know, brought me a second dry baloney sandwich and cold coffee. If I had been firing on all cylinders, I'd have noticed how preoccupied the kid was. I guess I ate the sandwich and went right back to sleep, because I don't remember anything else, and I never sleep that long at a stretch. The young cop woke me again at seven thirty Wednesday evening and said that I'd been sprung. My lawyer was waiting out front.

Trying to make myself presentable, I straightened my tie and buttoned my wrinkled double-breasted before I gimped through the busy station and down the steps to the cold, rainy street.

Outside, I expected to find my mouthpiece Ira Jacobson, but he wasn't there. Instead, Dixie Davis was standing on the sidewalk next to his car, an idling Packard with a driver at the wheel. That's when I got the first glimmer that I was involved in something bigger than a crazy cop locking down a righteous speak.

Befitting the best mob lawyer in the city, or at least the most expen-

sive, Dixie was decked out in a gray overcoat with a white silk muffler neatly crossed beneath the velvet collar. He wore a homburg and
leather gloves.

He didn't smile, but he sounded friendly enough. "Good to see
you, Jimmy, given the circumstances."

Dixie showed up at my place every now and again. He and Schultz
and his other clients were usually seen at flashier joints, but if he just
wanted a drink of good whiskey, straight off the boat, and a place to
talk in private, he came to Jimmy Quinn's.

"When Jacobson told me you'd been shut down, I called the Thirtieth Street station and they said you'd been brought here. They didn't
know anything about a raid. It took most of the day to chase down the
paperwork. All of the pertinent information on your arrest report was
incorrect, but don't worry, it's being taken care of."

"What's his name, the cop who brought me in?"

"The signature on the report was illegible."

"This is nuts. I think he's from the Bronx. At least I'm pretty sure he
was in my place before with some of the guys from the Bronx."

Dixie was unconcerned. "We'll figure it out. Don't worry."

Seemed like everybody was telling me that, not to worry.

Dixie went on. "In light of everything else that happened last night,
it wasn't too difficult to get all of the charges swept under the rug. Still,
might be a good idea to lay low for a day or so. Make sure there's nothing else going on before you open up again."

"Wait a minute, what do you mean 'everything else that happened
last night'? You mean something besides the bust-up at my place? And
what are *you* doing here, Dixie? Where's Jacobson?"

"I think your driver will explain everything. . . ."

Driver? What driver?

"Walter Spencer hired me. He's been looking for you. He called
Jacobson and when he learned that your place had been shut down
and Jacobson couldn't contact you, he came to me."

"Spence is behind this?"

Dixie nodded and took a cigarette out of a silver case. "He wanted
to find you as soon as he could."

A long, dark Duesenberg J pulled to a stop and double-parked beside Dixie's Packard. The chauffeur got out, carrying an overcoat and a cane. When he walked in front of the headlights, I saw that he was dressed in a black uniform with two rows of buttons on the jacket, polished boots, black cap, the whole megillah.

He stepped up onto the sidewalk and smiled. "Hiya, Jimmy, long time no see. Whassamatta, dontcha recognize me in this damn monkey suit?"

I looked more closely at the face under the cap. "Oh Boy? What the hell?" We shook hands. I'd grown up with Oh Boy Oliver, but it had been more than three years since I'd seen him. Since before Spence's wedding.

"Here." Oh Boy handed over my overcoat and stick. "Walter told me to go to the Chelsea and get your things. He needs you to come to his house."

"What the hell is going on? This doesn't make any . . ." I stammered, more confused than ever. "Why does Spence need to see me?"

Oh Boy sighed and said, "Oh boy, oh boy, because the Lindbergh baby has got snatched."

CHAPTER TWO

"You're pulling my leg. Sure, I got my brains scrambled, but I'm not falling for this crazy story."

"It's the truth, Jimmy." Dixie pulled a copy of the *Times* from under his arm and handed it to me.

It was just like in the movies, with headlines spinning around like they were going to fly right off the screen into your lap. That's what happened to me when I opened the paper.

LINDBERGH BABY KIDNAPPED FROM HOME

OF PARENTS ON FARM NEAR PRINCETON;

TAKEN FROM CRIB, WIDE SEARCH ON

As I read, it felt like the ground was shifting under my feet. I gripped the familiar handle of the cane and leaned on it. In that moment, everything changed. Later, people would be able to tell you exactly where they were and what they were doing when they learned about the kidnapping. I remember it fine, but for other reasons.

Not that I knew what was coming. First there was the impossibility of it. Lindbergh was the most famous man in the world. Something like this simply couldn't happen to him. He was too different from everybody else, too important.

I remembered when they held the big parade after he returned from flying solo to France, how the crowds filled the sidewalks, how all of swanky Fifth Avenue was closed off with all the confetti and ticker tape falling like snow. I also remembered how foully I cursed him then. I was supposed to make deliveries for Rothstein that day—payoffs to two important guys in the mayor's office and at police head-quarters. I had four good routes I could use when I carried cash to those addresses, and none of them would work with the huge crowds. That meant using the subway or the El, both confining and a lot riskier. And when I finally did make it to my delivery points, nobody was there. Because the whole town was watching the damn show on the street. I called Lindbergh every name I could think of, and it was well after dark when I made my last payoff.

But still, how could you not feel a little admiration for the son of a bitch for what he'd done? And then he married that beautiful, classy dame. The guy was made of gold. Kidnapping was something guys like Vinnie Coll did when they needed quick cash. It just didn't happen to Charles Lindbergh. And nobody kidnapped children. The world, as I knew it, didn't work that way.

I stared at the headlines, still unbelieving, until a loud car horn sounded in the street. Some guy in a Ford was pissed about the way Oh Boy was blocking traffic with the Duesy.

Dixie's driver stormed out of the Packard and had a quick talk with the guy in the Ford. Gears gnashed as the man shoved into reverse and backed down the street.

Dixie ground out his cigarette. "Look, Jimmy, I don't know why Walter wants to see you. That's his business. You want me to find out about this Bronx cop, I'll ask around. Dutch is thick with guys at the Morrisania station. Maybe they know something. Call me in a day or so."

Dixie got in the backseat of the Packard and it nosed smoothly past the Duesy and into the street.

Like the trained chauffeur he had become, Oh Boy went to the rear door and held it open for me.

I said, "Who the hell do you think I am?" and got in the front seat.

Oh Boy pointed the big car south and then west, making his way carefully to the tunnel. I thought it probably was some time since he had been in that part of town and so now the narrow streets bothered him. Why not? The Duesenberg was a one-car parade. Or maybe he was worried that some guy would chuck a rotten apple or a brick at us on general principle. After all, the car cost more than an ordinary Joe could expect to earn in a lifetime, even if he could find a job.

Oh Boy turned and stopped at the brightly lit tunnel plaza at Broome Street, and it was crazy, like nothing I'd never seen. Cops with flashlights and pistols were stationed at all eight tollbooths. More cops strode suspiciously through the clogged traffic, opening doors and trunks and rousting some people out of their cars. Oh Boy said, "You see. They're checking for the kid."

We eased forward. When we reached the gate, a plump patrolman held up a hand. I rolled down the window and said, "Top of the evening, Officer Lonergan."

He shined a flashlight at us. "Jimmy Quinn, how the hell are you? Heard there was some trouble at your place last night. Nothing serious, I hope."

"We're taking care of it. Come by this weekend."

His partner shined his flash into the deep backseat. Lonergan waved us on through and said, "No need to look in the trunk. See you soon, Jimmy."

Oh Boy rolled forward, paid his fifty cents, and accelerated quickly down into the tunnel. He relaxed once we were inside. The set of his shoulders softened and he eased back in the seat. "They really gave me a going-over on the Jersey side when I came in. Opened the trunk and everything. That's what they're really working on, all the people coming into the city."

"What do they know about this kidnapping? Gimme the whats and whens and wheres."

Oh Boy concentrated on the road and didn't turn his head as he spoke. "Happened last night at this place they built down south. I don't recall the name of the town. They weren't in the Englewood house. Just Lindbergh and his wife and kid and a couple of people who work for 'em. Maid goes upstairs to look in on the kid, and he's gone. They found a ladder and some tracks in the dirt around the house. They say there's a ransom note, but the cops deny it. Crazy, isn't it, something like that happening."

"So why does Spence want to see me?"

"I dunno. Flora, Mrs. Spencer, got the screaming meemies when she heard about the Lindberghs. She thinks that the same guys are gonna come after her kid. Or somebody else will do something, oh boy, I don't know."

"Spence has a kid?"

"Yeah." Oh Boy smiled. "Little Ethan, and that's why Flora is so upset. You listen to her for five seconds, you'd think that her and Anne Lindbergh were goddamn sisters." He affected a woman's high-pitched tone, "We went to the same school. She and Charles danced at our wedding . . . and that kinda stuff. Personally, I never saw no Lindberghs at the wedding, but what the hell do I know.

"Anyway, Walter'll tell you all about it. But you gotta understand, Jimmy, that she's got him by the balls. Whatever Flora wants, Flora gets."

Nothing too strange about that, I thought, and said, "What've you got to drink in this jalopy?"

"Jalopy, my ass." Oh Boy sniffed. "If you sat in the back like you're supposed to, there's a full bar back there, crystal, ginger ale, cracked ice, the works." Oh Boy always had a strong sense of the proper order of things.

"Then give me some of the Jameson you've got in your flask."

I could see Oh Boy's hint of a smile in the light reflected off the white tiles. He pulled a pewter flask from under his coat.

I had a long, warm sip. Moments later, we emerged at the plaza on the Jersey side of the river.

To one side, I could see construction work. I thought at first it was another tall office building like the ones going up in Manhattan. But then I realized I was seeing huge square concrete columns supporting a cantilevered span of steel girders looming more than a hundred feet tall. Welders' torches sparked high above us. "What the hell?" I leaned forward to see as much as I could. The structure stretched on into the night ahead of us. "What is it? An El?"

Oh Boy paid no attention. "More like a bridge, but for cars and trucks. When it's done, you'll be able to come out of the tunnel and go straight to Newark without stopping. Not like it used to be."

He reached for the flask, drank, and passed it back. "Remember that night?"

I took another slow sip. No need to answer.

There had been ten of us in three cars. Spence, Oh Boy, and me in the lead. Meyer Lansky, Siegel, and Charlie behind us. Frank Costello, Vinnie Coll, Sammy Spats Spatola, and a guy I didn't know in the third. We'd left Lansky's garage as soon as it was dark, heading for Egg Harbor, New Jersey. Spence and Oh Boy had shotguns for the close work. I was the best pistol shot so I had a Detective Special and a pocketful of bullets. Damn, that was a hell of a night. I was full of piss and fire, and felt like I was completely alive for the first time in my life, like I could do any damn thing I wanted. And that night I did. I was twelve years old.

I looked up at the strange new steel structure, thinking about how long it had been since I'd been out this way. It was a long time since I'd been out of the city at all. Spent all my spare time with Connie. Connie! Hell, that was the first time I'd thought about her since that business with the big cop. Marie Therese must have explained what happened. I told myself she'd understand, but I didn't really believe it.

And that was when I first realized how much I missed Connie. I missed being in bed with her, sure. But just as much I simply missed her, and wanted to talk to her, not on the phone but in person, to tell her about the cop in the ugly suit, and this madness with the Lindbergh kid, and find out what she was going to do the next day. The sudden strength of feeling surprised me. Troubled me. I'd never experienced it before.

I took another slow slug of whiskey and said, "How long till we get there? I gotta make a call."

Oh Boy gave the car some more gas, speeding smoothly along the wide road to Newark. "Little more than an hour, probably, depending on traffic. We've got paved roads for this sweetheart all the way."

Past Newark the streetlights thinned out but the road was still familiar. I'd been there before plenty of times, delivering booze with Spence for Longy Zwillman after he partnered up with Meyer and Charlie. Longy ran things in that part of Jersey. As often as not when we were working for him, we had a police escort. Longy didn't want anything to gum up the works when we were supplying the swells' parties in Morris and Somerset Counties.

Oh Boy drove through little towns with the occasional restaurant or gas station still open, and I saw a police car at most of them. Oh Boy kept his speed at the limit, neither fast nor slow enough to attract attention. The cops noticed us but didn't approach the expensive car. I guess they figured no kidnapper would be driving a Duesenberg J. We were almost to Morristown when we turned at a white metal sign that read: VALLEY GREEN BOROUGH 2 MILES. Oh, yes, I thought, Valley Green.

The big headlights revealed woods on both sides, white rail fences, and finally a stone wall. Yeah, I remembered that. The road curved, and the tall overhanging trees seemed to merge with the black asphalt to suck up the light. I guess that's what they meant in fairy tales about the forest being a dark and scary place.

Oh Boy turned at a stone gate and followed a gravel drive between rows of tall narrow trees. When lights appeared I could feel my neck stiffen. What the hell? Why was I getting all wound up about seeing Spence again? Walter Spencer was my friend, a pal who had invited me to join him at this very place years ago. If I'd said yes then, everything would have been different. But I didn't.

A large Tudor house loomed up ahead, though I've got to admit I didn't know the term "Tudor" at the time. It had steeply peaked roofs, dark timbers, light-colored stucco, and lots of chimneys. I thought the place looked like something in a movie where people get bumped off one at a time by a phantom killer.

Oh Boy pulled up at the front doors, where a white ambulance was parked. Spence and two other men stood beside it. They were in the middle of an intense conversation, maybe an argument. One guy was a tall, lean number with short blond hair and eyebrows, hollowed cheeks, and the thickest pair of glasses I'd ever seen. Beneath his overcoat, he wore a white medical smock with a stiff collar. The second guy was shorter and rounder and, to judge by his wide smile, happier. He was dressed in a dirty canvas coat and muddy rubber boots, and carried a single-shot .22 rifle snugged in the crook of his arm. A battered fedora was pushed back on his head, and he was smoking a curved briar. He had a bushy forked black beard, merry eyes, and apple cheeks.

When Oh Boy saw them, he muttered "Oh boy," in that worried way of his.

Spence hadn't changed much. He was still every inch the hero—tall, broad-shouldered, alert blue eyes, all of him brimming with confidence and strength. As long as I'd known him, he looked like Gary Cooper, even kept his hair combed the same way. He wore wingtips, a nubby tweed suit, light blue shirt with a white collar, maroon tie. Gary Cooper playing the country squire.

He recognized his Duesenberg and hurried over to pull me out. "Goddammit, you crazy Black Irish bastard, it's good to see you."

I was engulfed in a massive bear hug and then held up for inspection. He was about twice as big as me. Always had been. Embarrassed, I pulled loose and settled on my stick.

The goggle-eyed geek came closer, peering down at me like I was a mildly interesting insect pinned to a board. I had a sudden desire to belt him but Spence turned back to the guy. "I'll contact you as soon as I return. If we run into complications, I'll call." The man in the medical whites nodded and rubbed his pale, bony hands together as he got into the ambulance. When the car turned around in the driveway, I saw the medical snake symbol and the words "The Cloninger Sanatorium" on the door. The wild-looking little guy with the rifle had disappeared.

Spence wrapped a thick arm around my shoulder and guided me to the front doors. "Come on inside, Jimmy. Oliver, take his things to the guest room upstairs, the good one. Goddamn, it's good to see you."

So Spence called him "Oliver," not "Oh Boy" or even "Mr. Oliver." I guess that explained the monkey suit.

Inside, Spence led me across a wide L-shaped room with dark wood paneling and broad stairs at the back. Dark red and brown Persian rugs with complex patterns covered the floor. A couple of ornate black chairs and a matching table against one wall looked like they might have come from an old church or castle. An open balcony ran along three walls on the second floor, with a round wrought-iron chandelier hanging from the tall, arched ceiling. There was a massive fireplace, cold and dark, built into one wall. Across the room, in front of two closed doors, stood an older, stoop-shouldered guy with a walrus mustache. His watery eyes blinking rapidly, he clutched a Purdey shotgun by the barrels and stood straighter as we approached.

Spence took the gun and said, "That'll be all, Mears. Make sure that Mrs. Conway has prepared the room upstairs. My friend will be staying with us."

Mears nodded, then shuffled away. Spence slid open the doors and ushered me into the library. There were more intricate blood-red carpets, walnut paneling, walls lined with sets of books that looked like they'd never been touched, a fireplace banked down with a couple of logs, brown leather club chairs facing the fire. And a kid sleeping in a crib next to the desk. He was tightly tucked in, with the taut covers moving when he kicked and punched fitfully. Spence said, "Don't worry, he's out for the night. Dr. Cloninger gave him something." He leaned the shotgun against a wall and went straight to a cabinet that opened to reveal a fancy bar. He dumped chipped ice and whiskey into two crystal tumblers, giving each a splash from the soda siphon.

I took a sip. Canadian rye. The best. You never could fault Spence on his whiskey. I put the drink down on the desk beside the sleeping child and took the shells out of the shotgun. I've never been comfortable with loaded weapons around little kids. Even when the kids are doped up.

Spence was studying me. "I guess you're wondering what this is all about."

"You're about to tell me."

He started to say something but stopped. Then he said, "Where have you been, Jimmy? Why don't you come out here? I asked you more than once. Before the wedding and after. Don't blame your leg. I know it's not that."

He had me there. "I don't know, somehow it just didn't seem right. You left. You found what you wanted, and then there was this." I slapped my useless knee. "And then I had my place to run." I shrugged. "Whenever I thought about coming here, I thought about something else."

"For three years you thought about something else?" Spence tried to sound wounded, but it didn't wash.

"Has it been that long? And now you're completely legit and legal?"

Spence nodded. "Everything I saved when we were working for Meyer and Charlie and Longy is invested in Pennyweight Petroleum. I only see Longy when Flora decides to throw a party and we need extra liquor, but lately I haven't even seen him then. He's got a place near here but he's busy. Did you hear about that actress of his, the blonde? Jean Harlow? Yeah, Longy's putting the spurs to her."

"Yeah, I know. They've been in my place." I could tell that surprised him. "She's not bad, but to tell you the truth, she looks better in the movies. You and Longy always did have a way with the ladies. Both done pretty well for yourselves too."

Spence poured more whiskey and we sat in the chairs facing the fire. He said, "You remember the first day we came out here?"

Of course I remembered. That was the day everything changed. We'd taken one of the smaller trucks from the Newark warehouse around noon on a spring Saturday, 1928. Longy told us that they always wanted the best. We had to make sure that everything went smoothly, and we had to get payment in full before anything came off the truck because Mrs. Pennyweight was notoriously slow to settle up.

It was a hot day, and we both took off our suit jackets to keep them from getting wrinkled and sweaty. Whenever we were dealing with important customers, we tried to look like we belonged wherever we were going. No overalls, no loud colors or flashy suits, just businessmen's clothes. Made everybody more comfortable.

We drove out to Valley Green and turned at the long driveway. But well before we got to the house, we saw a sign that said DELIVERIES, directing us to a narrow road that brought us to the back of the place. The house was at the top of a slope leading down to a lake and the woods. There was a two-story boathouse at the water's edge, and the lawn between the two was filled with canopies, tables, and umbrellas.

A bandstand and dance floor had been set up near the boathouse. It was a hell of a nice spread, maybe not as grand as some of the joints we supplied out in Great Neck, but not bad.

A harried woman seemed to be in charge. She told me to unload the liquor behind the table at the big white canopy, but was unsure about who would be paying. I told her we had to take care of money before anything else. While she was dealing with me, half a dozen other people were wanting decisions about this and that. Sometime in there Spence wandered off and I waited thirty minutes before Mrs. Penny-weight herself showed up and took over. She was clearly a woman used to being obeyed, standing taller than she actually was in a light pleated dress, a wide hat, and sunglasses.

She held out an envelope of cash but demanded to see the invoice, checking off each case against it and opening the cases to make sure there were no broken or missing bottles inside. She kept me busy for the better part of two hours, more than enough time for Spence to wander up to the big house and meet her husband, Ethan Pennyweight.

The master of the house didn't hold with the damn fool parties his wife threw, so he and Spence hit it off right away. They were both war veterans, Spence of O'Ryan's Roughnecks and Pennyweight of Roosevelt's Rough Riders, and they both liked to drink.

Spence said to me now, reminiscing, "While she played hostess, we got drunk as lords in this very library. Ethan told me he'd never read any of these goddamn books. He didn't need no library when he had mineral rights. God, did we ever get plastered."

"I know. I was the one who tried to wake you up." And when I finally gave up and left him and drove the truck back to Longy's warehouse, I was about as pissed off as I'd ever been.

Spence said, "I stayed the night. The next day I met Ethan's daughter, and even as hungover as I was, I still fell for Flora. Fell hard."

That part, I remembered clearly. Two days after I left him at the Pennyweight mansion, Spence showed up, shamefaced as hell. He tried to act like he was sorry for getting so damn drunk and leaving me to handle all the work. But that wasn't really what he had on his mind. He said, "I've met this girl," as if that one sentence explained everything, and I guess it did. "She's young, beautiful, rich, and she's built in a way I can't describe." He had a dreamy look I didn't understand. After that, he spent most of his time in Jersey.

"Ethan approved," Spence told me now. "I think he knew what was going to happen before I did. Six months later we got married. You know that, too; you were invited but you didn't come." He sighed heavily. "A year after that the goddamn stock market collapsed.

"I'd put everything I had into Pennyweight Petroleum, and Ethan and I worked like crazy to keep the company running. We were hurt by the crash just like everybody else, and I know the strain took a toll. Ethan had a stroke and spent the rest of his days with Cloninger's sawbones poking at him. He died at the sanatorium. Now I'm in charge, and we're about to open three new parcels in Louisiana and south Texas. That's why I brought you here. Look at all this."

He went behind his big desk and rummaged through papers and unrolled maps that were weighed down at the sides. He held up two handfuls of official-looking documents. "Hydrologists' reports, leases, deeds, contracts. I don't understand half these goddamn things, and I've got to use them to make decisions that will keep this company going. Or ruin us." He shook his head and sighed again.

"I'm going to fly down to supervise the exploratory wells. I'd planned to leave this morning but Flora got hysterical when she heard about the Lindbergh kidnapping. She's convinced that we're next. And the only place little Ethan will be safe is here in this room, where the windows are all barred."

"That explains the duffer with the scattergun."

Spence rolled his eyes and nodded. "Flora believes that with her family's prominence and wealth and my 'underworld connections,' Ethan is the perfect target. I tried to tell her that nobody I knew had anything to do with the Lindbergh business. But by then she'd gotten herself so worked up, there was no talking to her. It got so bad, I had to call Dr. Cloninger to give her something to calm her down."

"Her and the kid?"

"The man's a genius. He's perfecting compounds with sedatives and stimulants that no one else is even thinking about. But she still demanded that I stay to protect them both, and I can't. I've got to go to Louisiana and Texas. Nobody else can handle this end of the business.

I'm responsible, and I can't put it off. So I'm asking you to stay here and make certain that nothing happens to my family."

"The hell you say. You don't understand, I'm not 'fast Jimmy Quinn' anymore. I'm a saloon keeper with a bad pin."

"You're the best shot I've ever known, and you're the only man I'd trust with my wife and son. You've got to do this for me, Jimmy, it's too important."

"Walter!" She shrieked his name as she pushed open the doors. "You absolutely cannot leave now! You promised me!"

Spence jumped up at the sound of that loud, panicked voice.

His wife was even more beautiful than the pictures I'd seen, and she was damn near naked.

CHAPTER THREE

In newspapers, she looked slender with a long, oval face, light hair, and the moony expression favored by wedding photographers. The rotogravure didn't come close to the truth. She was sixteen when they got married, and in three years she'd filled out sweetly under a loosely unbuttoned top of silvery satin. She was tall and she had a faint spray of freckles across her nose and cheekbones. Her face was glistening with fevered sweat, maybe from the spooky doctor's joy juice, and she was barefoot beneath loose pajama pants.

"Walter, they could be here." Her voice had a whispery quality. "Right now, they could be right outside." She grabbed her husband's coat sleeves at the biceps, her fingers digging in and twisting the material.

For the first time, I understood what had happened to Spence. I couldn't take my eyes off the woman.

"Don't worry, darling, I've taken care of everything. This is Jimmy Quinn, my old friend. I've told you all about him."

She turned and stared intently while I tried not to look down her loose pajama top.

"Will you protect little Ethan? Do you understand the danger he faces now? I'll have to trust you with my only son. Do you swear to me that you will do it? Do you swear that?"

At the time, I thought it must have been the dope that was making her lay on the drama so thick. I was wrong.

Spence put his arm around her shoulders and led her out of the room. "I'll explain everything to you in the morning, dear. Go back to sleep now. Jimmy's here, he's going to stay with the baby all night. There's nothing to be concerned about, nothing at all."

I poured another splash of rye and laid a log on the fire. A few minutes later, Spence came back in and sat behind his desk. "She'll be fine now. She was just more upset than Dr. Cloninger thought she was." He loaded a briefcase and rolled the maps into cardboard tubes. His voice took on the offhand tone he always used when he was trying to talk me into something.

"Look, Jimmy, I know this all sounds kind of crazy, but we don't know what's happened with Charles and Anne. You'll be doing me a great favor if you agree to stay here for few days and keep an eye on things. From what Dixie told me, your place is going to have to stay closed for a bit, so what do you say? I'll make it worth your while. That's a promise."

I stared into my whiskey, stalling for a few seconds. But by then we both knew what the answer was.

I finished the drink and said, "Why the hell not," and the deed was done.

Spence came around the desk and clapped me on the shoulder. "Good man."

"Where's the phone? I gotta make some calls."

Spence gestured to the telephone on his desk. "Use this line. I'll look in on Flora, and here . . ." He opened the top right-hand drawer and took out a little Mauser .25 automatic. "You'll want this."

As soon he left, I popped the clip out of the pistol and worked the slide to clear the chamber. Nothing there. I put the clip in the coat pocket with the shotgun shells, the pistol in the other. I dialed the operator and gave her the number of the Utley Hotel, where Connie stayed. The night man there told me that Miss Halloran wasn't in. I left a message with Walter's number. Then I called the Chelsea. She wasn't there, either.

I hung up the phone, pissed off and disappointed. Where the hell was she anyway? It was goddamn ten o'clock. She might be with Marie Therese and Frenchy, but they didn't have a telephone.

I took a slow drink, tried to calm down, and thought back to the first day that Marie Therese brought Connie in. It had been right before Thanksgiving last year, midafternoon when things were always slow. Marie Therese came out from behind the bar to hand me a cup of coffee. She sat down at the table and lit a cigarette, waiting for me to put down the newspaper.

"Jimmy," she said, "I'm going to do you a good turn today. I'm going to introduce you to your marvelous new waitress."

"Another marvelous new waitress? Didn't you say that about Dinah? And, before that, Gaby? They lasted less than a week between them. And what's-her-name, Bridgid something." Marie Therese was one of those kind souls who attracts strays. She brought in my marvelous new waitress or dishwasher every month or so.

She waved the names away with a plume of smoke. "They weren't serious, you know. This Connie's different. She's a good girl. She's new in town."

"And wait till you get a load of her porch," Frenchy interrupted. "This one's really put together."

She glared back at him. "Pay no attention to my pig of a husband. Trust me, you will like this girl and you know how busy we're going to be between now and New Year's. We need the help."

"OK, I'll talk to her. Tell her to come by."

Marie Therese called out, "Connie," and a girl came in from the front hallway, where she'd been waiting.

She was about five-foot-three, just my height, and Frenchy hadn't exaggerated about her shape. She was nice, very nice. I saw a dark-blue coat and skirt, bobbed blond-brown hair under a hat, and an uncertain, hopeful smile. She worried a small purse with both gloved hands.

Marie Therese pulled out a third chair. "Come over here, honey.

Have a seat. I told you, you don't have to worry about Jimmy. He won't bite. Unless you want him to." The girl blushed.

I liked her right away. But then Marie Therese knew I was a sucker for the girls she brought around. She wouldn't bring them if she didn't know that my speak was a good place to work. Things were tough then. There were a lot of places where guys would assume that any girl working there was a whore. But not mine. I hired nice-looking young women because they helped bring customers into a speak that didn't have a floor show or a dance band or ice to piss on. Instead, we had the best brand-name liquor from Canada and England, wine from France and Italy, and, when I could get it, beer that hadn't been needled with ether. All at top-drawer prices.

"What's your name?"

"Constance. Connie Halloran."

"Where're you from?"

"Yonkers."

"Are you an actress? You're pretty enough."

Another blush. "Oh, I don't know. I've thought about it and I sang in school."

"That's not why you came here? You're not planning to become a showgirl?"

"No, at least . . ." She shook her head, "No, I'm not a showgirl."

Marie Therese fired up another smoke. "Her boyfriend kept pushing her to settle down and she's not ready."

"Have you ever worked in a speak?"

"I was a waitress at the New Ideal diner last summer."

Marie Therese said, "She can start tonight."

She did. For the next two weeks, Connie Halloran showed up on time every night. She worked extra shifts whenever one of the other girls wanted time off. She didn't take any guff from the idiots, drunk or sober, and still did fine with tips. She volunteered to help me close up when Frenchy and Marie Therese left early on Christmas Eve. And then, to my happy surprise, she spent that night at the Chelsea Hotel with me. It was the best Christmas I ever had.

So now I asked the operator to call the private line at my speak. Frenchy picked up. "Boss, where the hell are you?"

"It's a long story. I'm in New Jersey, and it looks like I'm going to stay here for a while. What's going on?"

"Fat Joe and me came in this afternoon and cleaned up. There's not a lock or a seal on the door, so Marie Therese and I opened up late but only to regulars. No real business. What the hell went on last night?"

"I don't know. Dixie Davis sprung me and he said the paperwork on the bust was hinky. Did you recognize that guy? I think I remember him coming in with some other cops from the Bronx."

"Could be, yeah, now that you mention it, he was kinda familiar."

"All I know is that he was a damn sight more interested in working me over than making sure the place stayed closed. He left the station before they even finished taking my prints."

"Doesn't add up, Jimmy."

"No, it doesn't. Look, open like normal tomorrow. Has Connie been by?"

"No, want me to ask Marie Therese?"

"Sure."

I heard him talking in French and his wife answering, *"Je ne l'ai pas vu."*

"She ain't seen her," he said.

"OK, open up as usual tomorrow. But tell Fat Joe not to let in cops who aren't regulars. And if any cops do come by, find out if they know anything. You got last night's take, right?"

"Sure, boss."

"Hold on to it. I'll be in as soon as I can, and I'll call again tomorrow. And, oh yeah, here is my number in Jersey." I read it off from the tag under the glassine cover on the dial, then hung up.

The library doors slid open immediately, and Mrs. Pennyweight came in, leaning on a cane. I guessed she'd been listening at the door and was waiting until I hung up the phone. What did that mean? Was she being considerate or was she eavesdropping?

We looked each other over, checking out our sticks. Hers was ebony with an ornate, tarnished silver handle. Mine was made of wood, I don't know what kind, painted black with a curved handle.

She said, "You look like you slept in your suit. I'll take two fingers of that whiskey."

She was about as tall as her daughter and more angular. She had pale blue eyes, and was fond of tilting her head back and staring intently at anyone she was speaking to, daring them to disagree with any damn thing she said. Her hair was pinned up and she wore a thick, brown-gray belted sweater over loose trousers. Her brown leather shoes sported no heels. If she had on makeup, I couldn't tell.

I poured three fingers of whiskey neat.

"I know who you are, Mr. Quinn, and I know why Walter asked you to come. I'm not sure I approve. Still, after giving the matter full consideration, I believe he's right. If something that horrible can happen to a wonderful young couple like Charles and Anne, it can happen to anyone. We're taking reasonably prudent precautions. And unlike my daughter, who sometimes doesn't have a brain in her head, I understand exactly why Walter has to leave now and what he has to do. And how important the trip is to our family. These are hard times. Sometimes you don't have a meaningful choice."

"I've already told Spence that I'd stay, and I will."

"Fine." She gave me another long, cool look. "We've met before. Do you remember it?"

"Sure, the garden party. Spence, Mr. Pennyweight, the booze, and everything."

"Yes, getting drunk with my husband was not a difficult thing but Walter was better at it than most."

She frowned at the memory. Then her focus shifted and she looked toward the door. A second later, I heard the sound of an approaching car—the whining engine and a loud scatter of gravel as it slid to a stop. I could make out a loud, strident voice outside, and I picked up the shotgun. It was a man's voice, followed by a heavy fist pounding on the big front doors. I fed the shells into the Purdey. There was more bellowing from outside.

I held out the gun butt-first to Mrs. Pennyweight. "Can you use this?"

She reached out impatiently. "Of course." The front door banged open and the man yelled, still unintelligibly.

I snapped the clip into the Mauser, chambered a round, and gimped out into the main reception room.

A tall, potbellied man in a long black overcoat and tuxedo stood at the front door. He had a fringe of hair around his bald head and a smooth pale face with bulging eyes. He had a snootful, couldn't stand without weaving. When he saw me, he got angry as some drunks will do, and teetered forward. I thought I could hear the wail of an approaching police siren in the distance.

"My garden is properly tilled and the pigeons will soon be home to roost where's Walter I've got to talk to him it's critically important that he know about the hotel . . ." The man's babble had a weird lilting, hypnotic quality. He spoke carefully, each word clear and precise, but his big eyes snapped as he reeled forward, and his clawlike hands opened and closed mechanically. He reminded me of Lon Chaney in one of his really scary movies. The sound of the siren grew louder.

"You have a week and now no more no more . . ."

The man reeked of gin but his weird nonsense sounded like it was coming from dope. He lurched closer and clapped a paw on my shoulder. I twisted away and wondered why the hell everyone was so goddamned tall out there. I felt like I'd climbed up the beanstalk into the land of the giants. Who was this guy? By his clothes, he could be a rich neighbor. Should I try to jolly him back out the front door like a regular who's had one too many? Or shoot him in the heart?

"Spence'll be here in just a minute. Why don't you sit down and cool off."

"And I take everything into consideration for I have never wept nor damned the Roman kin, I am going to give you money if I can . . ."

He lunged forward clumsily, grabbing at me with both hands. I pivoted on my good leg and swung the cane around like a baseball bat at the back of his knees. He folded, knees hitting the carpet first, then hands, elbows, and finally his head. He shook it for a moment like a wet dog. Then he roared and rose up. When he turned, he was smiling madly, and his eyes bulged wider.

I was pulling the pistol out of my pocket when I heard Spence yell from above, "Don't shoot him, Jimmy."

"Fordham Evans, stop this instant." Mrs. Pennyweight's voice cut like a whip. The crazy guy turned to her, smiling, and his voice lost the weird drugged quality. "Ah, Catherine, there you are. Who's the runt?"

I looked up and saw Spence and Flora on a second-floor balcony.

Still falling out of her pajamas, she was excited by the fight, if you could call it that.

I pocketed the pistol as two cops sauntered in, one middle-aged, the other much younger, about my age. They wore snappy uniforms with black-peaked caps, dark-gray tunics, riding breeches, and tall leather boots. Fordham Evans raised his arms in welcome when he saw them. "Sheriff Kittner and Deputy . . . Deputy . . . what's your name? I know I know your name but it's flown straight out of my head. Fancy meeting you here. That little man hit me with something. My legs hurt. Let's have a drink."

The younger cop took the man's arm. "You're in the wrong house again, Mr. Evans. Let's go now, we'll get you back on the road." He stopped and both of them looked up at the balcony. "Hello, Flora . . . I mean, Mrs. Spencer." I was close enough to see a flush rise on his cheeks.

She smiled and waggled her fingers. "Hi, Jeff, good to see you."

As Spence led her away, the deputy stared after them. Well, he stared after her.

The sheriff paid no attention to the drunk. He touched his cap and said, "I hope he's not been too much trouble, Mrs. Pennyweight, but we can only do so much. Parker will make sure he gets home all right." The flesh of his thick neck strained against the high collar of the tunic. He hooked thumbs into his Sam Browne belt and rocked back on his boot heels. "With the kidnapping, we've had our hands full." He gave me his best hard cop stare but got no reaction.

"I'm sure you have. Here, let me see you out," said Mrs. Pennyweight, honey dripping from her lips.

He ignored her. "Who's this?"

"It's Mr. Quinn. He's staying with us for a few days."

The sheriff stepped up close and leaned in, smelling of cigar smoke and alcohol. Maybe he and Fordham Evans patronized the same bootlegger. "One of Mr. Spencer's old friends, is he? And just what were you doing with that piece you've got in your pocket?"

"I was going to shoot the fat drunk in the heart if he threatened Spence's kid. I didn't know that Valley Green's finest were in hot pursuit."

The sheriff sniffed. "A wiseguy, huh?" He leaned even closer, spit misting as he hissed. "Maybe that kind of talk buys you something in

New York, but you keep a civil tongue in your head in my county if you know what's good for you."

Before he finished, I turned and gimped back to the library for my drink. Mrs. Pennyweight steered him toward the front door.

If the sheriff thought it was unusual for her to be carrying a shotgun around the house, he didn't say anything.

When Mrs. Pennyweight came back into the library, she said, "It's not a good idea to anger Sheriff Kittner. He's often quite useful."

"What about the other guy?"

"Fordham lives down the road. He used to be in love with Flora. As often as not when he gets boiled, he stops by here. Last time he hit one of the trees by the drive. We didn't find him until the next morning when he'd stripped stark naked to take a swim in the lake. As you heard, he fancies himself a poet. The more he drinks, the more 'poetic' he becomes. At heart, he's just a harmless, crazy drunk."

Oh Boy came in and said, "I've put your stuff in your room."

Mrs. Pennyweight tucked the Purdey comfortably under her arm. "I think I can handle things here with little Ethan. Get settled in and tell Mears to have that suit cleaned. Oliver, show Mr. Quinn upstairs."

On the second floor, the stairs opened onto a balcony that overlooked the big room. Spence and Flora's rooms were on the other side. Through an open door, I could see them sitting on the bed in her room, Spence's shoulder and her hair reflected in a mirror that appeared to cover one wall. They were close together, arms around each other. He was still whispering to her.

Oh Boy said, "This way," and led me down another hall.

The room had a comfortable-looking bed, an armchair, a small table with a lamp and an ashtray, and a chest of drawers with a radio. A radiator ticked near the window. My Gladstone and spare cane, the heavier one I used outdoors, were on the bed. Some of my suits were hanging in the closet, along with a pair of shoes and my walking boots. A dark brown curtain with wide red stripes covered the window and looked heavy enough to darken the room during the day. A door on the wall opposite the bed led to a white-and-black tiled bathroom.

The tub had a shower enclosure. Both rooms smelled of a slightly dark odor, as if they'd been closed off for months.

I hooked my stick over the back of the chair and put Spence's Mauser on the chest. "Oh Boy, what the hell's going on here?"

"Don't worry about Mr. Evans, he's just a drunk."

"What about the guys out front when we came in?"

"Dr. Cloninger, he's another story. Oh boy, that man gives me the willies." Oh Boy shivered, his face twisting into a worried frown. I saw that his hairline had retreated to the top of his head and his ginger hair was cut short. The imprint of the chauffeur's cap still dented his forehead. And yet, except for the hair, he looked as young as I remembered.

"He and Spence have business together?"

Oh Boy shook his head. "I don't think so. He's got an office in the city, but his main place is close, on the other side of the lake."

"The sanatorium?"

Oh Boy snorted, "Yeah, the nuthouse. Rich drunks from the city go there to dry out." He hooked a thumb toward the window. "In the daytime you can see it from here."

"Who's the other guy? The one with the wild hair and the rifle."

"That's Dietz, the groundskeeper."

I opened the top of my bag and sorted through clothes, knee brace, and other stuff that Oh Boy had taken from the hotel, including my knucks and knife. "Did Spence tell you he was going to fly to Texas?"

"Yeah, he was supposed to leave today. They've got the Pennyweight Petroleum Tri-Motor over at the airfield. I don't know if Walter's going to want me to drive him there tonight or tomorrow." He looked even more worried than usual. "I guess I'll have to stay up tonight, too."

"How does a guy get something to eat around this joint?"

Oh Boy smiled at the mention of food. "That's easy. Come down to the kitchen after you clean up. The chow's good."

After Oh Boy left, I pulled open the curtains, turned off the table lamp, and waited for my eyes to adjust to the darkness. The sheer craziness of the past twenty-four hours was still too confused to figure. Maybe that damn big cop hit me harder than I thought. And why did he close me down in the first place, and then why did he do such a piss poor job of it? It's like he knew it wasn't going to stick but he did it anyway. If

Vinnie Coll was still alive, I'd think he was behind this scheme. I decided I'd call Dixie in the morning. And Lansky, if he was in town.

Shapes outside slowly became visible. Faint light from a ground-floor window fanned out over brown grass directly below. Beyond the light was the lake. I could make out the dark shape of Dr. Cloninger's sanatorium on the other side. Headlights were moving near it. I opened the window and heard the sound of an engine and transmission gears in the cold night air.

I closed the window and curtains. Who the hell would snatch the Lindbergh kid? More important, where was Connie?

I stood under the shower and let the water beat down on my head and neck for a long time. It revived me and sharpened my hunger.

I got out my razor and turned on the radio to warm up while I shaved. I twisted the tuning knob until I heard a man's voice.

". . . since yesterday. We know that this was not the first experience with kidnapping the family has dealt with. A year ago, Anne Morrow Lindbergh's sister Constance received a written threat that authorities took so seriously a false ransom payment was arranged while the colonel spirited the young woman to safety. No one was ever apprehended in that instance, and it is unknown whether the incident has any bearing on what happened yesterday."

The announcer had a crisp British accent but he also sounded tired. I wondered how long he'd been talking.

"For many of us, the reality of this crime is still hard to accept. You think that someone will step out from behind a curtain and explain that it did not really happen, but I'm afraid that's not the case.

"Colonel Lindbergh came to America's attention five years ago when he became the first man to fly solo across the Atlantic in the *Spirit of St. Louis*. He and his airplane returned on the USS *Memphis* to massive parades in Washington and New York, and then, of course, he was awarded the Congressional Medal of Honor. 'Lucky Lindy' became one of the most famous men in the world. He has used that fame to promote the cause of commercial aviation.

"In fact, he was doing just that when he flew to Mexico and met Anne Morrow, daughter of Ambassador Dwight Morrow. After their marriage, she came to share his passion for aviation, and they have literally circled the globe, seeking out and mapping new air routes. When Charles Jr. was born, they purchased several hundred acres of land in New Jersey's Somerset and Mercer Counties. Work on their graceful stone home was finished last year.

"So, to recapitulate the situation as we understand it now . . ."

When I finished shaving, I dug into my Gladstone for my notepad and fountain pen. I opened the pad to the first partially blank page and wrote *recapitulate*, sounding it out as I wrote the letters. Also on the page were

liminal
biddable
gormless
fasade façade.

The radio continued, "Police have identified two pairs of footprints, likely made by a man and his female accomplice. The wooded area around the house was thoroughly searched last night and today. Thinking that a stolen car might have been involved, law-enforcement agencies in New Jersey, New York, and Pennsylvania have identified sixteen stolen vehicles and are on the lookout for them."

The voice paused and the man said, "What?" and then "I don't think so," and "All right" to someone. "Here are the makes and models of those sixteen stolen cars. Police welcome any information the public can provide."

I finished shaving and thought that the guy had been right. I still couldn't believe what had happened to the Lindbergh kid. That feeling of things not being completely real was in the background of everything that happened for the next seven days at Valley Green, and the really strange stuff was just getting cranked up.

CHAPTER FOUR

I turned off the radio and started worrying about Connie Halloran again. Then I decided I was being a sap.

I didn't realize how she'd got under my skin. As I thought about it, for the first time, really, I remembered how little we actually spoke. At least, I didn't say much, and she wasn't a talker herself. For the most part, we screwed and walked and went to the movies. I thought it was great, and she hadn't complained about any of it. She was fascinated by stuff we saw on the crowded crush of city sidewalks—the charging kids, the peddlers, the pushcarts, all the tired guys looking for something to do, and the guys who had work and tried to look like they were heading somewhere important.

And she loved the movies, most of them anyway. Sometimes she surprised me by not liking the ones I thought she would, but that was OK because it was fun when she got bored. We always sat in double seats in the balcony, my arm over her shoulder, tickling her hair or her ear. Sometimes she'd brush my hand away. But if she really didn't like a movie, she'd slip off her coat to crawl over me. We could always go to the Chelsea of course, but there was something different in those dark seats where I could look up to see the gray smoky light playing over us. There was Connie on my lap, busy little hands working at the buttons of my shirt, and me tugging her blouse out of her skirt, carefully unbuttoning it from the bottom, one button after another, my hands rubbing across her soft stomach, fingers teasing at the edges of her brassiere, feeling her lips smiling against mine as she reached back to help me. I loved the smell of the stuff she put on her hair, the feel of it against my face. They don't make movies like that anymore.

I always tipped the usher on our way in to make sure we weren't disturbed. We never were.

Damn, where the hell was she?

I put on a black pinstripe single-breasted and a turtleneck sweater. It was too cold in that house for a shirt and tie. When I strapped on my watch, I was a little surprised to see the time: after midnight. I slipped my brass knucks into a pocket, notepad and pen into my coat, and bounced the little pistol in my hand. That's when I saw the stamp on the side. I held the gun closer to the light and realized that Spence had bought the piece at Abercrombie & Fitch. Well, hell, I guess he could afford the best, and even if the Mauser wasn't my first choice, it would do until I found something I was more familiar with. I slipped it into my coat pocket.

Then I picked up my everyday stick, checked the room one more time, and went out to find something to eat.

The stairs leading to the first floor were wide and easy. The servants' stairs at the far end of the hall were narrow, dim, and steep. I held on to the railing with my right hand, and took them carefully one at a time, leading with my right leg, the cane held in my left hand: "Good foot goes to heaven, bad foot goes to hell." That was the way Dr. Ricardo put it. "Stairs are easy if you do 'em right," he'd said, "but your right knee will never work the way it used to. The muscles will become stronger and support you most of the time. If you twist or put too much weight on that bad knee, it'll fold underneath you. So keep the cane on the same step with your right foot. When you have to support your weight on a bent knee, make sure it's your left. And when you're going upstairs, lead with your left, your good foot. Good foot goes to heaven, get it? Going downstairs is actually harder so you gotta be real careful. Bad foot goes to hell."

The doctor may have been a hophead but he was also right. And so Fast Jimmy Quinn, who'd been the quickest kid in the city, was reduced to going down stairs one step at a time. Thinking of Ricardo brought back the bad times and made me angry for feeling sorry for myself. That was pointless, and I thought I was done with it.

The stairs ended at a hall with the walls painted white. I could see and smell a kitchen at one end, and it made my mouth water, I was so hungry. It was a wide, warm room with a big rectangular table and half a dozen chairs in the middle.

A wiry, gray-haired woman banged pots at a stove and muttered to herself. Next to her stood an open pantry, a tall refrigerator, and a set of shelves stacked high with boxes and jars of baby food. It looked like there were a dozen different kinds.

Oh Boy sat at the table, hands warming around a mug of creamy coffee. The duffer who'd been guarding the library had a bottle of dago red and a half full glass in front of him. What was his name? Mears. And the wiry woman had to be the cook.

She turned around and nailed me with a gimlet glare.

Oh Boy stood, scraping his chair back. "Mrs. Conway, this is the guy I was telling you about, my pal Jimmy."

She sniffed. "The gunman." I guessed she was suspicious of anyone who came to Valley Green from the wicked city.

But I make it a rule to always stay on good terms with the cook.

I walked around the table and extended my hand. "I suppose you're right. I am a gunman, Mrs. Conway. That's what Spence thinks he needs right now. But I'm not a gangster. I'm just here to help an old friend. Do you think I could get something to eat, a sandwich maybe, and a thimble of Mr. Mears's wine?"

She sniffed again but I sensed a thaw. "Of course. Any guest in this house will have the full hospitality of the kitchen. Mears!" The old gent's head snapped up. "Another glass, if you please. We've some mutton left over that will do nicely."

The wine wasn't as bad as it could have been.

She sliced and buttered two pieces of bread and warmed them on the oven while she carved slices from a roast on the counter. As she worked, a dark-haired girl came in through a second doorway, pushing a cart full of dirty dishes and leftovers of what looked to be the same mutton.

"Constance," Oh Boy said, "this is my friend Jimmy Quinn."

She had glossy black hair, skin that was about the color of Oh Boy's light coffee, and a challenging look in her eyes. I couldn't tell about the rest of her under that frumpy black maid's dress. "Constance . . . ?" I held out my hand and she took it.

"Nix. And it's Connie."

Just what I needed, another Connie.

Mrs. Conway set down my sandwich and went around to the trays. One of them held a single pink rose in a narrow vase. She lifted the metal warmer lid from the plate and made a *tsk-tsk* cluck. "She barely touched her supper. Whatever is the matter with that girl?"

As she turned back to the sink, Oh Boy grabbed an untouched slice of devil's food from the tray before Mears could get to it. I tucked into the sandwich, carefully keeping myself from bolting down the excellent eats. Even so, as I was finishing, Mrs. Conway sliced more bread and mutton and made a second.

She poured tea for herself and sat at the table. "You know they're saying that gangsters from the city committed that unspeakable act on the poor little Lindbergh baby." Her eyes widened. "Or maybe it was that Purple Gang from Detroit or even Scarface Al Capone himself, ordering it from jail."

"I don't know anything about the Purple Gang or Capone," I told her, "but it wasn't any of the mugs I know in New York."

"And how can you be so sure of that . . . if you're not a gangster?" Her tone was sharp. Connie Nix, the maid, followed the conversation closely.

"I used to be a bootlegger. Now I run a speak." I saw the question in the younger woman's eyes. "A speakeasy. It's not a fancy nightclub or casino. It's just a place where a guy can get a drink of good whiskey and feel comfortable bringing his girlfriend or his wife. Or even a girl can come in alone and nobody will say boo. A nice place."

Mrs. Conway sniffed even more disapprovingly. A woman alone in a bar, the very idea!

"But I do know some of the guys you're talking about, the guys you read about in the papers, 'racketeers,' 'the underworld.' And they wouldn't do anything like that with a kid. They'll bust each other and they're not too careful about bystanders, adults who happen to be in the way. But they wouldn't go after a baby. Bad for business."

Everybody knew what happened to guys who hurt kids. "And even if they were gonna do something so stupid, they wouldn't come way the hell out here to do it, pardon my language."

"Is that so? Well, what do you think about this?" Mrs. Conway ruffled through a stack of newspapers.

"'Racketeer Murdered in Union City,'" she read aloud. "And over in Boonton, two men arrested on 'statutory charges,' and we know what those are, caught with two underage girls in a bungalow at the lake. Stanley Pawlikowski and Joseph Scerbo—Polacks no doubt, or worse. At least they didn't name the poor little girls who'd been led astray."

"Those girls weren't led too far astray," said Connie Nix. "I read that story. They ran away from the North Jersey Training School. I don't think they did anything they hadn't done before." She had a slight accent I couldn't place.

Mrs. Conway paid no attention to her. "And look at this: not one but three, mind you, three fires of mysterious origin in Cedar Knolls. And here, another gangster, Izzy Presser, murdered in a car owned by a woman lawyer. Imagine that! A woman lawyer—but then they were both Jews." She rummaged through more papers. "That sort of thing happens near any big city. But here? When I read this last week, a chill went straight up my spine, it did. Just look."

She read aloud again: "'Young Daughter Strangely Killed.' That's the headline."

She looked around to make sure she had everyone's attention. "'Three-Year-Old Girl Caught on Branch of Tree, Virtually Hanged. The unusual facts connected with the death of three-year-old Patricia Thomas Holmes, daughter of Mr. and Mrs. James Holmes, a prominent New York broker who resides at his country estate in Peapack, became known today. The little girl died on Wednesday.

"'According to the police, little Patricia, dressed from head to feet in a warm woolen suit, attempted to climb a tree. Her nurse, standing nearby, failed to notice the child's actions. Suddenly a scream was heard as the horrified nurse saw the fearsome spectacle of the little girl hanging from a branch of the tree. A part of her suit had caught on the branch, tightening around her throat.

"'The inert body was immediately taken into the house but efforts to resuscitate the child proved in vain. She died a few minutes later.'"

Mrs. Conway put down the paper and pointed at me like all of that had been my fault. "That's the mad world we live in today. Don't tell me a gangster from New York or Detroit might not come here to steal a child. We've been cursed ever since Miss Mandelina was taken from us."

The silence stretched out uncomfortably. Finally I said, "OK, I guess I'm the only one who doesn't know Miss Mandelina."

Something moved at the edge of my vision. A cat, a thick-bodied brindle that had crept out of a wooden box against the wall, stretched and sat beside me, leaning against my leg. It stared with a hunter's patience at the dark space beneath the stove. Mr. Mears poured more wine, keeping the bottle close this time.

Mrs. Conway busied herself with another cup of tea. "I probably shouldn't have said anything."

Oh Boy said, "She was Flora's sister."

The cook sat and silenced him with a sharp look. "Miss Mandelina was Flora's older sister, and you have never seen two girls more devoted to each other. When they were younger, the darlings were inseparable. For those little girls every day was a new adventure, both being so active and curious. You'd have thought they were boys, they were so full of energy, chasing each other from one end of the house to the other. And they were simply mad for horses from the day they could walk."

The woman's face fell, her tone darkened. "That was the problem. Horses. It's five years ago this autumn that Miss Mandelina had her accident as she and Miss Flora were riding between here and East Hanover. We don't know exactly what happened because no one saw it. I always suspected they were racing; it wouldn't have been the first time. They were arguing with each other over racing at lunch. Miss Flora was ahead, I'd wager, when Miss Mandelina's horse ran past her.

Flora rode back and found Mandelina on the ground unconscious. She was an excellent rider but even excellent riders can fall. Miss Flora did the only thing she could, and dashed home for help." She sniffed back a tear before she went on.

"We were so afraid that the child had broken her neck or her spine, and then thankful when we learned that wasn't so. But she was unconscious for three days, and the whole house was on a virtual death watch. Doctors came from New York, discussing concussion, shock, and then coma. That poor child just wouldn't come around. And even when she finally opened her eyes, she was never the same. For the first year or so, she was unusually quiet and still. And then she seemed to get better, more like her old self. But then she became . . . erratic. She laughed at the wrong things at the wrong time. Or she'd burst into tears for no reason. And then came the anger, the rages when the least little thing could set her off. And finally the wild stories. She accused her own father of nightly attacks in the most horrible way. And then she claimed that Mr. Evans tried to force himself on her."

Oh Boy nodded. "Yeah, she said that Clark Gable, Babe Ruth, and Bing Crosby came into her room one night."

"I loved those girls," Mrs. Conway muttered into her teacup, so low that almost no one heard. "I loved them more than their own mother."

"What happened to her?" Connie Nix asked.

"More doctors, the poor dear." Mrs. Conway paused, on the verge of tears. "Dementia praecox, they said. Completely untreatable. Incurable, too.

"Dr. Cloninger worked with her more than any of the others did. He came here every day, trying different combinations of drugs, and finally took her to his sanatorium."

Oh Boy shivered. "He gives me the creeps."

He was interrupted by the chiming of a loud electric bell. I looked up at the source of the sound and noticed a grid of numbered squares sitting high on the wall. The light on the number three shone brightly.

No one moved until Mrs. Conway tapped the old man's arm. Startled, he looked up from his wineglass. "Mr. Mears, it's Mr. Spencer for you." The old fellow stood, clearing his throat and pulling at his shirtfront before he shuffled out.

Mrs. Conway looked at the clock by the bell grid and frowned. "It's late for the master to ring. Oliver, did he say anything about going out tonight?"

"Yeah," Oh Boy said, and got up.

"Then you'd best see that the big car is ready."

Another bell sounded and the number-two light came on, then a third bell with the number-one light.

"Aye, that's it then." Mrs. Conway stood up too. "Nix, see to Mrs. Spencer and the baby. You, gunman, make yourself useful. Check on the baby."

The brindle cat stayed where it was.

Back in the library, Catherine Pennyweight was on the telephone. She said, "Yes . . . Fine . . . I'll take care of it," and hung up.

"There you are. Our pilot called about rough weather coming our way; he wants to leave as soon as possible."

Ten minutes later Oh Boy brought the Duesenberg around and loaded Spence's leather bags into the trunk. Flora, in a fur-trimmed jacket, fussed over the baby that Connie Nix carried. She wore a light coat over her uniform but didn't seem to mind the cold night air. Spence and his mother-in-law were in deep conversation. I sat in front with Oh Boy.

We drove for twenty minutes along dark country roads. I thought we were going to Newark until we came out of the trees to an open, foggy field, with the road leading to a small collection of buildings and a runway lined with lights. Oh Boy steered past the first place to a tall hangar behind it. A large monoplane with three engines rolled out onto the tarmac. It had a shiny, squarish aluminum body beneath the wide wing. The nose pointed skyward but the belly was low, barely clearing the ground. Even idling, the sound of engines hammered the air. Three guys in Pennyweight Petroleum coveralls busied themselves around it. I stared in absolute wonderment. I'd never seen a plane that close on the ground before, and I had no idea they were so damn big. When I got out of the car, I could smell gasoline, exhaust fumes, and motor oil, and I felt the engines' vibrations through the soles of my shoes.

A Cadillac with New York plates was parked nearby. Oh Boy

opened the back doors and the trunk of the Duesenberg and carried Spence's bags to an open door in the side of the plane. Two men, who had to be lawyers in their expensive overcoats, got out of the Caddy and huddled with Spence before they climbed aboard. Another chauffeur lugged their bags. Spence returned to his car to embrace Flora. He briefly took his son from Connie Nix and kissed him.

Then he grabbed my shoulder. "Keep my family safe, Jimmy. That's all I ask." He was yelling against the noise of the engines, and his voice sounded different. I saw that he blinked back tears before he turned and hurried to the plane.

The big plane lumbered into the darkness at the far end of the runway so slowly I couldn't believe it would ever leave the ground. But then the throb of the engines became much louder, and we watched as the glittering silvery thing turned around and rumbled back down the runway. The tail lifted slowly and the plane floated up into the night.

I was about to get into the front seat of the Duesenberg again when Mrs. Pennyweight gestured for me to sit in the back. I took the jump seat beside a polished wooden cabinet, facing the three women and the little boy. Flora fished a cigarette out of her purse. For a moment she seemed to be waiting for me to offer a light. Then her mother pinched her arm and demanded, "Give."

Flora winced, handed over a smoke, and they both fired up. Connie Nix shifted farther into the corner.

"Walter will be gone for at least five days, probably more. I believe that we're safe enough during daylight in our home," Mrs. Pennyweight told me.

"But at night . . ."

"Precisely."

"I'm used to night work. Flora, can you handle a gun?"

Her eyes widened in alarm, and her mother shook her head.

"Miss Nix?"

She cut her eyes to Mrs. Pennyweight, who nodded.

"Yes, a rifle. I'm not as familiar with pistols."

Mrs. Pennyweight said, "We have guns. Walter refurbished the shooting gallery."

I almost smiled. Of course. Spence would.

Oh Boy stopped in front of the house. Flora and her mother got out first and Flora immediately let out a shriek so loud it hurt my ears. Connie Nix held the baby close and sat tight. I hustled out and saw what had Flora so upset. It was a ladder, a tall ladder leaning against the side of the house and reaching up to an open second-story window. A white curtain was fluttering through it. I guess I should have stayed there, but I told Oh Boy and Connie Nix to lock the doors, and then followed Mrs. Pennyweight into the house. Flora kept screaming.

The older woman detoured into the library for the Purdey. I went straight upstairs. On the second floor I turned away from the hallway that led to my room and gimped to the balcony that overlooked the main room. There were more rooms on the other side. I thought that the closed door straight ahead led to the room with the open window. I had the little Mauser in my mitt when I threw open the door. It was dark and something smelled god-awful bad. Mrs. Pennyweight shoved me aside and hit the light switch.

In that first second when the light came on, I saw all the blood and what I thought was a dead baby. Gorge rose in my throat and I fought it back. The room was a nursery with a bed and an open cabinet with stacks of diapers, blankets, baby clothes, and more cardboard boxes of the baby food I'd seen in the kitchen. There was a waist-high table next to the open window. Sticky blackish red blood had soaked through a white blanket on the table and pooled on the floor beneath it. It also covered a doll, a headless doll that was pinned to the table with a knife through its belly. Bloody handprints were smeared on the wall, the windowsill, and the gauzy curtain.

Even across the room, I could see that the knife was a cheap piece of work with a fake mother-of-pearl handle. It folded down to about five inches long, easy to hide and easy to throw away. Just about every cheap mug who couldn't afford a piece carried something like it. At one time, so had I.

The doll and the blood and the slaughterhouse smell got to Mrs. Pennyweight the same way they got to me. I heard her sharp gasp when she saw it too. She recovered quickly and her expression settled into a hard, angry frown.

Sheriff Kittner and Deputy Parker showed up a few minutes after she called them. We were waiting outside. The sheriff looked like he'd been rousted from his bed or a barstool. He was boozy and bleary in a rumpled blue suit. Parker was still in his spiffy uniform. The sheriff wandered around with a flashlight at the foot of the ladder, pointing out things to Parker. Mrs. Pennyweight and I got bored watching them and went inside for a drink.

The lawmen found us in the library later.

The sheriff cleared his throat and held his hat in his hands as he made his report. By then he'd pulled himself together and tried to sound like he knew exactly what he was talking about. "I make out two sets of footprints outside. One of them goes out into the woods. The way I see it, they abandoned the ladder and took off when they saw your car approaching. They went down the service road around back to the driveway. There are fresh tire tracks there and we found something—a bloody steel pail.

"We talked to the staff. They were downstairs and didn't hear anything. According to Mrs. Conway, the doll isn't one of the boy's toys, and Dietz says the ladder doesn't belong here either.

"Now, you say that you were gone for an hour. Where were you—"

"That's right, about an hour," Catherine Pennyweight said before he could go on, and he knew not to ask where she'd been.

Deputy Parker took over, sounding embarrassed and unsure. "Mrs. Pennyweight, I've taken a look at the pail we found and I'm pretty sure it came from Bartham's Butcher Shop. He uses it for slop."

She gave him a sharp look.

"I hear talk in town," he continued. "Some of the merchants are unhappy. Well, they're more than unhappy, some of them, about payment. When they've had enough to drink, they talk about coming out here and getting what they're owed. Have any of them bothered you?"

She stared hard at both of them, letting them stew for a long moment before she snapped back, "I will not hear this kind of talk in my own home. Yes, it is true that the household finances have been a bit disorganized since my husband's death, but everyone knows that the Pennyweights pay their bills. We have been the best customers that many of these men have ever had and if they are displeased in any way,

I will be happy to take my business elsewhere. But I refuse to believe that any of them would do something this vicious, particularly Mr. Bartham."

The sheriff said, "We'll see what the state police think."

"No," she interrupted. "I will not have them trampling around my property. That's simply out of the question."

"But Mrs. Pennyweight," the sheriff protested, "we have to let them know about this. It's part of the Lindbergh investigation, I'm certain."

"No," she repeated, more firmly. By then, she'd lost patience with the man. "There's nothing more to be done here tonight. You may go now."

They left.

So, what did it mean? The first moment when I'd seen that damn doll and thought it was a real baby still churned my stomach. I didn't believe that the Lindbergh kidnappers had come out to Spence's place to steal little Ethan. Maybe, I thought, the deputy was right and somebody had bloodied up the room and the doll to scare Mrs. Pennyweight. But if that were so, all he'd done was make her really mad. Seemed more likely to me that it was just a threat, a damn nasty threat that I had to take seriously. But who'd done it and why?

For the moment, I didn't really care. I went downstairs to the kitchen, where I found Mr. Mears and asked him to take me around and show me all of the doors that gave access to the house.

Back up in the main room were the big double front doors. They were always kept locked unless visitors were expected. Smaller single doors off the conservatory and dining room opened onto porches and were always locked. Another set of wide double doors led to a ballroom. He opened them and I saw a wide, dim cold room with several sets of French doors on the far wall. The wind whistled through them, making the ballroom colder than the rest of the place.

He led me upstairs to the second floor. There was a porch off of Mrs. Pennyweight's rooms but other than that, no outside doors. Mears had already closed and locked the shutters of the nursery and the empty guest rooms. Servants' quarters were on the third floor. They had no outside access and small windows.

Downstairs in the kitchen, there was only one door. Oh Boy was sitting at the table. I asked him to show me the guns.

The gun room was at the far end of the basement, behind a wooden door thick enough to muffle the sound of gunshots. Like the kitchen, it had whitewashed walls. They were covered with mounted animal heads along with photographs, mostly of a smiling Mr. Pennyweight, his guns, and the dead trophies he'd shot with them. There were also pictures of a girl about twelve years old with a long, ruddy face. I guessed this was the older sister, Mandelina. She wore hunting clothes and posed with a deer or elk with a wide rack of antlers. She held a lever-action Winchester rifle, her father beaming proudly beside her. I studied the picture more closely. The resemblance to Flora was strong. But Mandelina seemed much more confident, almost cocky. You could tell that she was only a few years away from becoming a real looker.

Oh Boy took a key from a peg and unlocked the doors of a glass-fronted gun case. The racks inside held a collection of expensive shotguns and rifles. A second case held muzzle-loaders and older military pieces. Beside them was a workbench for cleaning the weapons and reloading ammunition.

Oh Boy opened a drawer and said, "Here's the pistols."

The drawer was lined with green felt, with spaces cut out for a dozen or so handguns. These were the familiar guns of my youth: Police Positive, Browning Hi-Power, and my own favorite, the Detective Special snub-nose .38. Another Mauser, the big broom-handle model, was in the center of the drawer. The largest cutout was empty. It was a simple angled shape meant for a Colt .45 automatic. I guessed that Spence had taken it on his trip.

I walked to the dark shooting range and hit one of two switches on the wall by the counter. Lights came down the narrow passageway. At the far end, a spotlight was aimed at a paper target already peppered with holes, suspended from an electric pulley-and-chain system. I snapped on the other switch. A motor whirred and the target glided back to me. I started counting the holes and stopped at thirty. There was a coffee can on the counter with a dozen or so .45 shell casings at the bottom. More littered the floor of the range. Spence had been practicing. "Oh Boy, what do you know about this trip?"

"Jeez, Walter's been working on it for almost a year now. We've been going into the city to meet with the company lawyers two, three times a week. Sometimes Saturday, too. Leave first thing in the morning, don't get back until after dark. Oh boy, do I hate those days. And the shysters have been coming out here, too. I talk to the other drivers, who say this is quite the big deal. I'll be glad when it's over, that's for sure."

I went back to the pistol drawer and found the cutout for the little Abercrombie & Fitch Mauser. Before I put it away, I offered it to Oh Boy.

He shook his head and frowned. "No, I don't like guns no more. You know that."

Some guys go a little nuts over guns. They've got to have the biggest, shiniest, loudest piece, wearing fancy shoulder holsters and such, making sure everybody sees what they're carrying, particularly women. You've got to watch out for guys like that. Oh Boy was just the opposite. Had been for years and he hadn't changed.

I took out the Detective Special. The compact weight was familiar but the grip felt different. It didn't have any friction tape or rubber bands holding it together. I opened the cylinder. Five rounds with an empty chamber under the hammer. If I was going to be carrying a pistol again, I wanted it to be something I was comfortable with. Probably wouldn't bring down an elk, but it didn't clump up my coat pocket.

We locked the gun cases and turned off the lights. Oh Boy said, "It brings back some memories, don't it?"

CHAPTER FIVE

On the third Tuesday of most months, Mother Moon left our building in Hell's Kitchen to meet Mother Fineman in a millinery shop on Second Avenue. Mother Fineman was a fence who knew that Mother Moon's mob of kids stole good merchandise. That Tuesday, I had been chosen to carry the bag of samples—a girl's dress and blouse from two racks of clothes that we'd picked clean, a can of Savarin Coffee from the five cases we'd boosted from a truck, and two men's pocket watches, one cheap and one good, part of a lot we'd bought from a jeweler's assistant who'd stolen them from his own boss.

At the millinery shop the women would spend a couple of pleasant hours examining the goods, haggling over prices, and drinking tea while complaining about the quality of the smoke at the Sans Souci opium parlor, their favorite. I could work the neighborhood if I wanted to, or make myself scarce if I stayed in the store. It was cold that day so I stayed. The place was warm and it smelled good, and looking at the shapely dress forms that the women used in sewing gave me a pleasant itchy feeling I didn't quite understand. Hell, I was seven years old, maybe eight. Bolts of cloth were stacked on the floor and shelves, and a small kid like me could work his way through them, tunnel toward the back, and find a comfortable place to curl up where no one would notice him but he could see everything that was going on. When you're my size, that's a useful skill.

I was stretched out on a shelf when the commotion started on the street. I heard yelling, a quick *pop-pop*, feet pounding on the sidewalk, and then saw the shop door slam open and bang against the wall. A fat little man crashed through, his straw-boater flying. He vaulted the first display and ducked behind it.

Another shot sounded. Louder, closer. A mirror in the back shattered. Two men with pistols shouldered through the doorway together. Mother Moon and Mother Fineman dove beneath the cash register, teacups forgotten.

The fat little man scuttled straight toward me. For a split second, we were eye to eye, and I flinched against the stench of spoiled garlic that surrounded him. I saw a shiny black suit and white shirt speckled with red and purple stains before he scurried away.

The gunmen turned in crazy circles. Where was their target? He knocked over a dress form and they both blazed away, running toward the headless model. The fat little guy bounced up, dashing across the store, ducking and twisting. One fellow emptied his pistol and reloaded. The other chased the fat man and kept firing. The bullets hit high on the wall and punched through the tin ceiling. The first guy rejoined the chase. The fat man bobbed and twirled and slid, his feet never still. The gunfire continued. I could see sweat pouring down their necks. One of the gunmen whirled and put a bullet through the store window. The gunfire abruptly stopped as his partner smacked him on the back of the head.

The fat little man peeked around the corner. The other two raised their pistols, but the hammers clicked on empty chambers.

The first gunman smacked his partner a second time. They rummaged through their coat and pants pockets. No more bullets. They looked at each other, one said something in Italian, and they disappeared out the front door.

The fat little man slowly stood, his breath huffing, eyes darting madly around the shop. At length, he retrieved his boater, and laughed a little when he stuck a finger through a bullet hole in the crown. After checking the street, he scurried out.

The women emerged from behind the cash register. Mother Fineman began to catalog losses, including the broken glass and mirror. Who could say how much of her stolen goods were damaged? She held up a bolt of dirty cloth. I stood in the middle of the floor and committed it all to memory so I'd be able to tell everyone about the wonders I'd witnessed.

Mother Moon appeared beside me. "Do you know who that was, lad?"

"Yes, ma'am. It was Joe 'The Boss' Masseria and those guys were working for Umberto Valenti, the guy that Joe tried to kill last week."

"And what did you learn from what you just saw?"

"Those guys can't shoot for shit."

She tousled my hair. "Aren't you smart. I think I see an opportunity here for us."

That very afternoon we started clearing one side of the basement in Mother Moon's building for a shooting gallery.

The project took more than a week to complete even after we emptied a narrow space along the back. Mother Moon found an article in *Modern Mechanix* magazine. She hired Mr. Merkl, the carpenter on the third floor, to frame up a wall of lath and plaster, and put in a waist-high counter at one end. Oh Boy and I rounded up bales of newspapers and stacked them from floor to ceiling outside for soundproofing. We rigged coal-oil lights, with sandbags reaching up the wall at the far end. Mother Moon bought targets and a couple of beat-up Colt revolvers, a sawed-off double-barreled shotgun, ammunition, and a gun-cleaning kit from a guy who worked at Frank Lava's gun shop.

The guy from Lava's told me about the rudiments of marksmanship, and showed me how to clean the pistols. I thought this was just about the greatest thing that ever happened, and I spent hours in the basement getting used to the big noise, the sudden power, and the recoil. I was able to make mistakes on my own, even when my grip wasn't strong enough and the Police Positive jumped out of my hand.

Or when I shot into the floor and almost hit my own damn foot. I learned to be careful, even when that meant going slow. For a little kid, I became unusually patient. I remembered the way the guys in the millinery shop acted, how fast and uncontrolled they'd been. If one of them had just stopped for a few seconds before he aimed, he'd have dropped the fat little man where he stood. But they were both too excited. Hell, I'd been excited watching them. I could still feel the leftover buzz, and I wanted to feel it again. But excitement didn't help when it came to hitting what you were aiming at. The trick, I came to learn, was not to hurry and not to hesitate.

I practiced for another week and then we spread the word. The target range was open for business. You could bring your own piece and ammo and rent the range, or Mother Moon would let you practice with her equipment, for a price. We always kept the money away from the shooting gallery, never allowing in more than one guy at a time.

One of our first customers was a gawky, skinny teen from a good neighborhood, not the kind of customer Mother Moon had in mind. She thought she'd attract mugs who wanted to get into local gangs. This was a working-class kid whose father had a good job at the Chelsea Piers. That didn't keep him from being drafted into the Army to fight in the Great War.

Mother Moon and I met the kid when he showed up on a gray cold afternoon, looking unhappy, hands stuffed into the pockets of his coat. He was pretty young but was already six feet tall, looming over both of us.

"Look," he said, "I gotta go for training in a couple of weeks, and then I'm sent overseas. They tell me they're gonna give me marksmanship training but I don't know from guns. So I figure to get a leg up here by learning to use a pistol, it can't hurt."

"A wise young man," Mother Moon said as she pocketed his money. "Are there other boys from your neighborhood in the same situation?"

"Sure. Dozens of 'em."

"If you recommend our little enterprise to your friends, I'll give you extra time with the instructor."

The deal was done on the spot, and I led him downstairs.

"You're the instructor?" the guy asked. From the tone of his voice, he was just curious. He didn't seem to care that I was so much younger and smaller. He stuck out his hand. "Walter Spencer. Spence."

"Jimmy Quinn. In here." I pointed the way.

I lit the acrid coal-oil lamps, got out the .32, and showed him how to open the cylinder and load the bullets.

"First, all the things you've seen in the movies, Tom Mix shooting guns out of guys' hands and stuff like that, it's crap. This," I said, like I knew exactly what I was talking about, "is a Colt Police Positive. You hold it in your right hand. Now, you can either pull the trigger or pull the hammer back and then squeeze the trigger. Either way, you need to hold it steady. You gotta use both hands or lean on something or kneel down and brace your elbow. Then you line up the sights right in the middle of whatever you're aiming at . . ." And on and on I went with my half-informed lessons.

Spence listened and watched, following everything I said. We spent the afternoon down there until the stink of the lamps and the gun smoke made it too hard to breathe. When we were done, we took the pistol and the remaining ammo back to Mother Moon and walked down Eighth Avenue in the cold evening to find something to eat.

"You're right," said Spence. "It ain't nothing like the movies. Why don't they ever have to reload?"

"That's the movies for you, I guess. You know, I was there when they tried to get Joe the Boss."

"Really? You saw it?"

"Yeah, let me tell you it was . . ."

And that was the beginning of a curious friendship that grew over the next three months. Somehow, the ten-year difference in age never mattered to either of us. Every now and again some guy would make a crack about Mutt and Jeff. If we could catch him, we'd beat the hell out of him. We went to the movies all the time, ate hot dogs and sandwiches at the deli, stayed up late, and rolled drunks for cash. I showed Spence the finer points of sizing up a properly boiled mark, and we regularly earned more than $100 each week. We sat up all night to watch the sun rise from the roof of Mother Moon's house. Spence said that his father worked extra hours at White Star Pier, drank a lot, and complained about his son. His mother drank too, and he thought that she worried about him, but he wasn't sure. That was all he ever said about his parents and his home. Both his mother and dad died while he was overseas.

Spence was a stand-up guy overall. He also delivered other boys from his neighborhood who wanted to play with guns. I provided the lessons, and Mother Moon prospered.

Spence shipped out for training in South Carolina in September. I got one letter saying that it was hot as hell down South, and most of the guys in his unit were apple-knockers from upstate. He hated them all, hated the Army and the whole goddamn thing.

CHAPTER SIX

It was almost four in the morning that first night, and I couldn't get the image of that damned bloody headless doll out of my mind. I went into the dim library, where Mrs. Pennyweight had fallen asleep. She was in the armchair in front of the fire with a thick lap robe tucked around her, shotgun across her legs. The baby was sleeping in his crib. Throughout the earlier commotion, little Ethan hadn't made a sound. Must have been pretty strong stuff that Dr. Cloninger doped him with.

I put a log on the glowing fire, mixed a weak rye, and searched the bookshelves for a dictionary. I found one on a stand in a corner and took out my notebook. Where was it? There: "recapitulate," the word I'd picked up earlier from the guy on the radio. I flipped the pages of the dictionary, running my finger down to where I needed to be. I was pleased that I'd spelled the word right, and that I'd almost known what it meant. *Repeat the principal points or stages of. Summarize.* Yeah, that made sense.

Mrs. Pennyweight stirred. "What are you doing?" she asked, her voice cross.

I gimped back to warm my butt by the fire that had crackled back into life. "Looking up a word. 'Recapitulate.' Do you know what it means?"

"Of course. What are you talking about?"

"I didn't last too long in school but I learned how to read and I enjoy it. Still, I have to look up words I don't know so I keep a list." I showed her the notebook. I've still got it and almost all of the others that I've kept over the years.

"How fascinating," she said, still cranky.

"Do people around here know about Spence?"

She shook her head. "They know he made money in the market."

That was true enough. Spence invested everything he made working for Lansky and Longy. They paid us pretty well and he turned his share into a nice little pile. I gave mine to Mother Moon. Most of it anyway. I always held on to a little something.

Mrs. Pennyweight said, "They don't know how he got it, but that's not really important. You see, Morris County used to be extremely wealthy. Vanderbilts and Rockefellers lived here. Not long ago, this was a place of mansions and luxury you couldn't believe." She stared into the fire. "We had our own train, the Millionaires' Express, so that the men who worked in the city but summered here could relax on the trip back and forth. Of course, that's gone now. Everybody lost their money in the crash. We're hanging on, and Walter is part of the reason. He was able to provide an infusion of capital when we needed it, and with my husband's help, he learned the business. Now, if he isn't able to bring in these new wells, I don't know what we'll do."

Her face had a haunted look in the firelight. "We've been through worse, but to have this come on top of this awful business with Anne and Charles . . ." She hugged herself and frowned at the flames. "Hell and damnation, if it were up to me, we'd sell this place and move to a cottage in New Hampshire. There's no reason for us to be here, but there's no one to buy the house."

Her voice and expression were bitter. "Perhaps we really are cursed."

Later, I stood at the window of my darkened room. Outside, the head-lights I'd seen before were still there. But were they the same lights? I couldn't really tell. They did seem to be moving at the same slow speed. Then the lights of a second vehicle appeared, approaching the first, and the second car stopped. It looked like the two drivers had stopped to talk to each other.

Then I heard, faintly, the grinding of gears as both cars began to roll slowly in opposite directions. I looked out, letting the damp wind chill my face. Ten minutes later, the cars passed again and stopped even more briefly. As I remembered the roads, they could be circling the house. About twelve minutes later, they approached, paused, and passed each other again.

I was still staring out when I saw movement in a shadow outside, at the edge of the light from the ground-floor windows. Then a figure in dark clothes stepped into the faint light, and a pale face looked up at me. At that distance it seemed to be a white mask, but it might have been a naked face staring upward. I couldn't make out the features or even much of the shape of the body. I opened the window for a better look, and the figure backed away and disappeared into the trees. I stared out the window for a while longer but didn't see anything else. Damn, I thought, this place is getting to me. First the crazy drunk waltzes in and then somebody stabs a doll and dumps a couple of gallons of blood and leaves it in the baby's room. Now there's somebody, maybe the same guy who did the doll, hanging around outside. This is just nuts.

I went back down to the kitchen and made another sandwich. That always calms me down. I ate standing over the sink and took a closer look at the incredible amount of strange foods they had for the baby. The shelves were filled with cereals and powders and medicines from Switzerland and Germany. There was even a box in the refrigerator labeled "Little Ethan" that had more stuff in bottles that I couldn't identify.

For the rest of the night I prowled the house and checked the locks on all the exterior doors and windows that Mears had shown me. Just before dawn, with the first faint gray on the horizon, I heard activity in the kitchen. I changed my shoes for sturdier boots, and grabbed my heavy cane, the one I used outdoors. I got my overcoat and hat, and went downstairs to the front doors. Outside, the ground sparkled with damp frost. I wanted to find the place where I'd seen the figure from the window.

The tree-lined drive stretched from the road to the house and on to a good-size garage that had been painted to match the house. I remember how cold that first morning felt. And how quiet it was compared to what I was used to every morning after I closed up the speak. I buttoned my coat and walked around the house on a wooden porch that led to the back.

On the other side, the land sloped down to the lake and the boathouse. In the faint light, I could see the shape of the sanatorium on the other side of the lake. It was a two-story stone building with some kind of tower and a stone wall that came to the water's edge. As I stood on the porch, I heard the slow *clop* of a draft horse's hooves and the rattle of a wagon. A moment later, it came into view, following a shallow rutted track. I realized it was on the same little road that Spence and I had taken on that first day, when we delivered the booze. The wagon was filled with coal. The driver, dressed in a mackinaw coat, muffler, and hat, got up close to the house and tugged lightly on the reins. He didn't need to. The big horse knew where to stop.

The man looped the reins around the hand brake, leaped down, and walked to the base of the house to lift up a small door. After propping it open, he pulled down a metal chute from the wagon and set it against the lip of the door. Back in the wagon, he shoveled coal down the chute. The pieces rattled loudly as they slid down into the basement even though the guy obviously tried to keep the noise down. It took him ten minutes to unload half the wagon.

As the driver was leaving, he saw me standing on the porch watching him. Obviously startled, he jerked on the reins. "G'morning, sir," he said, touching his hat. I nodded and watched the wagon until it disappeared in the back around the house.

I walked down the steps to the stubby grass and crossed to the tree line where I'd seen the figure a few hours earlier. The open space and bare woods spooked me. I was used to the noise and crowds and color of the city. Here, there was only the empty, washed-out winter landscape, all pale grays and browns. It was not my world. What the hell was I doing there, besides freezing my ass off? Was I was going to find footprints or a broken twig or a scrap of cloth caught on a branch like some Indian tracker in the movies? What a dope.

As I turned back to the house, I saw a fat man close by staring at me and smiling. It was Dietz, the groundskeeper I'd seen talking to Spence and Dr. Cloninger. He still had the little .22 rifle in the crook of his arm.

"A bit early for a walk, isn't it, Mr. Quinn?" He clamped a curving briar pipe between his teeth and fired a match on a cracked yellow thumbnail. Spit rattled in the barrel of the pipe as he lit the tobacco. Even in the cold air, a pungent mix of pipe smoke, horses, human sweat, and damp leaves wafted off him.

"I'm Dietz." He stuck out his hand. "And you're Mr. Spencer's gunman, here to keep little Ethan safe from your fellow desperadoes."

The accent might have been German or Danish but carried a cheerful lilt. "Best keep on your toes, city feller. There's many a strange beastie in these parts."

"Sure are. I saw one last night."

Dietz's eyes narrowed behind the smoke. "What's it you mean?"

"Just a few hours ago, I was in my room, looking out at the lake." I gestured with my stick. "I saw the lights of two cars. They might have been circling the house. And then I saw a person, right about here at the edge of the woods, watching the house."

"Must've been a deer, or just a city boy's eyes playing tricks on him. You never know what you're going to find in these woods."

"Wasn't a deer. It was a person. Any idea who might be casing the house at four in the morning?"

Dietz's voice took an edge. "You didn't see anyone. It's my business to know what happens on this property. I look after things. If there was a party creeping about in the night, I'd know about it, and I'm telling you there's no such thing." He chomped down on the pipe and glared, daring me to disagree with him. I wondered why he was so damned insistent about it.

"Come along now. Mrs. Conway will have our coffee ready."

We'd just started up the slope when the police car skidded to a stop and Deputy Parker jumped out and waved for us to come up.

We reached the driveway, and Parker said, "Get in. Sheriff wants to see you." He opened the rear door. "Not you, Dietz. I don't want you smelling up my cruiser. Just Quinn."

"What's going on?"

Parker was a young guy with a determined air, not as openly angry and obnoxious as his sheriff but experienced enough as a cop to expect to be obeyed.

"Get in," he barked once more.

I turned toward the house. "I haven't had my coffee."

"Goddammit, Quinn, this is important. If you don't want to be charged with murder, you'll get in the fucking car. Now."

Dietz said, "Maybe you better do as the man says, young fella."

I thought about my choices, then said to Dietz, "Tell Mrs. Pennyweight that I had to leave." I got in the front seat.

The deputy dropped the shift lever into first and took off as fast as he could without spraying gravel. Like the guy delivering the coal, he didn't want to disturb the rich folk. At the gate he turned right, still speeding as we hurried along narrow roads through thick woods.

Being in a disagreeable mood without my coffee, I was about to needle Parker about Flora, but he looked even more disagreeable than me. So I let it lie, and thought about Connie Halloran. It was too early for her to be up. Normally, this time of morning we'd be in my bed at the Chelsea. Frenchy'll know where she is, I thought, and she must've seen Marie Therese by now. Hell, where was she?

Parker slowed as we topped a low rise. Ahead, smudge pots and flares burned on the blacktop. The road curved sharply to the left. A red Marquette Roadster had missed the turn and gone straight, plowing a muddy fifteen-foot path through the underbrush. The grill was crunched between two trees, both scarred white where the fenders had sliced through the bark. Black evening clothes and white underwear were scattered around the car and in the branches.

Two police cars were parked on the side of the road. Parker stopped behind them and we got out. Sheriff Kittner stood where the Marquette had cut through the brush. He looked like he'd been up since the business with the blood and the doll, shoulders sagging under a shapeless coat, hat slipping down over his eyes.

Two other cops wearing bulky greatcoats came stumbling out of the woods. Their legs were wobbly and one of them was wiping his mouth like he'd just thrown up. Chief Kittner paid no attention to them. He said, "This way, Quinn," and marched toward the Marquette.

I followed slowly, picking the way with my cane, trying to keep the mud off my good boots. Kittner bellowed, "Hurry up, goddammit, we haven't got all day."

"Screw off, fatso," I said, and walked more slowly. The other three cops stopped what they were doing to see how the sheriff would react.

He blustered, "Parker, get him over here," stomping past the wrecked car as he marched into the woods. The deputy didn't move.

"Don't bother," I said, and followed the sheriff. Parker followed me.

Fordham Evans, last seen mumbling nonsense at the Pennyweight house, was naked, with rolls of fat gently swaying in the wind.

He'd been spread eagled against a wide tree, with his hands nailed to the trunk. His body had turned a cold bluish gray. His head lolled forward, a purple tongue protruding from purple lips. A damp wind kicked up, vibrating his pendulous lower lip slightly. There was a small black hole in his chest above the right nipple. An acorn-sized nubbin was visible in the shadow beneath his sagging belly. Not much blood, virtually none.

Parker walked over to the inert body as Sheriff Kittner lit a Lucky Strike. "You admitted threatening him last night. Said you were going to shoot him in the heart. That's just what happened. Maybe you decided to finish the job."

Kittner was so damn ridiculous, I almost laughed. "In a pig's ass. Did he make a habit of busting into other people's houses in the middle of the night or just the Pennyweight place?"

"That's none of your—"

"Did Deputy Parker follow him all the way home?" I continued. Parker shook his head, leaning down to study something on the ground by Evans's feet. The frozen mud was covered with horse tracks.

"I'll want to see the pistol you had last night," said Kittner.

"It's in the gun room." I saw no reason to mention the Detective Special in my pocket.

"What did he say last night before we got there?"

"A bunch of nonsense. Crazy jabber about hotels and money that he owed Spence and that Spence owed him. He was pretty well boiled, and I think he'd been dipping into something else besides alcohol."

Sheriff Kittner flushed, squaring his shoulders angrily. "If you mean narcotics, we don't have that kind of problem here. Maybe it's nothing to sneeze at where you come from, but not here, not in my jurisdiction. Anyway, that isn't important."

He peered at me more intently with an expression that was meant to be shrewd and cunning. It came off as a squint. "This homicide didn't have anything to do with drugs. Like the incident last night at the Pennyweights', it's part and parcel of the Lindbergh kidnapping."

I laughed, and Parker's head snapped up. This was news to the young deputy.

The sheriff was too pleased with himself to notice. "You think it's a coincidence that the most famous child in America is stolen from his parents' home and two days later, less than forty miles away, an attempt is made on another child and a man is murdered in this bizarre fashion? I doubt that Colonel Schwarzkopf and Lieutenant Keaten will see it that way."

I shook my head. "He wasn't murdered."

Kittner snorted an ugly laugh. "What are you saying? Did he nail himself to that tree?"

"I'm saying he isn't dead."

Parker turned to put two fingers on the blue man's throat. "He's right! Sweet Jesus, Evans is alive!"

The Cloninger Sanatorium ambulance got there twenty minutes later. By then, two deputies had used heavy pliers to pull the long nails out of Evans's hands, and one had donated his overcoat to cover the naked body. As they strapped the fat man onto a stretcher, his eyes popped open and then his mouth opened and closed like a fish. It took two male nurses and two deputies to get the stretcher onto the road.

Dr. Cloninger, still in his heavy overcoat, white smock, and thick glasses, watched them struggle. When they reached the ambulance, he examined the wound and then checked Evans's pupils. He said, "Wait one moment." Then he took a leather case from his breast pocket and unzipped it to reveal two glass syringes, one filled with a dark amber fluid, the other with some clear stuff.

He said, "Alcohol swab." One of the male nurses jumped to produce one. Cloninger gave Evans a quick wipe and shot before they loaded up the bluish body.

Cloninger turned to me and said, "You are Walter's friend, are you not?" He had a faint German accent. The daylight didn't do him any favors. His bloodless, corpselike face would give anyone nightmares. I figured he understood exactly what effect he had on people and liked it.

"That's right, I'm Jimmy Quinn."

"You had words with Evans last night. It appears that your aim was a little high. Better luck next time," he said with a chilly little smile as he got into the ambulance.

On the way back, Deputy Parker said, "You shouldn't talk to the sheriff like that, calling him 'fatso.' You'll make him mad."

"Who found the Marquette and the body? Kittner?"

The deputy's voice hardened. "All right, we made a mistake. He sure looked dead at first."

"What about Cloninger? Is he the borough coroner? That's why he was called in?"

"He's been here for years. He's always done these things."

So Parker was a local boy. Maybe that explained his interest in Flora. He was only a couple of years older than her. "What did the sheriff mean about Schwarzkopf and Keaten?"

"Bill Schwarzkopf is the superintendent of the State Police. Charlie Keaten is in charge of the kidnap investigation."

And we both knew that Kittner would do any damn thing to be part of such a big deal.

"What do you think about last night?" I asked him. "The doll and everything."

"It could be nothing. Mrs. Pennyweight is not popular with everyone around here. She can be highhanded and sometimes she's slow to pay. I'll check on the bucket. I'm sure it came from Bartham's Butcher Shop, but I doubt he had anything to do with it. He's not the kind of guy who'd do something like that with the doll just to scare her or make her mad. But there are other people in town who would do it."

"But what about Fordham Evans? If your sheriff really thinks he's involved with the Lindbergh business, why'd he drag me out here?"

The deputy gave me a nasty cop smile. "Maybe he thinks you shot Mr. Evans. I do."

It was so damned foolish I laughed again.

Parker said, "All I know is that nobody was stabbing dolls or nailing people to trees until you showed up."

"And for what it's worth, I saw somebody near the house early this morning, somebody in the woods watching the place."

Parker cut his eyes at me and said he'd talk to Dietz about it.

Word that Fordham Evans had been killed reached Mrs. Conway's kitchen before I got back. She was even more thrilled when she learned that he'd been shot, and frozen near death but survived. She turned down the radio while I gave her all the details, including the purple tongue.

"The sheriff's right. It must have had something to do with the kidnapping. Who'd have thought of it, poor Mr. Evans."

I drank a mug of strong black coffee as she made toast, spooned up scrambled eggs, and held forth on the latest Lindbergh news. The colonel was personally leading the search and hadn't slept since he discovered his son was gone. The newspapers reported $50,000 in reward money for the kidnapper and were confident that the child would be returned unharmed very soon. They wrote that Mrs. Lindbergh was bearing up bravely and calmly.

I ate my eggs and sympathized, wondering how long it had been since I'd slept. I couldn't remember, but it didn't matter. The eggs hit the spot. Mr. Mears worked on a bowl of oatmeal and a cup of coffee laced with aquavit. Connie Nix prepared two trays with white linen and bud vases. When she'd finished, she went to the shelves of baby food. She and Mrs. Conway put their heads together over a printed form. Apparently, they weren't sure what the kid was supposed to have for breakfast. It must have been really complicated because they had to open half a dozen jars and boxes before they got what they wanted on a tray.

"Did you actually see Mr. Evans?" Connie Nix asked.

"Yeah," I said between bites. "Looked to me like his car ran off the road in the woods not far from here, and then he took off all his clothes and ran into the woods."

Knowing looks passed between the two women.

"Damn cold night for that. Then somebody nailed him to a tree like this." I spread my arms wide. "And then they drilled him. One shot. Could have been a .32, nothing larger. Maybe even a .22. Or maybe they shot him and then nailed him up. Why does everybody think this shooting is involved with the Lindbergh business?"

"Well, Mr. Evans spent a lot of time in the city, and if it was the work of racketeers . . ."

I shook my head and repeated, "Nobody I know was in on this." Not after Vinnie.

"And now they've admitted that there is a ransom note . . ." Mrs. Conway rattled on about a bill in the New Jersey legislature that would give the death penalty to such heartless criminals. But, she argued with herself, that could force the kidnappers to kill the boy.

I got up and carried my coffee to Connie Nix, still fiddling with the trays.

I asked if she had time for a little talk, and she said yes, Mrs. Spencer probably wouldn't be up for hours. Of course, with Mrs. Pennyweight, you never could tell.

She poured a cup of tea and sat next to me at the big table. I could see that her hair and eyes were as dark as mine. She had thick eyebrows, wide cheekbones, and a sharp little nose. It was hard not to stare too closely at her face. I asked what kind of shooting she'd done.

"Target shooting with my father and brothers, and a little quail hunting with a shotgun. I never personally hit anything but I ate the quail. Tasty. Better than the ones they buy here." I liked her voice, too.

"Where was this?"

"California."

California? I didn't think I'd ever known anyone from California. That explained the accent. "Like we were saying last night, we might want another gun. Are you interested?"

She nodded. "I suppose so, but I haven't touched a gun in a pretty long time."

"You could practice. Spence has a good collection."

Mrs. Conway sniffed. "Actually, those are Mr. Pennyweight's guns."

"He won't be needing them. We do. It'll only take an hour or so."

"No," Mrs. Conway said. "Nix has her assigned tasks, breakfast and washing and I don't know what we're going to do about the nursery. I never heard of such a thing, a woman shouldn't be . . ." She banged a skillet into the sink.

"When?" said Connie Nix.

"No, never. She's not going to—"

"Mrs. Conway!" The girl raised her voice and the older woman piped down. "I can handle a gun. If that's what it's going to take to keep little Ethan safe, then Mrs. Pennyweight will want me to do it."

Mrs. Conway resumed muttering, but her heart wasn't in it.

I turned back to Connie. "When?"

"This evening."

"Fine," I said, yawning. "I'm bushed. Come down to the gun room later."

Upstairs, I stripped off my clothes, pulled the curtains closed, and crawled into bed. I was asleep immediately.

CHAPTER SEVEN

1919
NEW YORK CITY

I probably should have explained that Mother Moon was my aunt or great aunt or something. She always claimed we were related. You see, she was Mother Quinn until she married that Chinaman. At least, that was the story she told after she came back from a trip out west, from either San Francisco or Cleveland, depending on which version she chose. I heard both several times. She brought back an exotically dark-haired baby girl she called her daughter, Fantan Perfect Jasmine Moon, a couple of years older than me. Nobody had actually seen this Chinaman, but if anyone doubted the old gal, they didn't say so to her face. All that happened before I knew her anyway.

My parents came from Ireland, and went straight from immigration to an address they'd been given. It was a building on the south side of Hell's Kitchen. A relative back home had told them that another relative owned a tenement there, and she'd have a place for them. They moved into the building, and that's where I was born. My mother died of tuberculosis when I was too young to understand. Not long after, my father wandered away. The only thing I think I remember is being on the roof with my parents on a bright warm day, and their saying that this was the best place they'd ever found. But chances are that's only something I saw in a movie or made up.

Mother Moon took care of a mob of kids who lived in the building. We usually numbered between six and twenty. Some of us had parents or other relatives. But Mother Moon fed us regularly and provided beds to the ones who needed them. Every morning, she sent us out to school or to work or to steal. She'd made arrangements with Alderman Jimmy Hines's office as well as the local cops. They got a cut of everything we stole and on Election Day, Mother Moon's little street apes could be counted on to help deliver the vote. Hines also steered us toward shopkeepers and stores that weren't being cooperative enough with Tammany. We stole stuff or tore apart those places, depending on what we'd been told to do. In the rare cases when any of us got caught, the alderman contacted the cops and judges on our behalf, and had us sprung. If that didn't work, he'd see to it that we were represented by lawyer Ira Jacobson. We almost never went to court. When we did, the alderman and the counselor made sure that things were speedily settled.

I did well enough selling newspapers for a while. I was better at petty theft, but since I was always small, I got pounded regularly by the bigger boys. I can't tell you how frightened and ashamed I felt after each of those beatings, no matter how trivial, until one night when I came back bleeding, crying, and humiliated, and Mother Moon instructed me in the way of the world.

"You're never going to be the biggest boy in a fight," she said. "So if there's any way for you to get away, you take it and run. Remember, the last thing you want is a fair fight. Hell, there ain't such a thing. But you are quick, Jimmy. Speed is your gift, so you'll have to learn to use that. Do you understand?"

I didn't really understand but sniffed back those tears and said that I did. I'd figure it out later.

"You can *never* smoke, not ever. Not cigarettes, not cigars, not the weed, nor the dreamy pipe, bless it. Running fast is about all you can do, and smoke will ruin your lungs and your legs. Don't forget it.

"Now, the time will come when you find yourself in situations where you won't be able to run away and then you'll have to battle it out. When that happens, hit first and keep hitting. If you can put a guy on the ground, make sure he stays there. That's where these come into play." She handed me a set of joined metal rings.

"These are brass knuckles. If they're too big, we'll find another set. We'll also get you a knife. Here, your fingers go in this way. Now, knucks do two things. First, they protect your hand when you hit something hard like a skull. Second, if you hit a guy in the right place, around his eye or in the mouth, they'll draw a lot of blood and that's good in a fight. Scares 'em and then you can run."

I was a quick study. Soon enough the bigger boys picked easier, slower targets.

But bigger boys weren't the only bullies. Some of them were nuns. I hadn't been in school more than a year before I ran into this goddamn sister who loved nothing better than smacking kids with her goddamn whippy wooden switch. I'm not talking about a little smack on the back of your hands when you were doing something you shouldn't. She'd sneak up behind a kid and hit him right across the arm or the neck for no reason at all. I saw the sick smile on her face when she laid into one of the guys, and you'll never tell me she was just trying to keep her students in place. She liked to hit people, particularly people who were smaller. She did it to me once but I followed Mother Moon's advice and went after her with the knucks. I couldn't reach her face so I didn't draw blood. But I got in some good licks to her stomach and legs. That got me kicked out of school, and ended my formal education.

More or less the same thing happened when Oh Boy talked me into going to Mass, and some priest tried to handle my privates. I got him with the knucks too, but he never said anything to anybody. Those two things probably didn't happen as close together as I remember, but I think of them as one event after the other, and since then I've had no use for the Church.

Instead of school and godly pursuits, I applied myself to work. The shooting gallery was a good idea at first, but after the regular boys went "over there," most of the mugs refused to admit they needed any practice and so business slowed, which meant I had the place to myself. Mother Moon must have gotten a great deal on ammunition from her guy at the gun shop because she never complained about my using all those bullets. I could never claim to be a gifted marksman, so I practiced and practiced and practiced until I could aim and shoot several different pistols with either hand. From time to time, guys came messing around our building and I shot at them. I know I hit at least three, but I'm mostly sure I didn't kill anybody back then.

I also taught myself the geography of Midtown Manhattan and explored on foot as best I could the different neighborhoods around Hell's Kitchen and learned which ones to avoid, which ones were safe, and which ones you had to pay to use. I figured out that the streets changed literally from day to day. The alley that cut through from Thirty-Third to Thirty-Fourth one morning might be stacked high with trash cans the next. The open sidewalk I dashed down on Thursday could be blocked off and torn apart by Saturday, or covered with ice if the temperature dropped in winter.

On my feet, wearing the right shoes, I was fast, really fast, and the clogged sidewalks and city streets were perfect for someone my size.

Mother Moon soon realized how quickly a boy like me could cover any area, regardless of crowds. And besides being speedy, I was an obedient little squirt, always trying to do what she told me, and learning from what I saw. So she decided I could be more profitable to her in other areas.

One night, she told me we were going to meet someone important and I was to put on special clothes. She settled on my most comfortable pair of dungarees, a white shirt neatly buttoned to the neck, a jacket that wasn't too snug, a cap to tuck my unruly hair under, and my best Keds. She tried to make me put on a nice little tie but gave up when I kept pulling at it.

As we walked the long crosstown blocks, I could tell she was nervous. If I'd known she was nervous for me, I might have shared the feeling. But I had no idea what lay ahead even after we stopped outside Reuben's Deli on Broadway and Seventy-Third. She checked my clothes, roughly rebuttoning my shirt and explaining what to do even though she'd told me three times already. Reuben's was a busy, smoky place. Mother Moon pushed through a crowd of men to a table near the back stairs. And there he was, Arnold Rothstein. I recognized him right away. I didn't know exactly who he was or what he did, but all the older guys spoke his name with genuine respect. To them, Rothstein was simply "The Man." He wore a black wool suit and bow tie, his boater on the table beside an open paper bag. He had a long, rounded face and nose, a very high forehead, and tiny ears. He was talking to a massively muscled man with a bald bullet head. That was Monk Eastman. I was awed and frightened to see such legendary figures in the flesh.

The other men around Rothstein spoke to one another in low buzzing voices, waiting their turn for his attention. Some of them tipped their hats as Mother Moon approached. They paid no attention to me, but made room for another boy, a ragged-looking kid about my age who kicked up his legs in some kind of silly dance that made Mr. Rothstein smile. They stopped talking and he stopped smiling when Mother approached the table.

"Nice to see you," Rothstein said in a low voice that was hard to hear.

"A. R., this is the lad I told you about." She tapped my head, and I took my hat off before stepping up to the great man. I paid no attention to the others or to the foolish dancing boy, and tried not to look at Monk Eastman. Mother Moon had told me not to say a word unless I was asked a direct question.

Mr. Rothstein looked me up and down. I curled my fingers around the knucks in my pocket and stared back at him. In doing that, I forgot one of the things Mother Moon told me: "You can look at Mr. Rothstein, but you don't stare at him."

Now she said, "First, the boy won't steal from you. Not ever. I've taught him who he can steal from and who he can't. He's smart but not smart enough to be a problem. He can do sums with a scrap of paper and a pencil, even long division, and you can see this adorable little Mick phiz." She squeezed my cheek and turned my face so he could see that it was adorable. "He can walk into any office or station house and nobody will look at him twice. Anything you need delivered or retrieved, he's your boy. He hasn't done any work in Brooklyn. Doesn't know the streets but he's fine in most of the neighborhoods around here."

"I can always use another runner," Rothstein said. "And as it happens, I'm involved in an enterprise where such a lad might be useful."

I had no idea what they were talking about. But Mother Moon knew what he meant, and that was the reason she'd asked for the meeting. Later, I learned that the government was promoting the sale of Liberty Bonds to pay for the Great War. Everyone said the bonds were almost as easy to deal with as money, with hundreds of them moving between Wall Street banks and brokerage houses every week. A. R., as I came to call him, knew exactly which messengers were handling the transfers. For the right price, some of them tipped him off about their schedules and routes, later "suffering" mild beatings and robbery when they were held up. Rothstein and his partners had already made off with more than two million dollars. He didn't want a connection between the muscle who stole the bonds and the guy who cashed them in. That's where his runners came in.

A. R. leaned forward to whisper, "You know how much I hate violence, but these things get rough from time to time. Shots have been fired. I hesitate to involve such a young lad."

"Not to worry. He can take care of himself." Mother Moon shrugged. "And there are other boys."

Mr. Rothstein took a fig out of the open paper bag, chewed, and then swallowed. Turning to me, he said, "Do you know the Hotel President?"

"On Forty-Eighth."

"That's right. There's a man in Room 457. Go there and tell him that A. R. wants the second number. That's important, 'the second number.' He'll give you something. Bring it back here as fast as you can."

"Be quick," said Mother Moon.

I ran.

I couldn't understand what was so hard about this. Out the front door, go east, squeeze through the clotted sidewalk, always looking a few feet ahead, watch for cigars in hands that could burn, swivel around other kids who might stop in front of me. I knew I could move faster than foot traffic but only so much faster. I couldn't run at full speed when there were too many people. If I was too fast, I'd knock adults off balance, they'd yell, and that could get the cops involved. I never wanted that. But when I moved at a fairly quick pace, a sort of weaving trot, I could pass everyone on the sidewalk and most of the traffic in the street.

When one place became too thick with crowds, or the traffic slowed to a creep, I'd cut across to the other side, looking for an easier flow.

I was so engrossed that I didn't notice Monk Eastman and another guy following me out of Reuben's, trying to keep up for two blocks. After that, foot traffic thinned and I could really make time.

Then I was approaching the Hotel President, moving up the steps and through the doors into the busy lobby. What was that room number? Oh, yeah, 457. I slowed to a walk. Kids couldn't run in hotels without attracting attention, but I was still able to take the stairs two at a time.

The fourth-floor corridor was crowded with men and so at first I couldn't read the room numbers. It took long, frustrating minutes to reach 457. I knocked on the door and waited.

"Yeah," snarled the lanky young fellow who answered the knock. He wore a stained undershirt with loose suspenders hanging around his waist. He had a heavy stubble and a big plug of tobacco stuck in his right cheek. A card game was going on behind him.

"A. R. wants the second number."

"Huh! What the hell?" He was surprised to see a kid and hear the kid saying what I was saying.

I didn't know what else to do, so I kept my mouth shut, and stared fixedly at the man.

He scratched his blue jaw and looked down at me, probably wondering if someone was pulling his leg. He made a gruff noise and shut the door.

What to do? I hesitated, raising a hand to knock again when the door opened once more. The young man thrust a folded piece of paper at me. He muttered, "This better be on the level."

I grabbed the message and dashed down the corridor.

By the time I returned to Reuben's, both Monk and his associate were back inside the restaurant. The guys had tried to explain how I disappeared, slipping past everyone. And then I arrived and put the folded paper on the table.

Mother Moon allowed herself the smallest of smiles. "I can have him on call for a flat weekly rate, or would a per-job fee be more to your liking?"

I don't know what they agreed upon, but I soon became Mother's best earner. The work was wonderful and only sometimes terrifying. My part in the bonds business was simple.

I'd go to Reuben's around midnight and wait around until Mr. Rothstein called me to his table. A. R. would explain what to do the next day in a voice so soft I had to lean really close to hear.

He might say, "Be at the corner of Nassau and Pine tomorrow morning. Wear a tan cap. A man will give you a package. Take it to Room 715 at the Delmonico."

The next day I was at Nassau and Pine promptly at ten, with a tan cap and a bag of peanuts to stave off the constant hunger I felt in those days. I was eight, maybe nine. Shelling and eating the nuts also kept my hands busy and burned off the nerves. Countless hours later—that's what it felt like anyway—a blond guy who didn't look like much of anything sauntered out of a doorway. He was trying so hard to act nonchalant that everybody on the street gawked at him, or so I thought. He passed me a messily folded newspaper wrapped around a thick-clasp envelope and then ran like hell. So much for nonchalance.

I tucked the paper under my arm and melted into the crowd on the sidewalk. Moving fast, I felt through the newspaper without taking my eyes off the people around me. I found the envelope, and slipped the package into a wide pocket that Mother Moon had sewn inside my coat. I made sure it lay flat before buttoning the pocket. My pace quickened as I headed for the El.

I had no idea about what I was carrying, and didn't understand the business of negotiable bonds, but I knew they were valuable. Mother Moon told me some men might try to take these packages from me, and my inherently suspicious nature served me well. I noticed adult males who paid too much attention to me, or looked away too quickly when I stared at them. I learned different routes to get across town. Streetcars were better than subways. The El was OK but still a potential trap. I was most comfortable in my Keds on a crowded street, where no grown person had a hope of staying with me.

Three guys brought me the stuff, and it began to worry me that I recognized them so easily. If I knew who they were, so did other people. One of my contacts was a dark, hungry-looking young fellow with gaunt, hollow cheeks and eyes that were never still. Then there was the blond guy who didn't look like much of anything, always trying to be very cool, unruffled, and sure of himself. My third connection was a taller blond guy, very nervous, always chewing on a toothpick stuck between his teeth. He tried to act snappy and sharp but even I could tell he was afraid. Mr. Rothstein was sending me out three, four times a week. My part went off smoothly. One of my guys would show up at the right place within an hour or so of the proper time, and then I was off. It was all silky smooth—until one particular day.

I was waiting at the southeast corner of Union Square, bored with the posters in front of this movie theater, impatient and hungry as the sun rose higher and I was running out of peanuts. I was thinking, Just give me the damn thing so I can deliver it to the Chatham Hotel, which is twenty minutes away if traffic is what it ought to be on a Thursday. Then I can get something to eat, a dog with mustard, and a Coke. . . .

But there was a commotion on Seventeenth Street, and I saw my messenger stumbling forward, arms flailing with bright red blood on his face and his white shirt. Panicked, he ran straight into two old ladies and sprawled ass over elbows into the gutter not five feet away. I could see the wild look in his eyes and the bloody toothpick sticking through his upper lip. Two guys were chasing him, and they ran over the old ladies too. The women screamed as blood spurted from my man's face. His wide, frightened eyes locked on mine. The last thing I heard was the sickening crunch of a sap on a skull as I backed away.

The two men were ripping through my guy's clothes, evidently looking for the clasp envelope. But an outraged street crowd fell on them, helping the old ladies and yelling for the cops.

I threaded through groups of people, hopped the wall that bordered Union Square, and went straight to the room at the Chatham Hotel, where I was supposed to make the day's delivery. The place was empty, nobody there. It was too early to find Mr. Rothstein at Reuben's. But I knew he had offices on Fifty-Seventh Street, so I headed there, and found the Rothmore Investment Company on the building directory. I could read well enough for that.

Upstairs, a woman sat behind a desk in the front room. I knew her name was Freda Rosenberg, though I'd never met her before. She looked startled when I came through the door, like she knew who I was and what I did—and if she knew that, she also knew I wasn't supposed to be there. I could see Mr. Rothstein on the other side of a glass partition. He was talking urgently with a couple of other men. The woman at the desk nodded toward the door, meaning I should scram out of there. I did, with a crushing worry that gnawed at me all day. Had I screwed up? If I'd failed A. R., what would they do to me?

Around midnight, I went to Reuben's, trying to act like nothing unusual had happened during the day. I figured if I showed up with a long story of what I'd seen, I'd sound like a kid. Better to wait and be quiet, let the man ask what he wanted to know.

An hour later, the longest hour of my life, Rothstein beckoned me over to his table. He said, "I know what happened. Did you see it?"

"Yes."

"Did Berkowitz put up a fight?"

Berkowitz must have been the toothpick guy. "He was running but already bleeding when I saw him. He didn't have a chance."

He nodded, looking kind of sad. "Were they cops?"

I started to answer no, then stopped. "Yeah, they coulda been."

A. R. nodded again and murmured, "All right then." Relief washed over me though I tried not to let it show as he gave me a tightly folded bill from his vest pocket. "Tomorrow's going to be different. I've got something new for you. You know my friend Mr. Heller. Come here at two o'clock. He'll have something for you to deliver to Abe Attell at Jack's place. We've got a lot of work to do with the Series."

I didn't know what he meant, but the next month was really busy.

CHAPTER EIGHT

That evening, I woke up still seeing the bloody doll and the pale figure and Fordham Evans's cold, naked body hanging by his hands, and I was no closer to understanding what the hell any of it meant. Another hot shower and shave revived me, but I was still worried and confused. It was almost fully dark by the time I'd dressed in a warmer turtleneck and my good charcoal gray double-breasted. I put my notepad and fountain pen in a breast pocket, dropping the Detective Special in the right-hand coat pocket, knucks in the left pants pocket.

Mrs. Pennyweight called as I opened the door, and I went down the short hall to her suite. Across the balcony, the door to her daughter's room was open. I could see an empty bottle of Veuve Clicquot upturned in an ice bucket and two more on the floor.

The door to the nursery was open too. It looked and smelled like a cleaning crew had been at work. The bloody table and curtains were gone, and the wall had been scrubbed clean.

In Mrs. Pennyweight's rooms, a wall of louvered windows and French doors opened onto a terrace with a view of the lake. The wallpaper, furniture, and carpets were pale blue and light tan. Everything looked new. She had a desk, a low table, and a sideboard for her sherry and console radio. Her armchair faced a crackling fireplace. The tray that Connie Nix had been preparing that morning was on the table. Scattered around it were sections of the New York newspapers. I took the *Daily News*, the *Mirror,* and the *Times*. She had a robe tucked around her legs and wore a heavy sweater. She looked at me over glasses that had slipped down to the tip of her nose. I could see a bit of her bedroom through an open door. They'd moved the crib up to her room from the library. The baby was in it, playing with his feet.

The mantel was crowded with photographs. One was a formal portrait of an older woman draped in dark, heavy clothes. Given the style of her dress, I guessed she was Mrs. Pennyweight's mother. There was also a wedding picture of Spence and Flora. The largest photograph, in the center of the mantel, showed two dazzlingly pretty teenage girls, Flora and Mandelina. They were wearing light summer dresses and laughing in the sunshine. Arms around each other, they seemed simply to be two happy girls, not stiff young ladies posing for a photograph. Mandelina was slimmer and a little shorter than her younger sister. I was about to pick up the picture when Mrs. Pennyweight said, "Please don't touch that."

There was no trace of her recently departed husband anywhere in the room.

"Did you hear about your friend, Fordham Evans?" I asked.

"Yes, I've spoken to Sheriff Kittner. I can't for the life of me understand why anyone would want to mutilate that poor man."

"Yeah," I said, "took a pretty strong stomach."

"Fordham simply wasn't the type to inspire great passion. He pottered around with his poetry and drank far too much."

"And broke into houses, and stripped naked from time to time."

She waved me away. "He was simply befuddled by alcohol. The other thing was just eccentricity. Whatever may be threatening us, Fordham is not a part of it. Of that I am positive. What did you do to make the sheriff so angry at you?"

"I don't like bullies. I really don't like bullies with badges. What's the story with him? Why does a place as small as Valley Green have a sheriff's department?"

"Taxes. We weren't getting our money's worth from the county for services, so Ethan, Dr. Cloninger, and one or two of the other prominent landowners decided to carve the borough of Valley Green out of the county. There was a time when we could do things like that."

"So the department is your private police force?"

"I hadn't thought of it in those terms, but, yes, I suppose that's the case. Kittner makes sure that our needs are met. But as you saw with the business of the ladder and that hideous doll, he's overmatched. I discussed it all with Walter before he left. We agreed that we did not want Kittner and his clumsy deputies underfoot in this house."

I thought that if Spence had any sense, he wouldn't want young Parker around his wife, period.

"We needed someone we could trust, someone who was proficient with weapons. I don't know anyone who meets those qualifications."

"The trust or the guns?"

"Trust, of course." Her lips stretched in a tight smile and she sipped her sherry. "Mrs. Conway tells me that you're going ahead with your plan to instruct Nix in the use of firearms. That's probably a good idea. Like all servants, she's often lazy and requires supervision but she's not flighty. I think in this situation she can be trusted."

"Where's Flora?"

The question pissed her off. "Her old friend Cameron Rivers and some of their school chums came by to cheer her up. Lord knows when they'll be back."

"So she's got over being terrified of kidnappers?"

Mrs. Pennyweight rolled her eyes. "Apparently that's the case today. Tomorrow, who can say?"

Flora, it seemed, could turn from concerned mother to flaming youth without missing a beat.

As I left, I saw Connie Nix coming up the stairs with a tray of the weird foods for the baby. All business, she wouldn't meet my eyes as she passed. She paused at the door, tapped it lightly, and went in.

Mrs. Pennyweight sounded exasperated. "Finally. There you are.

Did you and Mrs. Conway make sure that these are the right supplements? We don't want a repeat of the last time."

Downstairs in the kitchen, Mrs. Conway banged her pots around the stove. She was not happy to see me. "The chicken won't be ready for another hour, so don't bother to ask. The soup is done but that's all."

I sat at the table and spread out the newspapers. "I see you've got some bread. If I could have a couple of slices and a bit of cheese, I'll be fine. And some mustard, please. And perhaps a drop of Mr. Mears's dago red." Mr. Mears, who'd been staring blankly at the table, looked up and cupped a hand protectively around his glass.

Mrs. Conway harrumphed but cut three slices of warm bread along with a wide wedge of cheddar. She also put a crock of mustard on the table before taking one of the newspapers. She read the latest kidnapping news avidly, following the words with her finger.

"Oh my dear sweet goodness, look at this, the baby's diet." Her voice was sad as she read aloud. "'A quart of milk, three tablespoons of cooked cereal twice a day, two tablespoons of cooked vegetables, an egg yolk, a baked potato or rice, two tablespoons of stewed fruit in the morning, half a cup of prune juice after his nap, fourteen drops of viosterol vitamins.' The poor dear."

She looked over at the shelves of imported baby food and muttered, "If Little Ethan were to be taken, it could be the death of him."

Oh Boy sidled inside, going directly, quietly, to the stove. Without looking up, Mrs. Conway said, "Stay away from there. It's not ready yet."

"Jimmy's having dinner," he complained.

"Bread and cheese. It's there on the counter."

"Is there any devil's food cake left?"

"Have you tended the furnace?"

"Oh, boy," he sighed theatrically, slumped his shoulders, and left.

Upstairs in the library, I lit a fire, poured a shot of Spence's rye, and added a splash of soda from the siphon. I picked up the telephone and asked the local operator for New York information. The operator connected me to J. Richard Davis, attorney at law. A woman answered. I asked to speak to Dixie. A few seconds later he said, "Jimmy, where the hell are you?"

"I'm at Spence's place in New Jersey. What have you found out?"

"A name. Hourigan. Detective Eustace Hourigan. Mean anything to you?"

"Nothing. He's not on my payoff list."

"He wouldn't be. You were right. He works out of the Bronx. Morrisania."

"Then where the hell does he get off trying to close down my place?"

"Nobody knows. He's a complete straight arrow, one of those guys you can't deal with. And now he's disappeared, nobody's seen him. He hasn't been back to his station house since Tuesday afternoon."

"Dixie, this doesn't make any damn sense. You're sure he's the guy?"

"Sure enough, yeah. Do you want me to keep working on it?"

"Of course, I gotta know why, and when I know why, I'll come back and do something about it."

"Be careful, Jimmy. He's a cop. He may have broken the rules by busting up your place but he's still a cop."

"I'll worry about that when I know what he's up to." I gave him Spence's number and hung up before I called my place.

"Frenchy, it's me."

"Hello, boss. You still in Jersey?"

Even through the long-distance static, I could hear the babble of conversation from the bar. Things usually picked up early on a Thursday, so word must've got out that the place had reopened.

"Yeah, I'm still here. How's the house?"

"Nice crowd. Nice." That probably meant that the bar was busy but not packed two-deep, also that maybe half the booths and tables were filled. On this dark evening, they'd have the lights turned up a little, but not much. Nobody wanted to see too clearly in Jimmy Quinn's.

"Any problems?"

"Nothing serious, boss. We replaced a table and three chairs from the stuff we had stored in the attic. Had to clean the carpet, too. Other than that, just the usual. Norris and Cheeks got their envelopes. Whaddya want me to do about Sergeant Marks?"

Norris and Cheeks were the beat cops who patrolled the neighborhood. Marks was their sergeant. Their captain's weekly payoff was included with Marks's money.

"Have Marks's envelope ready if he comes in tonight, and it's a good bet that he will. If he doesn't, he'll be in tomorrow. Did Pauley make his delivery?" Pauley was our beer guy.

"Uh-huh." Somebody close to the telephone laughed and others picked it up. The faint sounds cheered me. The laugh sounded like Kerwin, a reporter for the *Daily News* who held forth nightly, usually entertaining an appreciative crowd of regulars, lying to them about things he knew but couldn't print.

Of course, later in the night, some of those same guys would be puking in the potted palm or passing out in the bathroom. Even so, the good tended to outweigh the bad with the joint. At least, that's what I told myself after I finished cleaning the potted palm.

"I just talked to Dixie Davis. He says the cop who busted things up is named Hourigan, Detective Eustace Hourigan. Works out of the Morrisania station in the Bronx. That mean anything to you?"

After a thoughtful pause Frenchy said, "Nah, I don't think so, but like you said, I know I seen him before."

"That's all Dixie's got, so why don't you ask around. See if you can dig up anything else about the son of a bitch. You learn anything, call me."

"Will do, boss."

"Is Connie there?"

"Yeah."

She must've been standing right next to the telephone, and took it right away. "Jimmy, I've been so worried about you. Marie Therese told me what happened but I don't understand why you're in New Jersey and not here. They said a cop came in the other night and busted things up and they arrested you but then they didn't really arrest you. What's going on?"

She sounded worried, but I thought I heard something strained and nervous in her voice. "It was just a mistake with the cop. I'm taking care of it. I'm in New Jersey because of something else. Did I mention an old friend of mine, Walter Spencer? Spence? No? Well, from the time I was a kid, he and I have known each other. We were real close but then a few years ago, he married this rich girl out here in

New Jersey. They've got a swell place, I'll show it to you sometime. But, see, Spence had to go out of town for a few days, and this whole Lindbergh thing has got his wife so upset that he thought she and their kid needed some protection. So he asked me, as a friend, to stay out here while he's gone." Even as I was talking, it sounded crazy as hell. "It doesn't have anything to do with the cop."

"Is he coming back?"

"Nah, and even if he does, there's nothing to worry about. Fat Joe won't let him in again. What's the matter, you scared?"

"Well, I don't want to be arrested."

"I know, but I can't come back right now. Look, why don't you pack up your things and move into my room at the Chelsea. You'll feel better there, it's closer to work, and I'll feel better knowing you're comfortable. What do you say?"

She piped up right away. "Sure, Jimmy, I'd like that. I'd like it a lot."

"I'll call the front desk and tell 'em you're coming," I said, but I knew something was bothering her.

Still troubled, I mixed another rye and soda and took it downstairs to the gun room. Most of the rifles displayed in the glass case were hunting pieces, the kind that old Ethan Pennyweight used to bring down Cape buffalo and rhinos. A few showed some signs of wear. All were well-oiled and clean. None had been fired recently. They were powerful, heavy, and completely useless for my purposes.

I found what I was looking for on the workbench. It was a simple Winchester 92 carbine with a short barrel, probably the one that Mandelina was holding in the photograph. It was the least expensive, least exotic weapon of the bunch. It looked like someone had been cleaning the gun, and left it there on the bench with a cleaning rod, rags, solvent, and oil. The lever action seemed to work smoothly, but I couldn't really say because I'd never used a rifle myself.

I opened the pistol drawer and saw the box of .44–04 bullets right away. But the little Mauser pistol wasn't there. The cutout space was empty. I thought back to the night before. After the first crazy business with Fordham Evans and the ladder and the doll, we came down there and I offered it to Oh Boy but he said no, so I put it inside the cutout. I remembered doing it distinctly. Was there a chance that Oh Boy changed his mind and took it? No. I stared at the empty space.

What did this mean? Had the person I saw outside the house managed to sneak in, take the pistol, dash into the woods, and force Evans's Marquette off the road? Then had this same person made Evans take off his clothes, shot him, and then nailed the poor bastard to the tree? Oh, yeah, that made a hell of a lot of sense.

I was standing there, still confused, staring stupidly at the open drawer when Connie Nix came in. I asked her if she'd been in the room that day.

She shook her head. "No. This place is Mears's responsibility. I don't think he's been here for months."

"Dietz?"

"No, he just shows up for meals and to dip into the kitchen whiskey. His room is in the garage with Oliver."

"What about Flora and her friends?"

"No. Miss Rivers and the others were in Mrs. Spencer's room upstairs for a couple of hours before going out. I've never seen Mrs. Spencer here." Her eyes were wide, and I could tell that she was worried by my questions.

"OK." I explained that Spence had given me the small pistol, and now it had disappeared. "How difficult would it be for someone to get into this house?"

Connie Nix tapped her front tooth as she thought. "The kitchen door is locked at night. The doors to the terrace have been locked ever since I came to work for the Pennyweights. The only trouble we've had was last night."

"Yeah, I saw that it's been cleaned up. Was that your work?"

"No. Mrs. Pennyweight called some maids in Morristown."

"Did they come downstairs?"

"No, I don't think so."

"Well, hell, compared to the other crazy stuff that happens around here, I guess one missing pistol isn't that much to worry about." But I did worry.

"Speaking of that, was Mr. Evans really naked?"

"As the day he was born. Not even socks and garters."

"And he was *nailed* to a tree?"

I nodded and held my hands about six inches apart. "Nails about so long. They pulled 'em out with pliers."

"Really?" Her eyes were wide with amazement.

"Really." I gave her a few more of the details before we got down to business. When I showed her the rifle, she said, "That's a Winchester. My father has one, but his is different."

"Then you're more familiar with it than me. Know how to load it?" I turned on the lights in the shooting range and clipped a fresh target onto the pulley. She fed the bullets smoothly into the rifle, cocked it, and said, "What do you want me to do?"

"Just shoot. This is a pistol range, so it won't be hard."

She pulled the stock tight against her shoulder, sighted down the barrel, and pulled the trigger. Both of us flinched at the first sharp report. The rifle kicked but she held it firmly, cocked, and fired again. I admired the strong set of her shoulders and the curve of her waist and hips, or what I could see of her beneath the heavy black dress.

When she'd finished, I hit the switch and the target whirred back. All eight rounds hit the target, most near the center.

"Do you want to try the pistol?"

She looked hesitant. "Yes, I suppose so."

I gave her the Detective Special and showed her how to hold it. "Use your left hand to support your right. You sight it just like the rifle." I put a fresh target on the pulley and ran the cardboard figure back.

Her aim wasn't as sure as before but she hit the target with all five shots. She said she was more comfortable with the rifle.

As I reloaded, I said, "If anything happens and we have to break out the guns, you try to stay with the kid. They seem to think that the library is the safest place in the house. If that's where you wind up, put him in the corner farthest from the door and shoot whoever comes through the door. Unless it's me."

She smiled in a nice wicked way. "Oh, I know a better place to hide there."

Upstairs in the library, she went straight to a corner section of the bookcase near the fireplace. "I found this the first time I cleaned in here," she said, still smiling. "When the light hits the carpet in just the right spot, you can see the marks."

She reached around a book to the back of the case. I heard a click and a section of shelves popped open. She tugged with both hands so that a part of the cabinet pivoted away from the wall, revealing a dark, narrow doorway. She scrunched her shoulders to get through. I followed.

She hit a switch and warm light filled the hidden room. The lampshade was made of ornate colored glass suspended from the ceiling above a threadbare tasseled armchair and a footstool. Beside the chair was a table with a clean ashtray and a yellowed stack of *Police Gazette* magazines. In a corner stood a small sink and toilet, along with a second table holding a humidor, a bottle of brandy, and a dusty glass. One wall was made of brick. It was the side of the fireplace and the chimney. Roughly built shelves held more magazines, books, and stacks of photographs.

I picked up one of the books. It was filled with tinted pictures of naked women, very nice naked women. "So this is Spence's little hideaway."

"Oh, no," she said. "Mr. Spencer hardly ever uses the library. This was Mr. Pennyweight's room."

We were close together in the small space. She didn't try to back away. I leaned closer and tried to peer into the shadows.

"You're right. This is the place to stash the boy if anybody tries anything."

"Do you really think that's going to happen?" Her tone was serious, as was her face. I tried to concentrate but was sharply aware of her body.

"Hell, Spence has been gone less than twenty-four hours and somebody has tried to break into his house and somebody nailed one of his neighbors to a tree. Is there something else I should know?"

Her words came out rushed like she was afraid. "Something . . . something is wrong. I think I've known ever since I came here. It doesn't have anything to do with Lindbergh. It's just I'm worried and . . . something's wrong. I don't know what it is but . . . oh, forget it. I shouldn't have said anything."

She'd chosen a good time and place to make her case, whatever it was. Standing there in front of me, so close, her eyes were even with mine. If I'd thought about it, I might have remembered that I'd just told Connie Halloran to move into the Chelsea. But I didn't think about it.

We went back into the library, and I heard a loud thump outside, then the slow, haunted opening trumpet notes of "Meet Me in the Shadows" echoing on an Electrola.

I told Connie Nix to stay put until I knew what was going on, checked the Detective Special in my coat pocket, and hurried out.

The front door was closed. The wide double doors at the other side of the hall were open, with weak light and music flickering through from the big ballroom. The part of the floor I could see was big black-and-white squares of polished marble. The light came from wall fixtures. There was a dark chandelier above, with no bulbs. The room would nicely suit a jazz band. I could imagine fancy parties with flappers, dowagers dripping with diamonds, and stout gents smoking expensive cigars—the moneyed men who rode the Millionaires' Express into the city.

More light shone from candles on a piano in a corner of the room where Flora and another young woman were dancing. A couple of chairs and a chaise were carelessly strewn about like they'd been taken from another room. A slim young guy in a blue blazer and baggy Valentino slacks had four cocktails on a tray. Another man, a big long-haired guy, almost fat but not quite, stood by the Electrola cabinet, sorting through discs. He'd dragged the big record player in from another room, banging it across the threshold. That was the thump I'd heard.

Flora's friend, Cameron Rivers, was dressed as a man in a black-and-white striped jersey, tight black pants, and a beret over marcelled black hair. Flora wore a long yellow dress, slit up one leg past the knee, with a matching open jacket. The two women were doing a French Apache number. Even though Cameron was shorter, she whipped Flora around with exaggerated violence. She threw the other girl to her knees, grabbed her hair to pull her back, entwining their legs, and then flinging her away again. Both were breathing hard but seemed to be having a hell of a good time.

Something similar happened at my place one night when some guy started playing a squeezebox and two half-plastered women tangoed to the music. I remembered how the guys in the crowd got real quiet and intense as they held each other close. The women wanted attention and they got it. We had a couple of fights before closing that night. You run a speak, you see things like that.

Flora and her friend circled each other only to fall into a spinning embrace. The smaller woman grabbed Flora's head with both hands, pulling her into a slow open-mouthed kiss. They broke apart, staring at me as I approached, the sound of my cane on the marble floor muffled by its rubber tip.

All four in the group stared silently at me. The bigger guy had a football player's build, with wide shoulders that strained his jacket. Even loosened, his tie looked like it was too tight around his thick neck. He glared at me. The second man wasn't as large, with glistening fair hair and a dewy mustache. He passed the cocktails to the others. Both guys were familiar.

Several liquor and champagne bottles were scattered around the end of the hall. Remembering the ones I saw in Flora's room, I figured this group had been sucking it up all afternoon. The heavyset guy moved directly behind Flora, his hand resting on her shoulder. The smaller one drained his drink, fished out a cherry and chewed it. "You see, Cousin Titus, I told you it was him. I'll wager he doesn't even remember us." He had a mush-mouthed Southern accent.

Cousin Titus stepped away from Flora. He had a nasty look on his face. What the hell was going on? Flora's friend Cameron Rivers whispered in her ear, and they smiled at their shared secret. Flora's eyes were bright—too bright, I thought—and her lipstick was smudged. Her mother was right. The fear of kidnappers had been forgotten.

"We're looking for more champagne," Cameron Rivers said with a put-on British accent. "You're a bootlegger. You must know where it is. Teddy . . . that's Teddy over there. Teddy says that Walter keeps the best bottles in the butler's pantry. I think that's ridiculous. What do you think?"

I switched my cane to my right hand and leaned on it. Something phony was going on.

Teddy put an arm around Cameron Rivers's shoulder. "You don't remember us, do you, Quinn?"

The big one tried to look tough.

"Refresh my memory. Have you been in my place?"

Teddy said, "That's right. You threw us out over a silly little misunderstanding."

"I've thrown a lot of people out of my speak. I don't remember all of them."

Titus bunched his shoulders. "It wasn't right. I don't get thrown out of dumps like some common field nigger. I sit with Chink Sherman at the Swanee. Owney Madden saves his best table at the Cotton Club for me. It wasn't right what you did."

He was even more mush-mouthed than Teddy.

Teddy said, "I think he should apologize," walking quickly behind me so he stood between me and the door.

"An apology? That's what you're looking for?"

"No, I don't need no fucking apology. I just want a fair fight." Titus pulled off his jacket to reveal a shirt that was even tighter across his chest and shoulders.

I slipped my free hand into my pocket and strolled over to them. Flora looked hopeful, expectant, still flushed from her wild dance.

That's when I remembered them. "You're the assholes who were in blackface," I said, and the big guy got even angrier.

"That's why I didn't recognize you," I said. "You're Yale men, aren't you? Or you were. They kicked you out. It was a Friday night. You sang a song, something about the good times you had at a lynching. It was supposed to be funny, and that's when the trouble started. We told you to pipe down and then you"—I pointed my cane at Titus—"you tried to manhandle the cigarette girl." Connie was there that night. That's how it started.

"She was just a whore," Titus muttered. "And then the bartender sucker-punched me. None of you could have taken me man-to-man, not in a fair fight."

I ambled closer and said, "Now you want . . ."

"A fair fi—"

I smacked him in the mouth with the brass knucks. Blood and

teeth sprayed out. I came in as fast as I could and hit him again under his right eye. Choking up on the cane, I got him twice across the forehead and split the skin. More blood flowed into his eyes as he staggered backward. I shoved the big lug over a chair. He went down hard. His head cracked on the marble floor, and he stayed there.

I turned around and, sure enough, there was Teddy holding a champagne bottle by the neck. He danced in, nimble and light, and snapped the bottle at my face. He was fast, I'll give him that.

He connected, but he was so intent on bouncing out of range that the blow didn't really hurt. I still saw sparkles and stars, and lost my balance for a brief moment.

Teddy weaved from side to side, zipping in for another shot that came up short. I brought the cane tip in front of his face. The Detective Special was still in my pocket, but I knew if I pulled it out, I'd kill him. And I didn't want to do that. He wasn't threatening Spence's kid, and dealing with a body would be complicated.

So I moved in slowly, keeping my weight on my good leg. I feinted low with the cane, and when Teddy dropped his guard, I jabbed him hard in the throat. He gasped, dropping the bottle as he staggered back. I closed in with the knucks to his breadbasket. Three fast shots took the starch out of him. When he bent over, I straightened him with an upper cut and caught him again with the stick. That put him facedown on the marble floor.

It took a moment for the excitement to calm down. I felt it every time I had to get rough but took no pleasure from it. It's bad business to beat up your clientele, but then, they were assholes, so that made it kind of satisfying.

The women had been perched on the chaise. As soon as they realized that the rough stuff was over, they bounced up, jazzed by the action. I'd seen the same thing before. The girls pretended not to like it when boys mixed it up. But they caused most of the fights, and they enjoyed what came after. Flora tried to get the big guy to his feet, but he wasn't moving.

I slipped off the knucks and flexed my fingers. Everything was fine, but the big guy had gotten some blood on my sleeve and lapel—dammit.

Dr. Cloninger's ambulance arrived eight minutes after I called.

Nervous attendants scurried in with two canvas stretchers. Cloninger followed slowly, hands deep in his overcoat pockets.

The attendants struggled to get Titus's bulk strapped onto a stretcher. The right side of his face had swollen to the size and color of a grapefruit. The doctor strolled around the big hall, looking up at the dark chandelier.

"It's been years since I was in this room," he said. "I'd almost forgotten how grand it looks. A pity there's so little need for it now."

He turned to me. "You have had a busy day, Mr. Quinn. First Mr. Evans and now these two unfortunate young men."

I ignored the doctor's suggestion that I'd plugged Evans and asked how the half-frozen naked guy was doing.

"I predict he will make a full recovery. The cold kept him alive, you know. It slowed down the body's many functions. The wound itself was neither deep nor serious."

"You got the slug out of him then. What caliber?"

"Oh, I'm afraid I know nothing about firearms, but it was very small." He held two fingers close together.

So it could've been a .22, like Dietz's rifle, or a .25, like the missing Mauser.

They got Titus onto one stretcher and loaded Teddy onto the other. Cloninger turned to me again. "You haven't told me the nature of this altercation, but I must say that it strikes me as odd. Mr. Bullard is an excellent football player. Yet you seem to be unharmed. A slight scrape above one eyebrow perhaps."

He leaned down and pretended to examine my wound. I didn't flinch even though the doctor had a strong medicinal smell that made me a little sick. "Teddy Banks is exceptionally fast and proficient. And you are a cripple. Curious."

"They were drunk."

"As was Mr. Evans last night."

"I know. There's a parade of dipsomaniacs in this joint. Maybe that's why Spence asked me to keep an eye on things. He knows I'm experienced with uncooperative drunks."

The ambulance attendants returned to pick up Teddy. As they approached, Cloninger held up a hand and they stopped immediately.

Teddy stirred. His eyelids fluttered open, focusing on the doctor.

Then his chest heaved, his eyes bulged, and a panicked look came over his face. He strained against the leather straps.

Cloninger demanded another swab and whipped out his handy hypodermic to give Teddy a needle to the neck. The kid was out in a second.

While we were dealing with the injured, the two young women got into another bottle. But their whispers and giggles ended as Mrs. Pennyweight appeared in the doorway. Behind her, Connie Nix held the baby boy.

"Flora, come here. We need you upstairs. Cameron dear, I think it's time for you to say good night." Her tone was even, but she expected to be obeyed.

"It's far too late for Cameron to be driving," Flora slurred. "She's going to stay the night, aren't you, darling."

Cameron Rivers walked more steadily than Flora and stopped in front of me. She had a fine sparkle of sweat across her cheeks and her eyes were bright. She laid a warm hand on my chest. "Thank you for a wonderful ending to a wonderful day." The phony English accent had vanished. "I'm sure we'll be seeing each other again very soon. I can't believe that Walter knows someone like you. How did you ever become friends?"

CHAPTER NINE

1920
NEW YORK CITY

I probably wouldn't have got into the liquor business if it hadn't been for Spence. And of course Meyer Lansky. I was there at the creation, as they say.

Truth is, Lansky was the smartest man I ever knew. I met him for the first time on a Sunday afternoon in the fall of 1920.

By then I'd carried a lot of messages for A. R., and delivered enough bribes and payoffs to have a simple understanding of politics and economics. I knew which men were so secure that they didn't care if anyone saw them taking money. They'd tear open their envelopes right in front of me. Some would count carefully. Some thumbed through the tattered bills. I also knew men who were both embarrassed to be taking the money and thankful to see me. They tucked it away quickly and quietly.

Mother Moon had been right. My adorable little Mick mug made it easy for me to walk into any police station or Democratic Party office without drawing undue attention. Always polite and smiling, I could have been anyone's nephew or grandson. The men who knew what I was really doing made sure nobody bothered me. Rothstein was the important middleman that the Tammany boys used to keep their distance from the other, rougher racket guys.

I was also pretty good at fading into the woodwork. I could disappear in any crowd. My size helped. A. R. sometimes had me hang around during his marathon pool matches and poker games in case he had to conduct any of his other business dealings and needed a private message delivered. That's when I learned to read, picking up newspapers that were always lying around, first the funnies, then the sports pages, and finally the regular stories. That's also when I first started writing down words I didn't know, and looking them up in the dictionary at the public library. And that's where I watched A. R. become increasingly bitter and nasty during the games. My main work was carrying money and messages. I had nothing to do with Rothstein's casinos, and I never went with him to Saratoga or any other fancy places. I worked strictly in the city. Sure, there were other guys who did that too, but I was the best, and I'm not bragging when I say it. A. R. always made sure I was available for the most important jobs.

On the street, I was on my own. Word was out that I worked for Rothstein, and that meant I was carrying money or something else almost as valuable. I learned to be even more suspicious than I was during my Liberty Bond days, and I spent hours scouting out different routes to the places where Rothstein sent me. I can't say that I knew all of New York, but I was pretty familiar with a few hundred streets, alleys, sidewalks, hallways, back lots, broken fences, and walkways, all leading from one place to another. And I knew them in combinations most people never heard of. I was still most comfortable when I was on foot in moderate to heavy crowds. That's when a kid with my size and speed could really move. I figured that I was the fastest thing on the street, except maybe for a hungry dog. I could outrun and outmaneuver any adult.

And I loved it. Yes, there were times when I was scared. Once, when I wasn't paying proper attention, I almost ran into a bunch of older guys, four raw-boned brutes waiting for me outside Henri's Restaurant. I was carrying a packet from A. R. for the headwaiter. I saw the men too late to make a simple U-turn. They were right in front of me, only an arm's length away, the four of them fanning out across the sidewalk.

Without thinking, I sped from a trot to a run and cut toward the widest space I could see. One fellow reached out to grab at my coat and tore at the sleeve but hardly slowed me. I was weaving up the sidewalk when a chunk of pavement sailed past my head, and I heard running behind me.

I turned at the next cross-street and tried to figure out where I was and if there was anything close that I could use against these guys. Yes, the newsstand, just past the next corner. Without slowing too much, I reached into my pants pocket for the switchblade I carried along with the knucks. Not yet, I thought. Wait. I was tempted to look back to see if they were as close as they sounded, but that would have slowed me down. I rounded the corner at Third, and there it was—a long, open stand along the curb with hundreds of magazines and newspapers on display, and wooden boxes full of soft drinks on the ground.

As the first of the brutes barreled around the corner, I swept an armload of magazines at his feet. The guy slipped, and I closed in with the knife, slicing him across the face. I was aiming for the eyes but got him on the temple. He was bleeding but he didn't slow up until I smacked him in the mouth with my knucks. By then, the proprietor of the stand was yelling and I was half a block away.

I didn't deliver A. R.'s packet to Henri's until later that afternoon, and that night I went back to the magazine stand to give the guy a five-spot. Hell, fair's fair.

Rothstein had been in Europe for a month when I heard he was back and wanted to see me. Sunday afternoon, Room 502, Park Central Hotel.

I got there, and found a waiter was setting up a warming tray with half a dozen covered dishes, and a table for two with a heavy white tablecloth. A. R. was talking on the telephone, and motioned me to a chair by the window. I sat uncomfortably, my feet not quite reaching the floor. Rothstein wore a new dark-gray suit, a bow tie, and a white shirt with a collar that almost reached his round jowls and chin. His face was freshly shaved, and he smelled of something sweet and soapy. He finished his conversation and turned to me.

"How've you been, Jimmy? Listen, it's important that I break bread with the young man I'm meeting this evening. But I'm also expecting a call that I can't put off. Depending on what I hear, I'll need you to go down to Lindy's to deliver a message to Abe, then come right back."

I nodded. Simple enough, but as it turned out, the phone never rang that night.

"Did you eat?"

I shook my head.

"Fix yourself a plate. And by the way, pay attention, you might learn something."

I slid off the chair and carefully raised the polished metal covers from the dishes. I'd seen them before, looking through the front windows of lobster palaces and hotels, but I'd never actually handled such exotic food. There was something that looked like a little chicken and tasted just as good, cooked carrots, frilled browned mashed potatoes, and spinach—all delicious. I tried some kind of fish with the head still attached, then a small spongy cake. I piled a plate high, carried it back to my armchair, and dug in with a large spoon.

There was a knock at the door, and a wary young man of about eighteen came in. He held a hat and wore a herringbone overcoat. Rothstein greeted him all warm and friendly. "Mr. Lansky, so good to see you again. Let me help you with that."

Lansky's expression was guarded. He lit a cigarette, scanned the room, and stared at the kid balancing the full plate on his lap.

"That's Jimmy Quinn. He's all right. Runs Mother Moon's shooting gallery and takes care of things for me. We can talk freely in front of him. I'm afraid I have some other pressing business that can't be put off. I don't want us to be interrupted, but certain parties may need to speak to me. If they call, I'll have to get messages to other parties. Timing is essential. I'm sure you understand."

Lansky nodded. I knew enough to realize that this must be pretty important if A. R. was meeting this guy at the hotel instead of the deli, where he usually conducted business.

They sat across the white tablecloth but didn't eat. A. R. began by saying, "We're both sporting men, and I have a proposition that's going to change your life and make you wealthier than you ever dreamed."

I could tell that the younger man was interested but was trying not to let it show.

A. R. launched into his tale, all about laws that would make alcohol illegal. I couldn't believe what I was hearing. Close the saloons? Not sell beer? That made no sense. If anybody but Mr. Rothstein had said it, I'd have thought the guy was nuts. Remember, I was nine at the time, maybe ten. So I watched the two men and realized I'd never seen A. R. in such good light. I'd never heard him talk so much either. As I remember it, Lansky hardly said a word. Maybe he didn't need to since A. R. was doing the pitch.

"Somebody is going to sell liquor, and if that somebody corners the market on quality goods, he'll be able to charge just about as much as he wants to.

"I know you're working with Ben Siegel and Sal Lucania—"

This time Lansky interrupted, "Charlie Lucania. He don't like Sal, says it's a girl's name. He's Charlie now." This was years before he changed Lucania to Luciano.

Rothstein shrugged. So what? "But unlike other Italians, he doesn't mind working with us, or so I've heard."

Lansky nodded. "You heard right. Charlie's OK. We're interested in making money. The rest is bullshit."

"That's exactly what I want to hear, because there is more than enough to go around if everybody sticks to business."

A. R. described a new world I couldn't even imagine. They'd buy good liquor where it was legal, and bring it to New York in their own ships. They'd anchor offshore and carry the booze in on speedboats.

"Do you understand the quantities the public will demand? No matter what the law says, people are going to drink. You won't have trouble moving the stuff. You've already got the trucks at your garage. You'll have to take care of the cops in every city, but that's simply the price of doing business. You pass it along to your customers. It all comes down to money. Now, let me explain how this will work. . . ."

A. R. went into details about Cuba and Nassau and islands in

Canada and how they'd use them as their bases. I didn't understand a word of it. I knew that Brooklyn and New Jersey were on the other side of the bridges, but I'd never been to either one of them. The world beyond the Hudson and the East River was a complete mystery to me.

They talked for about six hours with Lansky raising occasional objections that A. R. easily answered. I listened to what they were saying the whole time, eating away at the food that the men simply ignored.

"If I'm wrong and people really don't want to drink anymore," A. R. said, sounding doubtful, "we'll go out of business right away. But if I'm right, the demand will be much more than one man can handle. I'll have to have partners."

And so he did, putting together Dutch Schultz, Longy Zwillman, even Capone—all helping to distribute the goods. And everything A. R. said about the demand for alcohol came to pass, and the market was so strong they cut stuff with other stuff you don't want to know about. Not that I had anything to do with that personally, you understand, but I know guys who did. Anyway, the point is Meyer Lansky said yes, and that's how I got into the bootlegging business. Eventually. About a year later, toward the end of the winter of 1921, I was in the basement shooting gallery practicing with a Browning Hi-Power when I heard a sharp rap on the thick door. It was Fanny—Fantan Perfect Jasmine Moon, Mother Moon's daughter.

Lately, I'd been getting odd pleasant feelings when I was around her, just like the feelings I experienced when looking at the dress forms that long-ago afternoon. Only, these sensations were much stronger and more distinct. But nobody messed with Fanny unless it involved business. She made the payoff to Patrolman Tommy O'Brien every Wednesday, the transaction taking place in her room in private.

That afternoon, when she opened the door in the basement, I saw that she had someone with her, a big shape that lumbered down the steps to the dimly lit gallery. It took me a moment to recognize Spence, returned from the Great War in France. This time Fanny didn't wander off to her movie magazines. Instead, she paid rapt attention to everything Spence said. If I hadn't been so happy to see him, and if I'd had any chance at all with her, I'd have been jealous. But then, he had that effect on most women.

"Goddamn, Spence." I grinned at the big guy. "Where the hell've you been? I went to the parade when your outfit came back. I looked real careful but didn't see you."

"Yeah, well." He ducked his head, looking a little sheepish. "I wasn't in that parade. There was this misunderstanding, you know how it is."

"We heard they'd locked you up. What'd'ya do?"

"It was nothing. It wasn't even me. There was this card game and some money went missing . . ."

"How much did you clear?"

He laughed. "Less than a yard. Damn, it's good to be back. Let's get the hell out of here and get something to eat." I locked up the automatic and the ammunition, and snuffed out the lamps. Fanny watched carefully as Spence and I left.

Out on the street, I could see that he'd filled out. In the years he'd been gone, he'd grown even taller and more solid through the chest. The unfocused teenager had become sharper, maybe even clever. But he still walked with that long, loping stride, his hands jammed in his coat pockets, and hunched against the cold.

It felt good, really good, just to be walking with my big pal. It made me feel grown-up, now that I was almost ten.

"What are you up to, Jimmy? I heard you been working for Arnold Rothstein. Not bad. Were you in on the Series fix?"

"I did my part. Carried messages back and forth. He told Mother Moon when to place bets so we made some side money too." Actually, she made a lot of money.

We went to Lindy's, A. R.'s new favorite deli, and had pastrami sandwiches and cheesecake. The waiter knew me, and so he treated us both with more abuse than usual, which was great. Spence was impressed. After we finished, I asked about the war.

He shook his head and said, "I can't tell you how bad it was. First they sent us down to South Carolina where it's hot as hell, and they made us march and train with machine guns, carrying all that goddamn equipment like mules. Then we go to France where the damn cooties give you scabies."

"Did you kill a bunch of krauts?"

"None that I know of. They had these high-pressure hoses that would spray burning gasoline across the trenches. I didn't get caught in any of them but saw guys who did. And the other gas, the mustard gas, that was worse. I've never seen so many men and animals slaughtered for nothing. I was about the shittiest soldier in the whole goddamn Army. That's why I kept getting busted, but," he brightened, "one good thing did happen."

"What's that?"

"I learned how to steal trucks."

"You did? That's great! I know a guy who'll take 'em off our hands if we can get good ones. Goddamn, let's do it! Right now."

Spence laughed and said, "Jimmy, you're a pip, you really are."

We paid and left. On the way to the Bronx, where traffic wasn't so clogged, Spence explained what we wanted to do. Ideally, we'd find a truck fully packed with valuables like cigarettes and tobacco, left idling while the driver chatted with a waitress in a café. We'd hop in and just drive away. Or we'd find trucks making deliveries. A lot of drivers were careless and left keys in the ignition. But, Spence said, Fords were easy enough to start without a key. All we really needed was a minute or so to jigger the ignition, and the balls to do it.

This was the first time I'd been out of Manhattan. We walked down a street of two-story houses and small stores, and passed several trucks before Spence settled on a green Brierley's Grocery delivery job. He said it was a half-ton Ford, and he'd worked on dozens of them. There were two guys in it, a driver and his assistant. We followed for a few blocks until they double-parked in front of a store.

Spence punched me on the arm and said this was it. The two guys opened the back, pulled out a hand truck, and loaded it with boxes. As soon as they were inside the store, Spence sauntered around to the passenger side, then slid over to the driver's seat. I stood by the open door, blocking Spence from the sidewalk. It seemed like he stayed under the steering wheel for an hour. Why was he taking so damn long? What the hell was he doing? Were there cops around? No, don't turn around, I told myself. Not now. No matter who's there, you'd never run out on Spence.

Then he was up, working the pedals and a lever as the engine coughed and caught. I jumped in. Spence signaled with his left hand, pulling smoothly away. I waited for someone to yell behind us, for loud orders to stop. But we drove on across the intersection and became part of the traffic. Several blocks later, I realized I had been holding my breath.

"Now, what do we do with this thing?" Spence asked.

"Go down to the Lower East Side."

We left the truck in a Ludlow Street lot and walked down Broome to Canal Street. The garage was on the corner, almost under the Williamsburg Bridge. The place looked to be closed but I could see lights through the worn areas of its black-painted windows and could hear the clatter of tools.

I rapped hard on the door and the noise stopped.

A guy opened up a little spy door to snarl, "Whaddayawant?"

"I need to talk to Mr. Lansky."

"Who's you?"

"Jimmy Quinn." The little spy door snapped shut.

Spence leaned over and whispered, "Who's Lansky?"

"Meyer Lansky. He works with Mr. Rothstein bootlegging booze. He also likes to work on cars. They say he can juice an engine and outrun anything the cops got."

"You and the goddamn Jews. I swear, Jimmy," he clapped me on the shoulder, "if I didn't know better, I'd think you was a hebe. But if you say Lansky is a right guy, that's good enough for me."

The door opened and a big man in dirty coveralls jerked his head for us to come in. There were about half a dozen cars in the place, most being worked on, and one being cleaned with a high-pressure hose. Lansky wore coveralls and wiped his hands with a rag. Three other guys in ties and shirtsleeves were playing cards at a desk, smoking cigars. I recognized Ben Siegel and Charlie Lucania. Siegel was a big teenager who looked at us suspiciously. Lucky seemed friendlier, with a pockmarked face that lit up when he smiled, and made you want to trust him. He used that smile a lot. The third guy was stocky, with a long weaselly face and weak eyes. He said, "Who's this fuckin' Mick kid?"

Lansky said, "It's OK, Vito. He's a runner for A. R. What's your business, kid?"

"My associate and I have come into possession of a half-ton

Ford truck, and we thought you might be interested in taking it off our hands."

"I might be," said Lansky. "How much are you asking for this vehicle?"

Spence said $300 and the card players busted out laughing. I elbowed my buddy in the side.

"Tell you what, Mr. Lansky. How about we bring it in and you give us whatever is fair. You tell us what other kinds of trucks—"

"And cars," Spence interrupted.

"Trucks and cars you might be in the market for, and we'll see what we can do." We settled on $50 for the grocery truck, but not until the guys playing cards had more laughs at our expense. "We've got a couple of real desperadoes here. . . . How many men did you have to kill to get this fucking thing? Did you have cops on your tail all the way from the Bronx?"

I could tell Spence was steamed, so I turned to Lansky for distraction.

"Tell us what you want. Name a car or truck that you can use and tell us what you'll pay for it."

The card players laughed even harder. Vito said, "Benny would look good in a Packard Twin Six. Hell, so would I."

I said, "We'll only steal one. How much?"

Lansky grinned a little, lit a cigarette, and said, "If you can get your hands on a Packard Twin Six, I'll give you a thousand." The card players laughed even harder. Spence said two thousand and we settled on twelve hundred.

Lansky had one of the other guys give us fifty bucks for the truck. By the time we left, the Brierley's Grocery lettering had been stripped off, with most of the green sides repainted shiny black.

The next day I told Mother Moon what Spence and I had done and gave her $15 out of my share of the truck money. I explained how we'd said we'd boost a Packard Twin Six but weren't sure how to go about it. Fords were everywhere but a Packard was a rich-man's car and a Twin Six was the top of the line. She pocketed the bills, fired up her pipe, and said, "The office where they sell 'em is up on Broadway at Sixty-First. Ought to find a few of them there."

That afternoon, we walked up to Columbus Circle, right across the street from a Packard dealership. Sure enough, they had the cars. We cased the joint for days without any luck or ideas for stealing such a fancy ride. Then Spence figured out a way.

We had to wait three days for the right guy in the right car. We saw some beautiful Twin Sixes but none of them were right for what Spence had in mind. That one showed up on Friday afternoon. It was about two years old and pretty dirty, with a dented rear fender where the spare tire was supposed to be. The spare was in the backseat. I pulled a big square of white cloth out of my pocket, folded it into a triangle, and tied two corners together. Spence put on his dark glasses, and we were off.

The guy with the dented Packard spent a half hour talking to a salesman, and was none too happy about what he heard. When he finally finished, he drove uptown on Broadway. We followed on the sidewalk until the car stopped at a light.

We approached the vehicle, the two of us being a tall guy in an overcoat and dark glasses carrying a kid in his arms. Spence said, "Sir, please can you help us, it's my son. If you could take us to a hospital."

I had my arm in a white sling and bawled like a baby.

"Get in." The man opened the rear door. Spence bundled me in the back next to the spare tire and hurried to the passenger seat, all the while muttering his thank-yous.

As the driver turned south, I pulled the pistol out of my sling and jammed the muzzle under his right ear.

Shrugging out of the overcoat, Spence said, "Pull over to the curb."

The car stopped and the shaken driver clambered out. Spence made his way around the gearshift to get behind the big wooden steering wheel. For a moment he looked confused, sweat beading his forehead as his hands lay helplessly beside the wheel. Then he grabbed the gearshift knob, shoving the lever toward the dash. The gears grated, and then the guy was back on the running board, grabbing at Spence.

He yelled that we couldn't steal his car in broad daylight and I reached over and smashed him in the nose with the butt of my Detective Special.

Spence got the car in gear and we lurched away from the curb into traffic. But that stubborn son of a bitch held on. I smashed at rigid fingers, and when he still wouldn't let go, I stuck the pistol in his face.

I had a fraction of a second to decide if I would pull the trigger on a man who'd done me no harm, and I think I'd actually cocked the pistol when he finally let go. At least, that's the way I remember it.

By then, Spence was pushing the car through traffic, swerving between lanes. I yelled out. "The hat! Put on the hat!"

Spence reached into his chauffeur's coat, and pulled out the matching cap we'd bought from Brill Brothers Uniforms. Maybe it was this obvious little disguise or maybe we'd gotten far enough away, but Spence was able to slow down, and then he looked like a real chauffeur driving an expensive car with a wealthy young brat in the back. We attracted no more attention, either from civilians or cops, as we zipped through Hell's Kitchen and into Chelsea. We stashed the Packard in an alley and called Lansky.

He knocked off $50 for the dented fender.

We busted our buttons that night, happy with the solid wad of bills in our pockets. Mother Moon had never been so glad to see me. She had a wonderful weekend with the pipe at the Sans Souci opium parlor.

But after the initial excitement had faded and I thought back on it, I realized that I was bothered by what we'd done. It was hard for me to figure, because the whole business of stealing cars was so exciting. But the man's frightened face came back to me too easily and too clearly, and I had to understand that I'd been ready to shoot him. But would I have pulled the trigger when it came to that? I couldn't say. It's one thing to steal a grocery truck or to fix the World Series or to bribe a cop who expects to be bribed, but it's another thing to shoot a guy because he has a car that you want.

I puzzled over that one for several years.

CHAPTER TEN

After Dr. Cloninger's ambulance took away the ex-Yale assholes, and Cameron and Flora had tottered upstairs, I tried to find Connie Nix. She wasn't in the kitchen or anywhere downstairs, so I figured it was best to leave her alone. It was well after midnight anyway. I returned to the library and Ethan Pennyweight's private reading room, where I got a clean glass and had a tot of brandy.

The ornate lamp cast a warm glow, and the chair sagged comfortably as I sat down to enjoy the drink. I could understand why even a rich guy like Spence's father-in-law would want this little secret place. As I was studying one of his French picture books, a small movement in the shadows distracted me. It sounded like the rats I remembered at Mother Moon's. I tilted the heavy glass lamp and the light revealed another part of the wall, a part that was made of sheet metal. I got up and gave it a tap. It made a hollow sound. A moment later I heard a vibration and then a grinding whir. I was looking at the outside of the dumbwaiter shaft that rose from the kitchen to the first floor and the family's rooms upstairs. We had a larger one like it at the speak, to move stuff from the basement.

I returned to the good brandy, sharp and smooth at the same time, and wondered if Connie Halloran had moved into the Chelsea yet. Probably. Should I call to find out? Probably not. Wait till tomorrow, during the day. Should I call my speak to find out if she was working that night? No, they'd be busy. No sense bothering anybody. But that was an excuse too. I was afraid if I called, I'd find that she wasn't there, and that Frenchy and Marie Therese didn't know where she was.

And then Connie Nix's face replaced Connie Halloran's, and I remembered how she stood so close to me in that same little room just a few hours earlier. I finished the brandy and went upstairs.

The doors to all the bedrooms were closed. Still, I could hear drunken laughter coming from Flora's room, and saw light under the door to Catherine Pennyweight's suite. I knocked. She told me to come in.

Baby Ethan was kicking around in his crib. Mrs. Pennyweight was in her chair with a cup of tea. She was watching the baby intently.

"You going to keep the kid up here or do you want me to move him to the library?" I said by way of hello.

"He'll stay with me tonight. Something's not agreeing with him. Flora and Cameron probably got him too excited this afternoon."

"OK, but you ought to know that I'm probably going to have to go back to the city soon. There are some things I need to take care of."

"Yes, I understand you had some unpleasantness with a policeman. It will be fine, I'm sure." She wasn't really paying any attention to me. She didn't care about anything but the kid.

As I left Mrs. Pennyweight's room, Cameron Rivers swung open Flora's door, and stood with one shoulder leaning on the frame. She wore a thin robe. The light reflected off the mirrored walls behind her was strong enough to reveal high, sharply pointed breasts, and a less focused pubic blur in the gap between her thighs. Her crooked leer was supposed to be sexy. Flora's laughter rang out, "Oh, Cammy, stop that. You are simply too wicked for words."

I tried not to smile as I walked toward the stairs. The woman blocked my way.

"You know, you were quite rude with Titus and Teddy. They were just having a little fun. We're trying to cheer up dear Flora now that her husband has so callously abandoned her. Don't you think a young woman like her needs friends to brighten her spirits?"

She leaned forward, fingered the edge of my lapel, and gave me a big-eyed look. Flora peeked around from behind her and giggled. I guess they thought I'd be embarrassed by standing so close to a half-naked woman as she caressed my chest. I returned the favor and gave her tit a friendly honk.

She squealed. Mrs. Pennyweight threw open her door and said sternly, "What's going on out here?"

Flora and Cameron laughed harder and jumped back into her room. Mrs. Pennyweight gave me an angry stare.

It was quiet for the rest of the night. The trouble started just before dawn.

In the library, I heard faint noises from upstairs. Some movement, doors opening, quick footsteps. The house had thick walls, so at first I didn't make anything of it, and then the sounds stopped. A minute or two later, a door slammed and I heard a woman's loud scream from upstairs. It was a young woman, either Flora or Cameron. I grabbed my stick and was out in the big room when Flora yelled, "He's gone! They've stolen little Ethan!"

She ran to the balcony railing and looked down, terrified and sobbing. "He's gone, he's gone. They've taken him!"

In that moment, I felt fear so pure and strong it cramped my stomach. Fuck, I'd failed. The goddamn bloody doll was for real. Spence had asked me to do this one thing, to protect his son, and I'd completely screwed it up, and there was nothing I'd ever be able to do to make it right. Ethan wasn't my kid but I was responsible, and right then, maybe I understood a little of the horror that the Lindberghs were going through. But for me, it only lasted for that short terrifying moment.

Before I could even move toward the stairs, Mrs. Pennyweight appeared at the far end of the room. She came up from the basement by the servants' stairs, moving fast, with something in her arms. I hoped like hell it was the kid and saw that it was.

She ignored her hysterical daughter and said sharply, "Quinn, come with me. This is an emergency," as she hurried past me to the front door.

We got outside as Oh Boy was swinging the big Duesenberg around a Pierce-Arrow that had been left out front. Oh Boy skidded to a stop, jumped out in his shirtsleeves, and flung open the back door. We piled in and were thrown back when he stomped on the gas.

She had the kid wrapped tightly in a blanket, so at first all I could see of him was a pale blue face, so blue it was scary. His eyes were closed and he was coughing or hiccupping and his breath was shallow.

"He's in distress," she said as she pulled the blanket away and twisted around to face me on the seat with the baby kicking on her lap. "This has happened before but never this seriously. Here, take these."

She unwrapped the blanket and gave me two corners to hold. Three crumpled empty boxes of the kid's special food fell to the floor. She turned Ethan over on his stomach and put her hands around his ribs. She squeezed and released then pulled his arms up and repeated the motions over and over again, as if she was forcing him to breathe evenly.

The big car skidded into a hard left turn when we got to the gate and Oh Boy gave it more gas and laid on the horn. A Model A truck appeared in the headlights, dead ahead of us. Oh Boy never flinched. He kept the Duesy steady right down the middle of the blacktop. The truck veered away and slid off the road.

When I looked through the back window, it was reversing onto the road and turning to follow us. More headlights appeared behind us and another car weaved on screeching tires around the Ford. It looked like both of them were trying to keep up with us.

The .38 in my coat pocket thumped against my leg. Everything was happening so fast that I didn't understand what was going on. Hell, right then all I felt was relief. The kid may have been sick but he hadn't been snatched. It didn't even occur to me to wonder where we were going.

Oh Boy swung into another hard left at a three-way intersection and we slid across the seat. Mrs. Pennyweight lost her rhythm with the breathing exercise and yelled, "Goddammit, Oliver, slow down! If you kill us, I'll fire you!"

He paid no attention. Oh Boy was like that. He may have been too much of a worrywart, but once he got set on a task, he stuck with it. He slowed to make another left-hand turn and then sped up again. Looking through the back window, I got the impression of a big metal gate and trees on both sides. A little later, the front of a building filled the windshield and Oh Boy slowed. He followed a curved drive around it to a narrow road.

We lurched to a stop and Mrs. Pennyweight was out the car before it had settled on its springs. She and Oh Boy ran to a set of double doors, where two nurses in white were waiting to take the kid. They all hustled inside.

I turned off the engine and pocketed the keys. A nurse came running out, grabbed the crumpled food boxes from the backseat, and ran back into the building. Moments later, I heard the sound of another car, and the Pierce-Arrow that I'd seen earlier slid around the corner to a stop. Flora and Cameron in nightclothes and long coats tumbled out of the car and ran into the building. I found my stick.

Inside was a kind of admitting room with a counter at the back and corridors on either side. It had the nasty alcohol-medicine smell of a hospital. There was nobody behind the counter. I heard voices down one of the corridors and followed them to a crowded white treatment room with bright lights and a bed, where Cloninger and the nurses buzzed over little Ethan.

I couldn't see him, of course, but through the babble I heard Mrs. Pennyweight say, "When you had him yesterday, did you feed him anything?"

Flora answered, her voice rising, "What are you talking about, he's my son. We only gave him some . . . and then you steal him right out from under me and frighten me nearly to death. Even *you* can't do that, Mother!"

Figuring that there was little chance anybody would try to kidnap the boy in that crowd, I wandered back outside and got my first good look at Cloninger's acorn academy in the early light. A massive, new-looking four-story building with narrow windows rose up on one side. It reminded me of the Tombs back in the city but not nearly as big. The grounds were as carefully tended as a golf course and I could see five or six smaller older redbrick buildings nearby. I couldn't tell what they were for. There was something cold and strange about the whole setup. It gave me the same creepy feeling I got when we first drove in through the dark woods. This was a place where bad things happened.

I was sitting in the Duesenberg when Oh Boy came out. He fumbled his makings from his shirt pocket, rolled a smoke, and explained.

Little Ethan had always been a sickly kid who sometimes couldn't keep his food down and had spells where he had trouble breathing. At least, he did until Cloninger put together a special diet that eliminated meats and butter and other stuff that everybody else ate. Cloninger actually went to Europe and brought the stuff back. They'd been testing various combinations for months to figure out what worked for the kid. At first, Oh Boy said, they thought that Mrs. Conway had got the days mixed up and little Ethan had his Saturday menu on Friday, or something. Or it may have been that he ate something he wasn't supposed to have when Flora was showing him off to Cameron Rivers.

That morning, as soon as Mrs. Pennyweight realized that he was having an attack of whatever it was, she called Cloninger. He said to get the kid right over and to bring the empty boxes from his dinner. She didn't even think to say anything to Flora. She just called Oh Boy for the car and took the kid down to the kitchen to fetch the boxes. That's about the time Flora checked her mother's rooms, saw that her son wasn't there, and started screaming. The thing that Mrs. Pennyweight had been doing in the car was a variation on the "Schaefer method" that Cloninger had taught her to use whenever things got really rough for the little booger.

Oh Boy was in the middle of explaining it all when Cloninger sidled up to us. Oh Boy shied away from him. "Our paths cross again, Mr. Quinn. Trouble seems to follow you. First, poor Mr. Evans, then the two unfortunate young men last night, and now this, not that you had anything to do with it. We have located the source of the youngster's problems."

"Yeah? And what was that?"

Cloninger didn't answer. Instead, he said, "Come, let me show you around my little establishment. There's something I want you to see."

Oh Boy took the opportunity to duck back into the Duesenberg. I went with Cloninger around to the other side of the big building, where a terrace faced the lake. On the other side of the water, a lot closer than I expected, was the Pennyweight house.

"You see," he said, "we're neighbors. It's a two-mile drive by car but only a hundred meters or so across the water. You need not worry. Most of our patients simply drink too much and we help them with that. Some have more serious problems, but this is not a place for 'homicidal maniacs' or anything else you might have seen in movies."

He pointed his cigarette at the other side of the terrace. "This way."

I've got to admit he was right about one thing. Everything I knew about loony bins came from the pictures. I imagined drooling people in straightjackets and padded cells, and I worried that somebody would find a way to lock me up in there and it scared the hell out of me. All I wanted to do was get away.

Cloninger went down a couple of steps to a path that led to more buildings in a grove of evergreen trees. When we got closer, I saw that one of them had a steeple. He said it had been a private chapel for the previous owners or something like that, I don't remember exactly. The important thing was the graveyard, anyway. He led the way past the older headstones to the newest and biggest, a polished slab flanked by two angry angels with swords in their hands. It read:

ETHAN PENNYWEIGHT
1861–1929

Beside it was a smaller simpler stone:

MANDELINA PENNYWEIGHT
1906–1931

Cloninger said, "Ethan was my benefactor, my partner, my friend, and finally my patient. He asked to be buried here. I know that your first loyalty is to your friend Walter. But you must understand that I have known the Pennyweight family for decades. I have seen to their medical needs for three generations, ever since I came to this country. I have no one left in Germany. They are my only family now and I will not allow them to be harmed in any way. I advise you to keep that in mind. But, of course, our interests are identical, are they not? And you and I are in agreement."

I shrugged. "I suppose so."

113

He smiled that thin, spooky smile. "Excellent. Let's go back. Catherine and Flora must be ready to leave."

As it turned out, we heard them before we saw them. Mrs. Pennyweight limped toward the car with the kid, who'd got his color back, while Flora followed beside her and screamed. Oh Boy held the car door open and watched helplessly.

"You're saying this is *my* fault?" Flora yelled. "Just because I gave him two maraschinos, maybe three." She stepped in front of her mother and screamed at her, "He loved them, he wanted more. I've never seen him like something so much and now you're acting like it's the end of the world."

For a time, Mrs. Pennyweight didn't react at all. For a time. Then she stared straight into her daughter's eyes and spoke slowly. "You were drunk. I know you haven't been as involved with Ethan's diet as Mrs. Conway and I, but there's no excuse for this. Don't you understand? Those cherries are preserved in alcohol. Alcohol! You might as well have given him strychnine. You could have killed him, you stupid, stupid girl."

"That's ridiculous. Nobody cares about me. Nobody cares that I'm miserable. I'm not *just* a mother, I'm still me. . . ."

Her friend Cameron stood to one side and didn't try to hide her bright enjoyment, until she saw that I'd noticed it. Then she looked concerned.

Flora went on, "First everyone was so sorry for poor Mandelina—"

Her mother slapped her cheek with a hard backhand, then got right up in her face. "Don't say that. Don't *ever* say that."

The slap brought tears to Flora's eyes and she reacted by shoving her mother angrily. The older woman's bad leg gave out on her and she fell, twisting to keep the boy from hitting the ground. He started bawling anyway. Flora didn't care. Ignoring her son, she stood over her mother and screamed, "I'm nothing but a goddamned brood mare for you! Once I'd provided the male heir, nobody wants me around anymore. Well, to hell with you, to hell with him, to hell with all of you."

She stalked back to the Pierce-Arrow. Cameron Rivers hurried after her and they drove away. Cloninger helped Mrs. Pennyweight to her feet and got her and little Ethan into the backseat of the Duesenberg. She brushed herself off and acted like absolutely nothing had happened. I sat up front with Oh Boy and figured the mother and daughter wouldn't have gotten so mad at each other if there weren't a lot of truth to what they'd said.

Mrs. Pennyweight and the male heir got out at the house. I rode with Oh Boy back to the garage. Like the main house, it was a tall building made of dark timbers and whitewashed walls. The place had been built as a carriage house. Stalls lined one wall, and you could still smell horses. But a concrete floor had been laid down, and riding gear had been replaced by car stuff. Dietz was bent over a motorcycle with a homemade sidecar that looked like it was meant for hauling tools. It was little more than a stout wooden box bolted to the bike with a big wheel on one side. The groundskeeper sat on a short three-legged stool, his .22 rifle against a wall, close at hand.

Oh Boy stopped in the back, right next to a sweet little green Ford coupe. There was virtually no mileage on the odometer and the interior was spotless. If I came into that garage to steal a car, I'd take the Ford over the Duesy any day. It was quicker, newer, and a hell of a lot easier to park.

Dietz was absorbed in cleaning a machine part from the motorcycle in a small can of gasoline. Smoke curled up from the briar clamped between his choppers. Without looking up, he said, "How's little Ethan? We hear you had to take him to the sawbones."

Oh Boy said he was OK and explained about Flora and the maraschino cherries. Dietz chuckled, set the can of gasoline on a shelf, and stood up. "Our Flora, she's a pip, she is." He tucked the rifle into the crook of his arm. "Let's have breakfast. Mrs. Conway should have the coffee ready by now."

He was right. In the kitchen, Connie Nix was fixing a tray with plates, silverware, and a flower. She shot me a quick look before turning away. Mears sat at his usual place at the end of the table nursing a large bowl of oatmeal, with a bottle of aquavit standing beside his coffee. Mrs. Conway's radio was turned low.

She poured two mugs and said, "Dietz, wash your hands. You stink of gasoline." He shuffled off obediently to sink and soap.

She put a mug on the table in front of me. "Mrs. Pennyweight said that little Ethan is going to be fine. I can't imagine what Flora was thinking when she gave him . . ." She shook her head and stopped before she said something she shouldn't in front of me. So she changed the topic.

"Before the commotion this morning, I understand we had more visitors last night. What happened in the ballroom?"

Dietz answered, "Those two overeducated bruisers Teddy Banks and Titus Bullard showed up again, and the woman, what's-her-name, she stayed the night."

My first sip of coffee was great. The thick-bodied brindle cat appeared from nowhere and pressed against my leg, still staring seriously at the space beneath the stove. When I scratched its neck, it bit me again.

The cook shook her head. "It's not right for a married woman with a child to behave in such a manner, not with trash like them."

Dietz sat down next to me. "Banks and Bullard are at Dr. Cloninger's place. They required medical attention after they tangled with our gunman here."

Connie Nix spoke up. "They ganged up on him. I think Mrs. Spencer and Miss Rivers knew it was going to happen."

So she'd been watching.

"It wasn't that serious. Sorry about the mess, it couldn't be helped. Mrs. Conway, is that salami on the counter? Could you slice a bit into my eggs?" Anything to get them off of the topic of the assholes.

"Salami and eggs? What in the world? . . ."

"Breakfast of champions."

Dietz said, "That sounds interesting. I'll try 'em, too." Minutes later, he was wolfing down a plate. Oh Boy had toast and jelly.

As we ate, the guy with the British accent, the same guy I'd heard on the radio that first night, started talking about the Lindbergh case. Mrs. Conway quickly turned up the volume.

". . . and as we told you, police still deny any contact with the kidnappers. But many within the official investigation suggest otherwise."

All activity in the kitchen came to a standstill. The men stopped eating, the women stopped working. All five of us focused on the news, curious about the Lindberghs. I realized the same thing was happening all over America—hell, all over the world. Everybody's attention was on this one crime, this one small child, and it was something that had happened just down the road to two people who were as scared as I had been.

After we'd finished, I was still jazzed up so I walked with Oh Boy back to the garage. He asked what had happened in the ballroom.

"The two college men showed up, Titus and Teddy. You know 'em?"

He nodded.

"Sometime back, we threw 'em out of my place. They're still pissed off, and they got a little rowdy. What's the story with those two anyway? The big one, Titus, said that he was a friend of Chink Sherman."

Oh Boy shook his head, looking uncomfortable. "I don't know nothing about that. I think they was at Spence's wedding, that's all. But since they got kicked out of Yale, something about gambling, we hadn't seen 'em much. It ain't right that Titus came here now, what with Walter being gone and everything."

"You mean he's sniffing around Flora." Like Deputy Parker.

"It's good you taught him a lesson. Walter'll be pleased."

I wondered if Oh Boy was right. Maybe Spence really wanted me to keep his wife in line, and not look after his son. "What the hell's going on, Oh Boy? Two nights in a row, guys showed up and tried to poke me in the nose and somebody acts like they're trying to take the kid. And there's something else I gotta ask you. I've seen and heard a couple of cars, or maybe a car and a truck, both circling the house at night. I think you ran one of them off the road this morning. And late the other night, I swear I saw somebody watching the house from the woods near the lake."

He shrugged, unconcerned. "I dunno, I hadn't seen nothing like that."

"OK, what's the story with Connie Nix?"

"She's a pip, isn't she, but kind of cold, too. She can remind you of Fanny Moon, huh? You know . . . serious. Sometimes she won't give a fella the time of day but at other times she'll be OK, even pretty nice."

"How long has she been working here?"

"Let's see . . ." Oh Boy scratched his head. "They hired her right before little Ethan was born. That would make it about a year, I guess."

We reached the garage and he invited me in to see his place, up a flight of stairs at the back. Oh Boy went ahead while I took the steps more slowly. He was holding open a door by the time I got to the top. "Isn't this swell? Look."

He had a pine-paneled room with a sofa, a hooked rug, three lamps, a table, a fireplace, and a kitchen area with a hot plate, sink, and icebox. One corner was his bedroom with a mirror and a wardrobe where his clothes were heaped, and a bathroom with a high-backed tub. Oh Boy showed off his empire proudly, his chest puffed out like it was a suite at the Ritz. "Hot and cold running water and everything. I got it lots better than the house staff. I told Spence I couldn't stay in one of those little attic rooms on the third floor, no sirree. Hotter'n hell in the summer, then you freeze your ass off in the winter. Hell, Dietz and me got a place around back, with a grill where we cook steaks and drink beer whenever we feel like it."

"He lives here too?"

"Downstairs. He had a groundskeeper's house out in the woods, but in the cold weather he stays here. I tell you this is a great place, Jimmy. I hope you decide to stay. Oh boy, wouldn't it be great to have you with me and Spence again. I mean, after all the stuff we done together, did you ever think we'd wind up in a swell joint like this?"

CHAPTER ELEVEN

1923
NEW YORK

Oh Boy took over the day-to-day running of the shooting gallery. Spence and I stole cars. We used Mother Moon's connections with the police to figure out which neighborhoods were safe and worked out payoffs with beat cops, desk sergeants, and party bosses. They told us which cars were good for us to take. I assumed that the owners had done something to piss them off, but I never really knew.

As Lansky and Lucania's booze business prospered, they accepted every car and truck Spence and I could provide. Things changed in the fall of 1923. We'd just brought in another Ford half-ton and found Lansky, Siegel, and Lucania looking grim in the garage. Charlie brightened when he saw us. "Jimmy, Walter, you come at the right time. Meyer, what do you think, should we let them in on this deal?"

That was Charlie Lucky, always trying to charm you.

Meyer said, "No need for the soft soap. This is the situation, boys.

We know that two trucks full of scotch will be leaving Atlantic City late tonight heading for Philly. We're going to take them."

Lucky muttered, "We gotta."

Lansky glared at him. "Yeah, because of Mr. Bigshot here, we're low on cash and product."

I knew what he was talking about. Charlie was in hot water with a lot of people, including the high-society golf buddies he'd been hanging out with. Since he became one of the city's better-known bootleggers, he was a popular guy for the muckety-mucks to be seen with. But he was also one of the city's better-known dope dealers, and the cops had caught him with a dozen packs of heroin. To keep his ass out of jail, Charlie made a deal. He told them where Chink Sherman's stash was hidden, in a closet in a Mulberry Street basement. This turned into a double good move. The cops let him go while he screwed his biggest competitor. But when word got out about the double-cross, he had to buy two hundred ringside tickets at top dollar for the Dempsey-Firpo fight, and he passed them out to anybody who could help rebuild his reputation.

"Hey, you agreed we had to do it," he protested now, unembarrassed, still smiling. "And those tickets worked, didn't they?"

"Yeah, they did, and now Charlie's so popular that both Masseria and Maranzano want him."

Joe "The Boss" Masseria, the guy I'd seen dodging bullets years before, and Salvatore Maranzano both wanted to be the boss of all the Italians in New York. They'd been fighting each other for years and both of them wanted Charlie and his booze business as part of their operation. He had held them off so far, but they wouldn't wait any longer.

"So now he's got both goddamn old bastards mad at us," Lansky complained, "and it's no coincidence that three of our liquor shipments were hijacked in New Jersey."

"Four," said Charlie.

"Four shipments of scotch," Lansky repeated. "And two of our warehouses were raided by the goddamn feds. We need more whiskey right away."

"And we know where to get it. It's coming in to Atlantic City tonight."

They were like an old married couple, finishing each other's sentences. Lansky said they already paid two thousand dollars for the route that two trucks would take to Philadelphia, where the booze would be cut. He and Charlie meant to knock over the shipment before it got there.

Spence piped up, "I know Philly."

Lansky looked doubtful. "You know the best roads, both to Atlantic City and to Philadelphia?"

Spence said he did. So Lansky handed over a hand-drawn map that showed an unnamed road that ran between Washington Avenue and Cape May Avenue, on the way to Egg Harbor City.

He gave me a notepad, the first one I ever had, actually, and said, "Drive down there. Write down the landmarks and turns, and find a good place where we can stop the trucks. We'll be taking three cars, and we have to drive the trucks back here. I don't want anybody getting lost."

Lansky gave Spence the keys to a Dodge roadster. We took the Weehawken Ferry into Jersey and he made two wrong turns right away. As Spence got us straightened out, I figured what he was up to and said, "You don't know how to get to Atlantic City."

"Sure I do," Spence said. "You go south. There's signs everywhere. We'll figure it out. You just write it down and we'll be fine." That was Spence for you, never more confident than when he didn't know a damn thing about what he was doing. At least, that's the way he was then.

As it turned out, he was right . . . well, right enough, anyway. There were signs to Atlantic City, but everything changed once we were past Newark. It was the first time I had crossed the Hudson River. The air was hot, still, and dusty, and it looked to me like all of New Jersey was flat and empty. We drove through little towns—West Keyport, Wickatunk Station, Tuckerton—with mostly empty fields between them. I couldn't imagine what people did there. I wrote down careful directions, remembering that we'd be driving back at night, assuming Lansky invited us along. "Go around horse fountain in middle of town square and straight," I noted. And then, "Turn hard left 1/4 mile past New Gretna church."

Not counting all the wrong turns and time spent backtracking, it took us almost four hours, mostly on unpaved roads, to find the road on Lansky's map. It was marked with a hand-painted wooden sign that read EGG HARBOR CITY—3 MILES, and it wasn't much more than two rutted tracks through a sandy pine forest, so narrow that when two cars approached each other, you had to slow down and pull to the right.

We drove it all the way, then I told Spence to turn around and go back the way we'd just come. That pissed him off. "The hell you say. It's hot, we've seen what Lansky wanted us to see. It'll add another goddamn hour to the trip back."

"Look, we need to find exactly the right spot. I think I saw it, but we've got to be sure and we've got to mark it. We can't screw this up, Spence, it could be our big break."

He grumbled, but he knew I was right and turned the Dodge around.

Five hours later, with wheels still turning in our heads, we made it back to Lansky's garage. Lucky and Siegel were still there, with a bunch of other guys I didn't know at the time. One was the flaming needledick Vincent Coll, and another was his watery-shit friend, Sammy Spats Spatola. Coll was a redhead and Spatola had greasy black hair. Except for that, they could've been brothers, both tall, lanky, and rough-featured.

I don't remember exactly how it happened but as we were walking past them, I bumped into Spatola and he said something like, "Watch where you're going, shorty," and slapped my hat off. Instead of ignoring him, or telling him to fuck off like I should've done, I got mad and belted him in the kisser with my knucks. He fell flat on his ass, and I was about to split his head open when Coll laid into me. Then Spence waded in and went off on Coll and we all mixed it up until Siegel and Lansky broke things up. They didn't want anybody fighting there with a big deal in the works. When we finally shook hands as Lansky demanded, we knew it didn't mean a damn thing.

Lansky told me to show him what we'd found. I opened the notebook and explained how the road turned at this one place. "They won't be able to see us, and it won't be hard to make them stop."

Lansky thought it over for a second and said, "Do you want to be in on this?"

Spence and I said yes together.

"We could use another gun. Know anybody who'd like to earn half a yard?"

"How about Oh Boy? He knows how to shoot. He'll be scared but he won't run."

"All right. Be here at nine tonight. Bring masks."

"You got pieces or should we bring our own?"

"We got guns."

That night, Spence took a short-barreled pump, and I gave Oh Boy a sawed-off double-barreled like the one he carried at the shooting gallery. He was sweating when he took it. I said, "Don't worry. This'll be easy."

Oh Boy didn't believe me for a second.

Around ten o'clock, Lansky said to Siegel, "OK, these guys"—he jerked a thumb toward Spence and me—"know where we're going. Stay close but not so close that any cops should think we're together. Don't speed. Don't give them any reason to look at us."

We loaded guns, bats, clubs, and flashlights into the trunks of our cars and left. I remember how I could hardly contain my excitement during that second drive through Jersey. This was the greatest thing I'd ever done. At least, I hoped it would be. I was thrilled to be in on it and scared that I'd screw up.

It took three hours, with no wrong turns this time, to get to the place I'd marked with two branches that I'd leaned against the base of a tree in an X shape.

The autumn night was windy, thick with the smell of pine. There was some nervous laughter when we got out of the cars, and several guys went straight into the woods to piss, loud and long.

Lansky handed me a flashlight and said, "OK, kid, show me."

I shined the light on the dogleg turn in front of us, where the sandy road curved around a briar thicket.

"They'll be coming the other way and they've got to slow down for this. If we cut down a tree or a big branch and put it across the road, they'll stop to move it. They won't try to drive around it."

Lansky nodded. "Yeah, that's smart. But pull off more of these little branches and put them in the road on the other side of the curve, like they got blown down by the wind. Then they won't think it's a trap."

He pulled out a pocket watch and said, "We've got time, but be fast anyway."

I got sticky sap all over my hands pulling the boughs off and I was still trying to rub it off an hour later. Oh Boy, Spence, and I stayed beside the Dodge on one side of the road. One of the touring cars, the one with Coll and Spatola, was parked on the other side, angled toward the dogleg. Lansky's car stood in the middle of the road, pointed at the curve. Oh Boy was shivering, he was that scared. So was I, truth be told. Spence's hands were steady as he lit a tailor-made cigarette.

Oh Boy said, "I guess you saw worse stuff in the war."

"Yeah." Spence spit a fleck of tobacco off his tongue. "You know, it's funny, but the reason I met you guys is because I thought it'd help me over there to know how to shoot a pistol. Well, that was wrong. You can be the best shot in the world and it won't do you a damn bit of good when they're shooting cannon shells and mustard gas at you. Compared to that, this'll be easy as pie."

Oh Boy muttered, "Oh boy, oh boy, oh boy." Then we saw a flicker of headlights from the oncoming trucks and heard the groaning engines.

I said to Oh Boy, "Just stay here. When the shooting starts, point the gun up and pull the trigger."

He nodded, still shivering.

The sound of approaching engines became louder, with the lights brightening behind the briars as the trucks entered the turn. Lansky had ordered everyone to stay still until he hit his lights and fired the first shot. Spence tapped me on the arm and said, "Put on your mask."

I hurriedly pulled the bandana over my nose and it stuck to my sweaty skin. I tried to force my breathing and heartbeat to normal and ordered myself not to act too fast. Make every movement smooth. See what you're shooting at. Don't hurry, don't hesitate.

Then we saw the first truck, a dark mass behind the headlights, as it rounded the turn and stopped. The lights of the second truck were behind it.

Lansky waited until the second vehicle came into view and skidded on the sand, nearly rear-ending the first as it stopped. The driver and his guard jumped out. Then somebody yelled, and fired a shot, and started running. It sounded like Siegel. Lansky hit his car's lights, and everything went crazy.

It was too dark to see where to shoot. I rested the pistol on the hood of our Dodge, trying to find something to aim at. I got a moving figure in my sights, fired, and missed. To my left, I could hear the sharp crack of pistols and the deeper boom of shotguns, and I caught muzzle flashes in the corner of my eye. I sensed movement close by and realized that Spence was running across the road where the other guys were. Without thinking about what I was doing, I edged around to the front of the Dodge and stepped forward slowly. I wanted to run but knew that was wrong. I couldn't run and shoot with any accuracy. I held my pistol in both hands as I watched guys fighting by the glare of headlights.

Clubs and bats were swinging, with men from the trucks on the ground as three others ran from the back. They had shotguns and clubs. A man in a derby raised his club, and I shot him in the chest. He crumpled to the ground. Still without thinking, I shot the guy behind him.

But he did not fall. Even as his white shirt turned red, he aimed his pistol at me. A full load of buckshot knocked him off his feet. He disappeared in the harsh light and shadows. Then Oh Boy stood by my right shoulder, and Siegel was showing why they called him Bugsy, going bat-shit crazy with fists and a short club.

As we got closer, the scene became clearer. There were half a dozen guys on the ground, some sprawled, others kneeling. Men still standing all wore masks. Except for Oh Boy. I grabbed his bandana and pulled it over his face. But he pushed it down and turned away to heave.

We were on the road when I sensed something beside me and turned to see Spats Spatola leveling a nickel-plated automatic at my face, and in the same moment, Spence jumped between us and smashed the butt of his shotgun into Spatola's jaw. The greasy-headed bastard went down like a tenpin. Spence turned and sprinted toward the trucks.

By then, things began to settle down. Lansky made sure everyone on our side was accounted for. None of our guys was seriously hurt, but two of the others were dead or dying and the rest were bleeding. I couldn't tell if the fellow in the derby I had shot was dead. There weren't any derbies on the ground. I probably should've been more upset than I was.

Spence climbed into the cab of the closest truck and yelled, "This one's ready to go!" He started the engine and was the first one to leave. Oh Boy and I followed in the Dodge.

We rode in silence for a long time as the adrenaline rush settled down. I savored the night, the wild wind blowing in through the open windows, the feel of the car on the road. I'd wanted to drive it ever since we saw it in Lansky's garage.

Oh Boy said, "This was bad, Jimmy. I feel sick."

"What're you talking about?"

"I didn't do what you said. After Spence ran off, I followed you. When you shot that guy, I shot the guy behind him. I didn't mean to do it, I swear, but I did. I think I'm gonna puke again."

"You're not gonna puke. Spence was looking out for us. I think he figured that Coll and Spatola would maybe shoot the wrong guys in the dark, he made sure they didn't hit us. I owe him one, and I guess I owe you, too. Thanks, man."

In the dim light, I could see Oh Boy smiling weakly as he sat up a little straighter.

After that night, things changed. Lansky and Lucania knew they could trust us. Spence and I started delivering booze to speaks and parties, and we made pickups from the boats from time to time. Then when they partnered up with Longy Zwillman, we worked for him, too. In the years that followed, we all made a lot of money.

CHAPTER TWELVE

I was yawning when I left Oh Boy's apartment over the garage and walked back to the house. I met Dietz on the way.

The fat man struck a kitchen match with a grimy thumbnail and fired up his briar. Squinting up at the slate-gray sky, he said, "Bad weather on the way, gunman. Best fasten the shutters and lock the windows. You never know what these spring storms will bring."

I smelled the damp air and picked up something different, something that might have been snow but not the kind we got in the city. Everything smelled different here, looked different too, and sounded different in the cold gray wilderness. Why the hell anybody would want to live there when he could live in the city was a mystery to me.

"You're probably right, groundskeeper." I turned up the collar of my overcoat and went back to my room. After the set-to with the Yale assholes and little Ethan's emergency, sleep came fast, and it took a long shower that afternoon to wake me up.

I turned on the radio as I dressed but there was no further news of the kidnapping. After I put on my charcoal double-breasted, I checked the load in the Detective Special and saw that it needed cleaning. Before leaving the room, I gathered my knucks, notepad and pen, and my indoor stick. From the balcony I could see that Flora's bedroom door was open, and clothes were strewn everywhere. It looked like she and Cameron Rivers had departed for another evening of high spirits. No surprise. After the scene at Dr. Cloninger's, she'd probably do just about anything to get away from her mother.

Downstairs in the kitchen, Mrs. Conway and Connie Nix were working on dinner, a ham by the wonderful smell of it. The cook said I could have leftover mutton for my sandwich, or the ham if I wanted to wait. I asked for the mutton, with permission to get into the ham later. Newspapers were scattered about on the big table. I found the first section of the *Times*. The headlines proclaimed:

NO TRACE OF LINDBERGH KIDNAPPERS;

300 QUESTIONED, SERVANTS EXONERATED;

PARENTS BY RADIO ASK RETURN OF BOY

Kidnappers of Lindbergh Baby an Organized Gang

Mrs. Conway gestured at the paper. "You see, it says professional kidnappers."

"Maybe so." I shrugged. "But like I said, none of the guys I know would've done it."

"And how can you be so sure of that?"

"Because last summer a redheaded son of a bitch, pardon my language, killed a kid by accident. His name was Vincent Coll, and the whole city went nuts."

The cook's eyes widened. "The Mad Dog?"

"And you know what happened to him."

She nodded, silenced for the moment.

"Some guys are crazy," I said. "They enjoy hurting people. Guys like Vincent Coll and his pal Sammy Spatola, they'd rather beat up a guy and take his money than just take his money. I try to stay away from people like that.

"Now, the guys I used to work with, Meyer Lansky and his mob, they're nothing like Coll and Spatola. They'll hurt anybody who gets in their way but they're in the business of making money. There's a lot to be made in liquor, even more in drugs. But that's a different game, and the cops take it seriously. For me, the risk isn't worth the profits. I stick with booze."

Connie Nix nodded. "My dad grows grapes. But instead of making wine, he turns it into something called Vine-Glo. People use it to make their own wine at home. He says the stuff's terrible. But it's legal and it's selling like crazy."

I was intrigued.

After dinner, I went down to the gun room and took some target practice with the Detective Special. It had been a while since I'd fired one of the things, but the weeks and months of practice in Mother Moon's basement came back. I could still aim it comfortably with either hand and put the rounds close to the center of the target. When I'd finished, I cleaned the pistol and the Winchester that Connie Nix had used the night before.

Upstairs in the library, I called the Chelsea Hotel and learned from the deskman said that Connie Halloran had moved into my room. But she wasn't there, so I called the speak. Frenchy reported that Connie had been there, and she'd talked to Marie Therese for a long time before she left. But it was a busy Friday night and he didn't really have time to talk. I poured some of Spence's rye and wondered where the hell she was and why she wasn't at work.

Still, there was nothing to be done about it, so I went back to the kidnapping news in the papers. A rumrunner had told a guy at a Coast Guard station that he'd heard a baby cry on a dirty white boat with a green stripe. The bishop of New York wanted all churches to have special prayers for the missing Lindbergh boy. So did the president of the school board, and the Companions of the Forest of America. The Changchow Merchants' Guild in Peiping sent a message about all China being shocked. Mrs. Hoover personally ordered a sailor ashore from her yacht to get the latest word about the kidnapping.

When I'd finished with the papers, I'd written *boatswain, gleanings, dissemination,* and *wainscoting* in my notepad. I looked them up in the big dictionary and found that I'd been right about *gleanings* and *dissemination,* sort of right about *boatswain,* and I still wasn't sure about *wainscoting.*

I was at the dictionary when Catherine Pennyweight came into the library, followed by Connie Nix carrying the woman's grandson, who had half his little fist crammed into his mouth. He seemed to be completely recovered from whatever had upset his stomach that morning.

"Still working on your vocabulary, Mr. Quinn?" Her tone was light, not mocking.

"Just killing time until the next belligerent drunk shows up. Join me in a drink?"

"That's why I'm here. You'll find the good scotch on the bottom shelf."

Connie Nix put down the boy, cute as a little bug. He burped and crawled across the carpet toward the fireplace. Folding her legs, she sat on the carpet in front of him to block the way, careful about his well-being. Outside, the wind had kicked up, thudding heavily against the house.

"Miss Nix, what'll you have?" I asked.

"Nix is on duty," said Mrs. Pennyweight.

I ignored her. "You look like a rye and ginger girl, and it's my business to know."

I mixed the drinks, enjoying Mrs. Pennyweight's irritation. I gave her three fingers of the good scotch from the bottom shelf, mixed a weak ginger ale and rye over cracked ice, and poured another rye for myself.

"We shouldn't have any visitors tonight," Mrs. Pennyweight said as she took her drink. "Has my daughter come back?"

"Haven't seen her," I said.

"That girl." Catherine Pennyweight drank, scowling. "Motherhood changes some women. I thought it would change her. Cameron Rivers is a bad influence. Always was."

She acted like the big blow-up hadn't happened at all, but I couldn't help but wonder about the timing. As soon as Spence left, Cameron Rivers and the assholes showed up. It might have been a coincidence, or maybe Flora invited them.

"How's the boy?"

"Right as rain. Once again, Ernst has worked a miracle. Now," she said, "there's something I've got to ask you."

"OK."

"I know you've been very close to Walter, and I know that before he married my daughter he asked you to work for him at Pennyweight Petroleum."

I nodded, not liking where this was going.

"You turned him down. Actually, you never answered him at all. I'm sure he was hurt. Will you tell me why?"

Why? Hell of a question. "How much do you know about what Spence and I used to do?"

Firelight softened the woman's features as she smiled, and I could see how beautiful she'd once been. And how much her daughters resembled their mother.

"I'm sure Walter wouldn't have told me anything that was too incriminating. I know you stole cars and trucks, and transported liquor from rum row. And that you worked with Longy Zwillman, a charming man. I know him socially."

"Yes, he is, I suppose. He reads books and goes to the opera. I've also seen him beat a man nearly to death with his fists."

She was neither shocked nor impressed. "Did this man deserve it?"

"He tried to steal from us. He knew what would happen if Longy found out, and Longy found out. Spence and I got to know him through a couple of New York guys in the same racket, Meyer Lansky and Charlie Luciano."

Connie Nix asked, "Are they gangsters?"

"Yeah, but not like Al Capone, getting his name in the papers all the time,dressing wild and flashy, or actors in movies, shooting it out with the cops, Charlie and Meyer ain't . . . aren't like that. Charlie has a taste for the limelight, but not Meyer and he's the real boss. They learned from Arnold Rothstein. So did I. Our business is selling booze.

We don't shoot cops, we make deals with them whenever we can. Hell, pardon my language, but when we delivered booze for Longy, we had a police escort. There's been times when things got a little out of hand, and people spent some time in jail. But that didn't happen very often. It's not profitable and not good for business."

The Egg Harbor knockover had changed things. Soon after it, Charlie Lucky became a real man about town and moved into the Waldorf Towers. I started delivering bribes and payoffs for him and Lansky as the work with Rothstein tailed off. A. R. abandoned booze for the heroin and morphine business, which he worked with Chink Sherman.

And after that, I was only with Rothstein for two or three of his famous marathon poker games, and he lost both times, mumbling that the bastards would just have to wait until he was goddamn ready to pay. By then, I was old enough to know how these things worked and understood that A. R. was breaking the rules. But he was still Rothstein, "The Brain," and he was treated with respect. The guys at Lansky's garage said he was stretched too thin. Two of his men had been arrested with a big shipment of heroin, and he had to make bail. Nobody had ever seen A. R. like that.

"Something else you need to understand is that before I was hurt," I explained, holding up my cane, "I was the best runner in the city—or courier, if you want to make it sound more legit. I delivered more money and private messages than anyone else. I was never caught or ambushed. Guys chased me, sure. They hit me and shot at me, but they never stopped me or stole my stuff."

I felt good in that warm library with two women listening as I bragged on myself. I realized I'd better not like it too much or I'd say something I shouldn't.

Working for Meyer and then Longy meant that Spence and I went everywhere, from Long Island to New Jersey, with fine-looking women flocking to us, two successful young gents in sharp suits. We brought them alcohol and we carried guns. OK, the truth is the women flocked to Spence, but he made sure some flocked my way. Spence also gave me rubbers and explained how to use them. "The one good thing I learned overseas," he said. "There's all kinds of nasty bugs out there. You'd think these society girls wouldn't have anything to do with it but they do."

But I figured Mrs. Pennyweight and Connie Nix didn't need to know about that part, so I didn't mention it.

Mrs. Pennyweight looked amused. "So you and Walter worked for Mr. Rothstein and Mr. Meyer and Mr. . . . Luciano. Did you do well?"

"Can't complain. But I worked so hard and I got so tired that I didn't get to spend much of what I earned."

Actually, I still turned over most of everything to Mother Moon. She gave me back what she thought I needed and moved me and Oh Boy into one of the big rooms. She and Fanny also bought us good suits and work clothes from Brooks Brothers and other classy places.

Mrs. Pennyweight said, "Yes, Walter told us much the same. He thought his horizons were too limited and that Prohibition was sure to end. I ask you again, why didn't you take him up on his offer to work for Pennyweight Petroleum?"

I thought for a moment and told half the truth. "I probably should have, but I just couldn't imagine leaving the neighborhood where I grew up. It was the only world I knew. Walter had been to France. He wasn't afraid to go anywhere. When he and I came here that afternoon, he found something he wanted more than what we were doing."

"And you felt what . . . betrayed?" Her smile was mocking.

"I guess I did. I was still a kid then."

"Is that all? You were miffed at your old friend and so you turned down a good position?"

How to explain? I poured another drink, knowing it was probably not the right thing to do, and finally said, "I've never told anyone about this, because it's not a good story. I guess it goes back to Arnold Rothstein.

"It was the first Sunday in November, three years ago, in 1928. Around ten, ten thirty that night, I went to Lindy's deli where A. R. conducted his business. He was at his booth in the back, shuffling through a stack of papers and notes. That was the way he worked. He told me to go to the Drake apartment building on Fifty-Sixth. Back then it was a new place. I knew where it was but I'd never been there. A. R. wrote a note, folded it once, and told me to take it to Stanislaw, the doorman. I had to make sure it wasn't Edward the doorman. Stanislaw would give me something to bring back. As I was leaving, he told me that he might have to go out later. If he wasn't there when I got back, I should hang on to whatever I got from Stanislaw and give it to him the next day."

That kind of thing had happened before, lots of times.

"So off I went, a couple of long blocks east and few blocks north. Stanislaw was on duty. I gave him the note from A. R. He said wait a minute, went inside to his little office, and came back with a sealed envelope. I put it in my inside coat pocket, and went back on Fifty-Sixth the way I came. As I was coming up to Seventh, what did I see but A. R. crossing the street, and going into the service entrance of the Park Central Hotel. I was too far away for him to see me, and anyway, you didn't yell in the street to Mr. Rothstein. Actually, you didn't yell at Mr. Rothstein anywhere. I figured that maybe he knew I'd be coming this way and he'd been waiting for me. I know that doesn't make a lot of sense now, but at the time it did."

I didn't tell them that this was the same hotel where I listened while Rothstein predicted Prohibition to Meyer Lansky.

"Later I heard that A. R. was at Lindy's when he got a call and told the guys there he was going to the Park Central. He sent his car away and told his bodyguard he wouldn't need protection. Nobody knows why he did that. It doesn't make any sense. And then he walked to the Park Central by himself.

"I went through the service door and took the back stairs. I figured I'd just take a look, see if he was around, maybe in a card game. He was known to play there. I went down the hall on the second floor. Nothing. I went up one more flight and I was in the stairwell when I heard men's voices arguing, and then a shot, a pistol shot close to where I was standing. I pulled open the door just far enough to see another door open slowly, two guys sticking their heads out to check if anybody was around. A second later a third man came out, and they all started down the hall toward me. I ran like hell."

The first two were Vinnie Coll and Sammy Spats Spatola. I didn't know the third guy by name but I'd seen him playing cards with A. R. and knew he held A. R.'s markers.

I charged down the stairs, hanging on to the metal handrail as I ran. I might have heard footsteps behind me or I might have imagined them. I was never sure about that part. Seconds later, I was back out on Fifty-Sixth Street. Without breaking stride, I turned left and then right, heading downhill on Seventh Avenue.

Later, I'd tell myself that I wasn't running because I was scared. I was getting out because I knew I wasn't supposed to be there. I had no idea if A. R. had been shot. I'd been told to go to Lindy's, and that's what I was doing. But I knew the truth even if I didn't admit it to myself. I was frightened. I panicked and I ran. I was nothing more than a terrified, foolish boy.

Something went wrong as I turned on Seventh Avenue. Maybe my shoe caught against a curb, on a step, or a break in the pavement. Whatever it was, as I twisted, flinging myself around the corner, I felt a sharp pop in my right knee. My leg collapsed, and I crumpled into a useless tangle of flailing limbs.

Nobody had hit me. Nobody pushed me. Nobody touched me. There was nobody to blame but my own damn fool self.

That's what happened. But all I said to Connie Nix and Mrs. Pennyweight was, "When I got to the street, I fell and tore up my knee."

I don't remember how I managed to get back to Mother Moon's house, only that my knee hurt like hell. I was crying from the pain, and also because I knew I'd done something seriously wrong to myself. Even then, I knew I would never run again.

"About an hour later, they found A. R. in the same stairwell with a bullet in his gut. He died two days after that, and never spoke a word about who shot him.

"Like I said, this all happened on the first Sunday in November. The next Friday or Saturday, your daughter and Spence got married. I still couldn't walk, and by then there had been another death in the family."

CHAPTER THIRTEEN

I have never been so goddamn miserable and sorry for myself as I was in the days after A. R. was shot. My knee swelled up like a water balloon and wouldn't support me at all. I was still wallowing in pain and confusion when Fanny and Dr. Ricardo came into my room. The doc looked shaky, like he was overdue for a smoke. Fanny looked serious, but then she almost always did.

I twisted around on the bed, reaching for the crutches Ricardo had sold me.

Fanny said, "She's dead," and I knew what she meant. Mother Moon had stopped frequenting her opium parlor and had taken to the pipe almost every day in her room. We could tell she wasn't her normal self, even if we didn't really mention it to each other.

Ricardo said, "It was a cancer. You can get a real doctor to check it if you want, but I've seen it before."

I swung my legs over carefully and sat up using the crutches. The bitterness, self-pity, and anger were as strong as they'd been, and the news of Mother Moon's death did nothing to change that.

Fanny said, "Jacobson told me she had him draw up a will, all legal and proper. She left me the building. I've got the money she saved for you."

"How much?"

"Ten thousand."

"The hell you say. It should be four, five times that." I pulled the notepad out of my coat pocket. "I've got a record of every penny I gave her." I was getting really steamed, but I could tell there was something else. Fanny might not be lying but she wasn't telling the whole truth. Not that I was either. I hadn't told anyone about the money I'd been holding back for years, or about hiding A. R.'s last envelope. It was still snug against my ribs, there in my coat pocket, unopened.

"Show me her strongbox."

We went to Mother Moon's room. Ricardo had covered her body, and with the heavy drapes closed and all windows shuttered, the room remained thick with fruity opium fumes. Mother Moon lay on her daybed, banked with cushions and swayed by years of use.

Fanny said, "I told Tommy . . . Patrolman O'Brien what happened. He's sending a car for her." She stopped, chewing on a fingernail. "Tommy wants me to move in with him, to sell this place, and move in with him. What do you think I should do, Jimmy?"

Fanny was still taller than me. But as Mother Moon's health declined, she'd treated me more as an equal.

"O'Brien? He's married."

She shrugged. "I dunno, he says he loves me. And he's nice, and he's gonna leave her. So I think I'm going to sell this place. You know Oh Boy is working for Spence now, don't you? Yeah, he's moving to Jersey."

That surprised and stunned me almost as much as Mother Moon's death. I stood openmouthed, trying not to fall off my crutches. Dr. Ricardo pulled the strongbox out from under the bed and ignored us.

When I returned to my room, still reeling, I rolled up my pant leg for Ricardo. He was a pale guy who never liked to go outdoors. Some people said he'd been a real doctor once, and others that he was a medical student when he started smoking hop. Didn't matter much to us.

He knew about drugs and injuries and wounds and women's problems. And he lived in the building.

He said, "Can you stand up?"

When I pushed up from the bed, the knee bent to one side in a way that made both of us sick to see. I sat back down fast.

Dr. Ricardo shook his head and told me to take off my shoe. "See how your heel is bruised all the way around the sides and at the back? You were turning but somehow your foot planted down solid, and your leg twisted too far. When you do that, something's got to give. In your case, it was your knee. You see, you've got these four big ligaments that hold everything together . . . no, it's three ligaments that hold your knees together, or four, yeah four. . . . Anyway, you broke one of them, tore it right in half."

"How do I get it fixed?" I asked, knowing what the answer was going to be.

"You can't fix it. The muscles will grow stronger, and you can get a brace that will keep your leg straight. I know a man in Chinatown who can make one for you. That will help. So will a cane."

"Will I be able to run?"

"A little, maybe, but not very well."

It was all I could do not to cry like a damn baby.

I waited until Patrolman O'Brien showed up with the hearse that took Mother Moon away. The mortuary gave him a kickback for every customer he delivered. When he and Fanny left with the body, I went back to Mother's room and used my duplicate key to open her strongbox. The upper tray held letters, some in Chinese, along with a box of jewelry and folded documents I couldn't understand. Below this stuff were folded silk scarves, three tins of opium pills, a switchblade, a straight razor, and a collection of small blue glass bottles. All the stuff that Fanny, Ricardo and I had just gone through.

For years, I'd seen Mother Moon put things inside that box, and take things out too. I figured that it had to hold special secrets. It didn't take long to release the false bottom where I found eight banded stacks of cash.

There was another $2,000 loosely stuffed in a tasseled pillow at the foot of the daybed. Deep inside the fat silk pillow that had fit the small of her back, I found a couple dozen folded pieces of white paper. Each held a stone. Some were clear, some green.

Back in my room, exhausted by the stairs, I collapsed on the bed and opened my own stash of cash that I kept behind a section of loosened baseboard. But such a simple hiding place wouldn't do any longer. Putting the money I'd taken from Mother Moon's room in one stack, I clicked open the switchblade to slice open A. R.'s envelope, never returned to its rightful owner. It held more cash, mostly hundred-dollar bills. I counted quickly: $6,772. The money from Mother Moon's strongbox came to $5,440. Toting up the numbers in my notepad, I found a total of $16,436. Combined with the money from Meyer and A. R. that I'd been holding back from Mother Moon, I had $22,874. Plus the stones in folded paper.

I stared at the bundles of cash and wondered what I would do. It was a complicated question. When Fanny sold the building, where would I live? What would I do with all that money? Where could I keep the cash? What would I do for work? A better man than me might have tried to get Rothstein's money to his widow or his girlfriend. A better man might have tried to arrange some kind of split with Fanny and Oh Boy and Dr. Ricardo. I didn't even think about it.

All I knew was that I still had one good leg, $22,874 and twenty-four stones that might be diamonds and emeralds. The world was changing around me, and I couldn't do a damn thing about it. Mother Moon was dead. Spence was gone. Oh Boy and Fanny were leaving. And A. R. had been killed.

First thing, I got the Detective Special and checked the load. I found a suit that wasn't too sharp or too shabby. I filled my pockets with the stones and as about half the cash. The rest of the money went into a brown paper bag.

Outside, on crutches with the paper bag under one arm and the pistol in my coat pocket, I tried not to look like I was rushing anywhere. People knew me in that neighborhood, so I told myself that this was just another day and I was just heading out to steal another car. But I knew that now I really had something to lose. It wasn't A. R.'s money I was carrying anymore—it was mine, and it was all I had in the world.

I walked until the sidewalks got wider and the people were better dressed. Then I hailed a cab to the Harriman National Bank on Fifth Avenue. Mother Moon had never trusted banks, but A. R. kept a safe-deposit box at the Harriman. If the place was good enough for him, it was good enough for me.

I remember feeling enormous relief after I paid for the box, took the key, and locked up the stones and most of the money. As I left the bank, I began to realize how ignorant I was about these things. I knew what a meal cost at a deli, but $22,874 didn't have any real meaning. It was just a lot of money. I didn't know what I could do with it, or even what I wanted to do. That's what I'd have to figure out. The next morning I moved into the Chelsea Hotel.

Two days later I took a cab to Chinatown and swung my crutches down Mott Street. I'd been in the neighborhood often enough that it didn't seem foreign or particularly exotic. I knew you didn't steal from Chinese shopkeepers. They saw everything and smacked you on the head as hard as hell if you even thought about putting the pinch on something in their places.

Dr. Ricardo had told me to go to the fifth door past the intersection with Grand Street. The place wasn't easy to spot behind racks of vegetables, fish, and stuff I couldn't name. But then there it was, a narrow green door, just two steps below the sidewalk. I fumbled down clumsily, almost toppling over on the stairs. Then I walked down a dim hall with a faint light at the far end. I was sweating despite the cold by the time I reached a second door, and I smelled burning charcoal as I entered.

Inside I found a room with a rough plank floor that opened onto a courtyard bordered by alleys and the backs of neighboring buildings. It had probably been a stable at one time. Harnesses and strangely shaped pieces of metal that might have been weapons were hanging on the wall. All had paper price tags. Outside in the courtyard, a Chinaman worked with hammer and tongs at a circular piece of metal on an anvil by a forge. He was a young guy with a wide face and massive shoulders. He wore a leather apron over a black robe, felt slippers, and some kind of wooden clogs.

He looked at my crutches and said, "What kind of brace do you need?"

I said, "You don't sound Chinese."

"I'm Japanese. Who sent you to me? Christiansen?"

I didn't know that Japs could speak such good English. "No, Ricardo. It's, uh, my knee."

He set his tools aside, came inside, and cleared some stuff from a small bench. "Sit down and roll up your pant leg."

For the next twenty minutes he worked with a tape measure and calipers, and wrote down numbers. When he finished he said, "What kind of brace do you want? I can make one that will keep your knee from buckling for ten dollars. I can make one that will last for years and it will be so light you'll hardly notice it but that's a hundred dollars, and I can give you anything in between." He took a long look at my suit, overcoat, and hat, saying, "I imagine a man in your position will want the best. I also have some canes you might be interested in."

"I might be. What's your name?"

He rattled off a mouthful and then said, "But everybody calls me Sam."

"OK, Sam, here's fifty bucks to get started. Make me your best, and tell me what you've got in the way of sticks."

Six days later, the brace was ready. It was made of metal, lined with leather, and hinged in the middle, kind of like a small version of what polio victims wore on their legs. Five belts held the thing in place. Sam had me try it on to check the fit, then removed the contraption when I said it felt too tight at the top. He worked with the part that curved across the front of the thigh. When I tried it again, the gizmo felt much better.

"You can't twist your knee," Sam told me. "The hinge won't let you have full flexibility, but the knee won't pop out the way it does now. Now, for a cane, I recommend one or both of these."

He handed me two black canes, one with a metal collar near the handle.

"That one is what you probably expect, a sword."

With a quick twist, the body of the cane unlocked from the pistol grip, slipping off to reveal a mottled blade about two feet long and razor sharp.

Sam said, "Do you have any training with a blade?"

I shook my head. "A little, but with a knife. If I get into a scrape, I prefer my knucks." I pulled them out of my pocket. "At least, I used to. I don't know if they'll do me much good now."

"Once you're accustomed to the brace, you'll be able to use them. I can make you a set that's better than what you've got. Thicker at the top to give your knuckles and fingers more protection. And they won't hang up in your pocket. Are you interested?"

"You bet."

"You can do a lot with a regular cane, too, like this one." The second cane must have been made of denser wood. It was heavier, with a simple curved handle.

"Can you teach me?"

"No, but my father can. Come back tomorrow. Wear old clothes."

The next day I put on coveralls and walked with the brace and the cane for the first time. The pain was about half as bad as it had been at its worst; the brace didn't chafe as much as I'd feared. I managed to get up and down the steps to the El all right. None of that changed the fact that I couldn't run. I was trapped at a turtle's clumsy pace. In my days of working for Rothstein and Lansky, I'd been Fast Jimmy Quinn. From now on, I'd be Jimmy the Stick.

Inside Sam's shop I found that the floor had been cleared. Sam said, "Good morning, Jimmy San. Father, your new pupil is here."

A grouchy-looking old man and a kid entered from a side door. The boy wore short pants, a white shirt, and a tie. The old guy had on a dark-blue robe and carried a short cane. The boy translated. "Grandfather says that the price of a lesson is ten dollars and you're using the cane wrong. Keep it in your left hand."

I shifted the stick to my left, watching as the old guy circled me.

"He says the basic rule of fighting with the cane is to strike at the hard places." The old man's cane was a blur as he rapped me sharply on the upper arm. "And jab to the soft." He reversed the cane in his hands and stabbed the tip into the center of my chest. I yelled and took a wild swing that didn't even come close to the old guy.

So the lessons began.

I went to Sam's shop every day for two weeks and spent a lot of time on my ass. But I learned. The old man and the boy showed me how to keep my feet apart at shoulder width and my weight balanced over them. They taught me how to use small steps to move forward and side to side. I learned how to break a headlock, to hook an ankle, to use the stick along with my wonderful new knucks. By the time I was finished, I'd shelled out another $150, and it was money well spent. I wasn't quite as crippled as I had been before.

After that, I worked to strengthen the knee by walking. I walked everywhere in any weather. Sometimes I stayed by the rattling El. Sometimes I followed the lighted subway globes for miles, all the time chewing over the big question. What was I going to do?

I was wandering around brooding late one afternoon when a guy tried to mug me. It was really my fault. I wasn't paying attention to what was going on around me and the cane made me an easy mark. The guy rushed up behind me and shoved me into an alley and slammed me against a wall. I never really got a look at his face. He just grunted "Gimme your wallet" and slapped me open-handed across the face. If I'd been a civilian, that might have shocked me into obedience but in that moment of bright pain, I remembered what I'd been taught.

I grabbed the cane with both hands and jabbed it straight up. The handle caught the guy under his chin and snapped his jaw shut. As he stumbled back clutching his throat, I hit him hard across the temple. He staggered across the alley and thought about coming after me again until he saw that I had the cane up. He ran and, damn, did it ever feel good to see him turn tail.

I was still pleased with myself later when I gimped into Carl Spinoza's place, sat at the bar, and ordered a celebratory beer.

In the mirror, I could see Carl at a table in the back. He was talking to Vincent Coll and Sammy Spats Spatola. Actually, he was doing more listening than talking, and it looked like he didn't care for what he was hearing.

Coll and Spatola had gone to work for Dutch Schultz by then, trying to intimidate speaks into buying his crappy beer. If their "salesmanship" didn't work, they beat up reluctant bar owners. I'd heard they were sticking to the Bronx, where Dutch did most of his business. Nobody said anything about Manhattan.

When they got up to leave, Coll said, "We'll come back next week. You can tell us then." Carl looked like he'd eaten something that disagreed with him.

I turned on the barstool, and they saw me for the first time. Spatola paid no attention and there was only the smallest hint of recognition on Coll's face. It had been five years since Egg Harbor.

"Jimmy Quinn, what the hell are you doing here?" Vinnie finally said, smiling like he was trying to be friendly.

I smiled back just as sincerely. "Having a beer."

"You still work with the Bug and Meyer mob?"

"Now and then."

Spatola took another look, and I could tell he remembered who I was. "Guess you ain't delivering any more messages for Rothstein." He and Coll snickered at what they thought was a private joke.

After they left, I talked to Carl Spinoza for a long time.

The next day, I went to Lansky's garage and sat down with him in his office.

He said, "Hell of a thing about A. R.," and we commiserated for a while about him and Mother Moon. Nobody was sure whether Rothstein was shot because he'd welshed on a bet or been in on a heroin deal that went bad. It could have been either. I didn't say anything about what I had seen.

Lansky nodded at my stick. "I heard you busted your leg. That's a tough break too."

"My running days are over but I can still get around. Do you want me to make my deliveries?"

"Sure. It doesn't matter that you can't run. Use a car and a driver from now on."

That's more or less what I expected him to say. Lansky and I weren't exactly friends, not like he and Charlie were friends, but we always got along and somehow understood each other. Part of it was because we were both short. We knew what it was like to be the smallest guy in the room and what you had to do to keep the big guys in line. The other part of it was that I never stole from him. Over the years, he had me deliver hundreds of packages of cash, maybe thousands. I have no idea how much money it added up to. But Mother Moon taught me well. There are some people you can steal from and there are some you don't steal from. I knew the difference, and I knew that nobody ever made a living stealing from Lansky.

"There's something else I need to talk to you about," I said.

"Yeah?"

"I talked to Carl Spinoza last night. He's ready to sell his place and retire. I'd like to buy it from him."

Lansky looked skeptical. "Why? I hear he's losing money."

"He is. There's nothing special about his joint, and I'll change that. I think it could do pretty good if the booze was improved, you know, nothing but the best. I mean if you want a fancy floor show or an expensive dinner and dancing, there are dozens of places right there in the neighborhood and a hundred more uptown. But if word got out that Spinoza's speak was under new management, serving nothing but the best, straight off the boat . . ."

Lansky nodded. "Yeah, you might have something there."

"Could I buy direct from you and Charlie?"

He thought before he answered. "Sure, but don't expect much of a discount. Do you have any idea how much we make when we cut this stuff?"

"Hell, I'm going to charge whatever the market will bear. When can I take my first shipment?"

Thus I came to own a speak.

But first I asked around at some of the jewelers on Canal Street, and I got about eleven grand for some of Mother Moon's stones. They turned out to be uncut diamonds. I had some membership cards printed that said "Quinn's Place" even though most people kept calling it Spinoza's. I talked to cops who patrolled the street, and told them I'd be adding an extra fin to what Carl had been handing over. Of course, they were welcome inside anytime. I wanted them to know I was planning to run a quiet place, just like Carl. So Frenchy, Fat Joe, and I went over the inventory and threw out the worst of the rotgut after we got the first truckload from Lansky. Then we figured out new prices, cut the fare on the old but drinkable stuff, and jacked it up for the new name brands. Funny thing, we wound up keeping King's Ransom scotch, one of the most heavily doctored brands, because so many guys had developed a taste for the stuff.

I figured I had a decent shot at making a go of it. After all, the standard complaint about neighborhood speaks was "the liquor's rotten but it's easy to get to." This place was less than half a block off Broadway. Everybody knew it.

When Vinnie Coll and Spats Spatola returned, they weren't happy. That happened the next Monday afternoon. I was at the back table with my newspapers spread out in front of me.

"You still here, Quinn?" Spatola said as they sat down without being asked to. "Where's Spinoza? We got business to discuss."

Vinnie's suit was muddy brown, Spats's was a big blue-and-white houndstooth pattern. It hurt your eyes to look at them sitting close together.

I put down the paper. "Carl decided to retire. I'm the new owner. What'll you have? First round's on the house. Frenchy, bring these gents a couple of Bushmills."

Smiling, Frenchy brought over three drinks, then busied himself behind the bar. I raised my glass. "*Salut.*"

Coll tossed back the whiskey and was surprised by it. "Hey, this is the real McCoy."

"We're only selling the best."

"Who's your supplier?"

"I'm buying direct from Lansky and Luciano."

Coll said, "We had a deal with Spinoza. He was going to take our beer."

"I'm sticking with Owney. We've got Madden's No. 1."

Spatola unbuttoned his coat, leaning back in his chair, letting the coat fall open to show off two big shiny .45s in shoulder holsters. He and Coll grinned at each other.

"You should give our beer a try. That's what Carl was gonna do."

"No."

"You're not giving us a fair shot. That's not good business." Spatola flipped his coat open wider.

"What the hell is this, Vinnie? You think Spats showing off his big guns is gonna scare me into buying your cheap-ass needled beer?"

I picked up the Detective Special I had under the newspapers and pointed it at Spats's head.

"You've got one second to close your coat." I cocked the pistol. Behind the bar, Frenchy pulled back the hammer on his hog leg.

Coll turned around to find himself looking down the business end of the huge pistol. He said, "Button your coat, Spats."

"Now," I said reasonably, "I plan to run a nice quiet place here.

You're welcome to come back as customers; just leave your guns outside. We got the same rules Owney sets at the Cotton Club. No guns, no fighting. Patrolman Norris and Patrolman Cheeks cover this block. They're outside now, looking after your car. I told them you'd be coming, and I wanted to be sure they know who you were."

Now, I've got to admit, that was a really stupid, show-off move. You don't pull a gun on a guy to threaten him. You pull a gun on a guy to shoot him. But in those days, Vinnie hadn't yet gone completely crazy, and if you could get him to pay attention, you could reason with him. He didn't have anything to gain by shooting me that afternoon, and within weeks he had broken with the Dutchman anyway. He tried to set up his own beer business and started the war that would get him killed.

That was the last time I saw Coll until the night I fingered him to Owney. Spats and I weren't done with each other yet.

CHAPTER FOURTEEN

Mrs. Pennyweight sipped her scotch and said, "So you turned down Walter because you hurt your leg. And then your mother died and you opened a speakeasy. Did Mr. Coll and, what was his name, Mr. Spatini, threaten you again?"

"Spatola. No, not long after his visit to me, Vinnie Coll and Dutch Schultz parted company, and then it became clear to everybody that Vinnie was nuts, completely crazy."

"Is he the 'Mad Dog' you and Mrs. Conway were talking about?" Connie Nix said, finally tasting her drink.

"Yeah, and everybody knows what happened to him."

"I don't."

"Neither do I," said Mrs. Pennyweight, holding out her glass. I made another drink and refreshed Connie's with a little ginger ale.

"OK, Vinnie got arrested on a Sullivan Act beef. The cops caught him with a concealed weapon. Dutch made the ten-thousand-dollar bail for him, but Vinnie skipped, and Dutch was out ten G's. At the same time, if you can believe this, Vinnie demanded a cut of Dutch's beer business. He wanted to be a partner! I know it makes no sense, but that's the way Vinnie was. Dutch told him to screw off, pardon my language, and Vinnie answered by killing one of his top guys, Vincent Barelli, and his girlfriend, May. That did it for the Dutchman, who's pretty close to full-tilt crazy himself. He sent some guys to Harlem looking for Coll. When they couldn't find him, they killed his brother Pete. Vinnie went even more nuts when he heard about it. After his brother got clipped, Vinnie declared war on Dutch's operation and killed about half a dozen of Dutch's guys."

Both women looked horrified.

"Dutch put a fifty-thousand-dollar price tag on Vinnie's head. Dead only. Now it was serious. One day Vinnie spotted Joey Rao, one of Dutch's men, on the sidewalk in Spanish Harlem. So Vinnie and two other guys drove by in a car and opened up with everything they had, spraying the whole street with shotguns and pistols. Only, Joey had already seen Vinnie's car, and ducked out of sight. So Vinnie and his guys hit five kids playing on the sidewalk. Four of 'em were wounded, some pretty bad. One was killed, a kid named Mikey something."

I heard Connie Nix catch her breath.

"Now, even with Dutch's guys killing Vinnie's guys and vice versa, neither the cops nor the politicians really cared. Another dead bootlegger, no great loss. But when a kid gets killed, everything changes. This guy named Brecht claimed to have seen it all and fingered Vinnie. The papers started calling him a baby killer, and the mayor said he was a mad dog. And then everybody was looking for him. A sane person might have decided this was a good time to head for Canada or Mexico. But not Vinnie. Instead, he kidnapped Owney Madden's pal, Big Frenchy DeMange, and ransomed him back to Owney for thirty-five grand."

I turned to Connie Nix. "That's what I was saying before. Vinnie and some other guys I know would kidnap people. But never anybody who might call the cops. You snatch somebody who's already in the business, has the money close at hand, and doesn't want local police or the federal guys involved. For his part, Owney knew that if he came up with the cash, Vinnie would let Big Frenchy go. So he paid up. Vinnie used that money to hire Sam Liebowitz, maybe the best mouthpiece in town, except for Dixie Davis. That was after he got nabbed. They caught up with him and the rest of his guys in a hotel upstate."

I poured another drink for myself. "So anyway, Vinnie goes to trial. And Liebowitz, the mouthpiece, turned Brecht, the eyewitness, inside out. He convinced the jury that Brecht was lying, that he only wanted the thirty-thousand-dollar reward. Turns out that Brecht had done the same thing in another case, identifying the wrong guy. When it was all over, Brecht was committed to Bellevue and Vinnie walked away a free man. The Reds and the reformers accused the DA's office of intentionally sabotaging their own case. Other guys said that Owney had arranged for Vinnie to get off so he could take care of the Mad Dog himself. I don't know if that's true, but I do know that the word was out, if you saw Vinnie, you called Owney PDQ. And that's what somebody did about a month ago."

They didn't need to know exactly who that somebody was.

"Again, you'd think that with everybody looking for him, Vinnie would have left town, but he didn't. He stuck around and got spotted one night when he was making a phone call from a drugstore. One of Owney's guys with a Tommy gun caught up with him. According to the papers," I lied, "he just about cut Vinnie in half right there in the phone booth, before he got in a car and drove away. And the next day, two more of Vinnie's mugs were killed. So after that, do you think anybody in the 'underworld,' as the papers and radio like to call it, would harm a kid, particularly the Lindbergh baby?"

Mrs. Pennyweight said, "I suppose not."

Connie Nix said, "For somebody who says he's not a gangster, you sure know a lot of people who get shot."

I'd never thought of it that way.

CHAPTER FIFTEEN

Flora Spencer and Cameron Rivers rolled in at dawn.

I heard the whine of an over-revved engine and was waiting outside the front door when the Pierce-Arrow slid to a stop. Deputy Parker's patrol car was behind them.

Cameron Rivers tottered out first, hoisting another bottle of Veuve Clicquot, and bowed in my direction. "The Sisters of Isadora salute the approaching sunrice . . . sunrise."

The passenger door banged open. Laughing, Flora tumbled through it, stumbling a bit until she got her balance. She wore a cloche hat and a tan coat with a thick fur collar. When she saw me, she stopped laughing.

"So, you're still here, Walter's little watchdog. I think Teddy and Titus were right about you. I know whose side you're on. Don't think you can pull the wool over my eyes."

She was as drunk as Cameron Rivers, and like a lot of drunks, she thought she had everything figured out.

"Well, you don't know anything," she slurred. "None of you know anything about what's going on, but you'll see, yes you will."

She wagged a finger at me. Cameron Rivers took her arm and whispered something that made her smile in a snotty, childish way. I realized again how incredibly young she was.

The deputy's eyes never left Flora as the two women weaved their way inside. He was stuck on Flora, all right. I leaned on his open window and said, "Did you find anything about that bucket that came from the butcher?"

"Yeah," he glanced over at me. "Bartham says somebody stole it from his shop, and I believe him."

"So you think it was somebody local who's pissed at the Penny-weights?"

He shrugged. "Probably."

"OK, there's something else. The other night I saw someone watching the house from the trees down by the lake."

"Did he try to get in?"

"No, he backed off when I opened the window."

"Did you tell Dietz about it?"

"Yeah, he said I saw a deer."

"Then you saw a deer. Nothing goes on around these woods that Dietz doesn't know about."

I still didn't buy that, so I told Parker about the car and truck I'd seen circling the house for the past two nights. "Could they be cops? Would Kittner have men patrolling these roads?"

He frowned. "No. The sheriff is in Hopewell," he said, sounding tired and resigned. "I'm in charge while he's gone. These vehicles, where do you see them?"

"The lake side of the house." I didn't mention the one that Oh Boy ran off the road yesterday morning.

"That's the township road," he said. "Always has traffic."

"No, they show up every ten, fifteen minutes or so, moving in opposite directions. Sometimes they stop together."

The deputy shoved the column shift of his car into reverse. "I'll swing by tonight. Probably nothing." He turned around and left.

154

All the headlines in the *Times* covered kidnapping news. I read them over coffee as Mrs. Conway fried eggs and turned up the radio.

Oh Boy had brought in four of the New York papers along with the local *Daily Record*. Taken together, the stories remained mystifying. Nobody knew what was really going on.

There was "Red" Johnson, palling around with Betty Gow, the Lindberghs' nurse, the young woman who had discovered the disappearance of the baby. According to the *Times*, Johnson was about to confess. But the *Daily Record* said that the police had cleared him completely.

Suspicious customers were everywhere. In Chicago, a bunch of detectives called "the Secret Six" busted into a rooming house to question people but were unable to beat useful answers out of anybody. New York cops got a tip that the kid was with the hobos in the Hooverville at Thirty-Ninth Street and Twelfth Avenue. They rousted everybody, with no results. New Jersey cops suspected a gypsy camp in Linden and gave it a thorough going-over. The gypsies were probably used to it. They sympathized with the Lindberghs, and offered one of their own babies to replace the missing boy.

I still hoped a woman was involved, as they'd first reported. I know some women can be as murderous as men but it still seemed to me then that the kid had a better chance if he was with a woman. If only one guy, or even a couple of guys did the job, they had probably already killed the little boy.

Connie Nix was putting another breakfast tray together. Oh Boy and Mr. Mears spooned sugar and cream into their coffee. Mrs. Conway cut a slice of last night's ham and put it on my plate with eggs and toast. The brindle cat showed up and bit me again. I left it alone after that.

Mrs. Conway sat down across the table. "Did I hear Flora and Cameron coming home just now?"

"It looked like they had a long night."

Oh Boy said, "Did they leave the car in front of the house?"

I nodded. Oh Boy shook his head and muttered, "Oh boy, oh boy," and got up to move the Pierce-Arrow into the garage.

"Deputy Parker followed them in," I added. Another distressed look passed across Mrs. Conway's face. "He said that Sheriff Kittner has gone to Hopewell to lend his vast crime-fighting experience to the investigation. One way or another, he'll prove that Fordham Evans was part of the Lindbergh kidnapping."

Mrs. Conway just shook her head. "Saints preserve us."

A bell sounded and the number one lit up. Connie Nix jumped up to answer. I went out with her and followed her up the servants' stairs. She stopped at the first floor and said, "You should use the front stairs. These are for staff."

"So what? Do you think I'm not working? Don't I eat in the kitchen? C'mon, I'm tired. Let's go."

The servants' stairs reached the second floor at the far end of the hall, away from Mrs. Pennyweight's rooms. The dim steps went on up to the third floor and the staff quarters, but I was in no mood to explore.

In my room, I stretched out under the covers but sleep came slowly. The wind was still rattling around, and I couldn't get images of Vinnie Coll out of my head. Him slamming against the back of the bloody phone booth. Vinnie and Spats that first day in Lansky's garage. The picture in the *Daily News* of four guys standing in the rainy mud of St. Raymond's cemetery with Vinnie's coffin on their shoulders. And there was Mandelina's gravestone beside them. Then Vinnie became little Ethan with his sweating red face in the car, and that turned into the Lindbergh baby and the bloody doll in the nursery, and then Connie Halloran and Connie Nix were part of it too.

When I finally did get to sleep, I didn't dream.

That evening, I put on my oldest and most comfortable light-gray suit, another turtleneck, and loaded my pockets with pad, pen, knucks, and pistol before I headed downstairs. The kitchen was filled with the warm, wonderful smell of a meaty stew.

On the shelf where Mr. Mears kept his wine, a new jug of dago red had appeared. I poured a glass and refreshed Mr. Mears's. The old guy smiled for the first time since I'd been there, raising his glass with a shaky hand.

Connie Nix was preparing two trays that appeared to hold only tomato juice, dry white toast, and two large carafes of water. For the Sisters of Isadora when they awoke, no doubt.

Mrs. Conway said, "There you are, Quinn. It's customary for the staff to gather for dinner on Saturday night. You're welcome to join if you like." She looked at the clock over the numbered grid. "We'll serve in half an hour."

"Thanks." I turned to Mears and said, "Two days ago, I saw a man delivering coal in the morning. Is the furnace on this floor?"

He nodded.

"Show it to me."

Mears drained his wine, then stood, leaning heavily on the table. He straightened his tie and shirtfront, and pulled at his coat as he shuffled off.

We went down a short hall to a door. He opened it with a key that was in the lock and pulled a cord to turn on a hanging bulb. Two wooden steps led down to a windowless furnace room. The smelly coal was piled on one side, with the furnace, boiler, and water heater taking up the rest of the space. Near the ceiling a little door, measuring about eighteen inches square, was shut tight.

I asked if it could be locked. Mears shook his head. "But that larger door is locked?"

He nodded.

"Always?"

The old man's eyebrows rose as he started to get steamed at the obvious question, and he nodded again.

Back in the kitchen, we met Connie Nix hurrying to deliver trays to Flora and Cameron. The big kitchen table was set for six, and Dietz and Oh Boy were hovering near the stove. Mrs. Conway pulled loaves of bread out of the oven as Mears headed for his dago red and poured two glasses.

I looked at my watch. Things would be jumping at my place now, on a Saturday night. I wondered if Connie Halloran was there, and somehow knew that she wasn't. I hadn't seen her since Tuesday, hadn't talked to her since Thursday afternoon. Best to call Frenchy later, see if he'd found out anything.

Dietz pulled a blue flask out of his coat and filled a glass with something yellowish and oily-looking. "Want a *real* drink, gunman?" He laughed and knocked back the coffin varnish.

"I'll call Cloninger when you're struck blind, groundskeeper," I said.

Dietz smiled, revealing gaps between his teeth. "I've no need of his mercies."

Connie Nix came in, wiping both hands on her apron, and went straight to the stove, where she picked up the stew pot to set it in front of Mr. Mears's chair. I reached for a slice of bread but Mrs. Conway slapped my hand. "Mr. Mears will say grace."

The old guy mumbled something while Dietz and Oh Boy bowed their heads and closed their eyes. Connie Nix and I looked at each other. Mrs. Conway peeked up at us and frowned. The brindle cat bumped my leg and stared at the stove.

It was the best stew I ever tasted, with onions, potatoes, carrots, and turnips, and seasoning I couldn't recognize. I stopped at two bowls. After the meal, Mrs. Conway poured coffee and tea. Dietz fired up his pipe. Mr. Mears lit a stogie, and Oh Boy rolled a cigarette. I took my coffee to the sink, where Connie Nix washed dishes.

"I see that you delivered trays to the two party girls. How are they doing?" I asked.

Before she could answer, Mrs. Conway snapped, "And what business is it of yours? We don't gossip about our betters."

"Betters? Hah! Are they going out or staying in? That's all I care about, how many people are going to be in the house tonight."

Connie Nix looked at Mrs. Conway. The older woman nodded. "They're staying here, as far as I know."

Up in the library, I poured some of Spence's rye, and took the word list I'd made from the day's newspapers over to the big dictionary.

unavailing

proffers

reticent

scantlings

I'd guessed right, more or less, on the first three, but "scantlings," that was a pip. The papers had said that a lumber expert examined the ladder the kidnapper had used to get to the Lindbergh baby's bedroom. It had been hammered together from "scantlings of yellow pine." A scantling turned out to be "a measured or prescribed size, especially of timber or stone."

Nice word, that, I thought as I finished my drink. Then, since I couldn't put it off any longer, I had the operator call my speak in New York.

Frenchy answered and it sounded loud and profitable. He yelled, "Boss, how the hell are you?"

"I'm fine. Have you got any news?"

"Yeah, Dixie was in earlier. He says that everything about what happened here on Tuesday has vanished from the police record."

"Good. What else?"

"He says Hourigan is a bull out of the Morrisania station in the Bronx, forty-one years old, married. Back when Dutch and Vinnie were going at it, Dutch promised the Bronx cops that if one of 'em killed Vinnie, he'd give that guy a nice house in Westchester. Apparently Hourigan was interested."

"Well, he wasn't there when Vinnie got killed, I can tell you that. Anything else?"

"Yeah, Sergeant Marks said he'd heard that a cop—and he wasn't sure it was the same guy—was drinking at the Drum, in the Bowery."

"Christ, that dump?"

The Drum served the cheapest slop you could pour out of a bottle, worse than Dietz's swill. Half the guys you'd see there looked like they'd be dead by morning.

Frenchy said, "The cop's been in there every night this week and he's spoiling for a fight, challenging the rummies to take him on."

Finally I asked about Connie, and he said she hadn't been at work. I told him to have Marie Therese call me when things slowed down. I was working on a second rye when the phone rang about forty-five minutes later.

Marie Therese hemmed and hawed for a few minutes before she explained. "Connie's scared about what happened the other night. She said she thinks she ought to go back home until you're here again."

I told her I'd given Spence my word that I'd stay at his house. But then I started to get mad. Goddammit, why couldn't the woman understand simple facts. "There's nothing to be scared of."

"I'll talk to her," Marie Therese said, and then, "if I can find her."

"If you can find her? Isn't she at the Chelsea?"

"Yeah, she moved her things in. But she hasn't spent much time there."

I hung up the phone, as troubled as I'd ever been. And I realized that I could think about it all night and be no better off than I was. Hell, hell, hell.

Later, when I'd checked all the doors again and climbed the stairs to my room, I could hear music from Flora's room, a radio or phonograph playing "Meet Me in the Shadows," again.

I stood by the window, staring at nothing until I finally knew what I had to do.

CHAPTER SIXTEEN

I knocked on Catherine Pennyweight's door a few minutes later. She was by the fireplace with the kid on the carpet near her feet. She turned down the radio music as I entered the room.

"I told you I've got problems with a cop. Well, I think I know where he is now and maybe I can take care of it tonight, but I promised Spence I'd look after little what's-his-name here. So," I said, "grab your coat, wrap the boy in his woolies, tell Oh Boy to bring the Duesenberg, and we'll go into the city."

Her eyes lit up. She clapped her hands and said, "What a wonderful idea! An adventure." She pushed a button on a box on her desk, calling Oh Boy, I guessed. "Where are we going?"

"To the Bowery, but we gotta make other stops first."

"Lovely."

Back in my room, I found my lug-soled shoes and opened the Gladstone for the brace Sam had made for me. I hadn't worn it much in the past year. As long as I wasn't lifting stuff or moving heavy things, I didn't need it. The stick was enough to get around. But not tonight. I sat on the bed, took off my right shoe, and rolled up my pant leg to fasten all the straps and buckles. When I stood up, the brace felt fine. Creaked a little when I walked, but it felt fine.

Gathering the rest of my things—the Detective Special, knucks, money clip, scarf, hat—I realized I was smiling. I really felt excited and charged up because I was doing something I knew how to do. Maybe it was all wrong, but dammit, I was doing something at last.

I heard Catherine Pennyweight open her daughter's door, and listened to their voices. They rose in argument until Flora's door slammed. I met Mrs. Pennyweight in the hall. Looking severe, she said, "Flora will not be joining us. She has other plans." Her disapproval couldn't have been any more obvious. "Nix will look after little Ethan."

"Fine. You got a gun?"

She patted her pocket. "Of course."

I took a flashlight from the library, and waited outside in the cold wind until Oh Boy wheeled the big Duesenberg up to the front door.

Looking confused, he got out of the car still buttoning his black monkey suit and squaring the cap.

"What's going on, Jimmy?"

"I've got some business in town. Mrs. Pennyweight and little Ethan are coming along for the ride. Miss Nix, too."

That didn't clear things up. "But what're we doing?"

I clapped my old friend on the shoulder. "Take us into the city and we'll work it out from there."

Mrs. Pennyweight came out, her eyes bright and her cane barely touching the ground as she hurried along. She wore a long overcoat, trousers, and a brimmed hat. Carrying the boy in her arms, Connie Nix had to run to keep up with her. She wore a dark coat and cloche hat. The big car rocked slightly in the cold, hammering wind as Oh Boy held the door open for them.

I got in the back, sitting in the jump seat, a good place to see if anybody followed us. Nobody did on the way out. Connie Nix was wide-eyed and curious. The baby was restless at first, but settled back smiling after his grandmother gave him some drops from a small brown bottle.

She put the stopper back in and said, "Nix, Mr. Quinn has pressing business in the city. I thought it was safer for Ethan to stay with us than to remain in Valley Green. I'm not precisely sure what it is that Mr. Quinn has in mind."

The two women looked at me for an answer.

It was impossible to explain so I said, "I gotta see a guy and explain some things. Once he understands that I'm on the up and up in resolving this beef I have, he'll say OK and I'll take care of it, maybe tonight, maybe some other time."

Connie Nix looked like she wasn't buying it. "Does this have anything to do with what you told us last night about Mad Dog Coll?"

"Not that I know of. If I was you two, I would take a powder at a nice place while I—"

"Nonsense," said Mrs. Pennyweight. "We'll stay with you. I've been assuming that we'd see your speakeasy."

Oh hell, I thought. It wasn't supposed to happen like this. But I knew damn well that if she wanted to go to my place, she'd go to my place.

Oh Boy retraced the route we'd taken on Wednesday night, through Newark and past the construction of the elevated highway. It started to rain as we entered the tunnel. When we got into the city, I slid open a section of the dividing glass, and told him to go north. It felt familiar and kind of comforting to be back in the slow, honking traffic.

We went uptown on Broadway. The electric signs got larger, taller, and brighter until they almost created a false daylight. Even Mrs. Pennyweight gawked like a tourist. Holding the happy boy tightly, Connie Nix leaned forward, craning her neck to see as much as she could through the light rain. To me that night, imagining the gaudy clutter through her eyes, the city looked a little cheap and bedraggled. For the first time, I didn't see the glittering theater marquees and looming commercial signs. Instead there were chop-suey joints that claimed to be nightclubs, with crowded penny-a-dance halls, cheap pitchmen, and screwy preachers in front of the arcades.

We passed dozens of movie theaters, half of them, it seemed, turned into grind houses that were open twenty-four hours a day, still showing stuff I'd watched years before. And there, in Times Square, the middle of the famous Great White Way, Minsky had turned the Republic Theater into a burlesque house. If only she'd seen the place a few years ago when it was really something. The only thing that remained as impressive as it had ever been was the Wrigley's sign— a full block long, filled with neon peacocks, fountains, and chewing gum. To me, it had always been the grandest thing on the street and it still looked pretty damned good.

We drove by two places where Charlie Lucky and Lansky sometimes hung out, a drugstore and an office building. But they weren't there, so I told Oh Boy to head for the Waldorf-Astoria.

Sounding impatient, Mrs. Pennyweight said, "What *are* you doing?"

I leaned forward and tried to explain. "The people I work with, we've got ways of doing business. I don't belong to anybody's mob, but like I told you, I do a fair amount of work with a couple of guys named Charlie Luciano and Meyer Lansky. I don't exactly have to get their OK to take care of my problem, but they need to know what I'm doing. It wouldn't be so good if they were surprised to hear about it after the fact. That's just the way things are handled."

She didn't seem to understand but I couldn't make it any clearer.

The Duesenberg pulled up in front of the hotel, with bellboys in monkey suits even fancier than Oh Boy's dashing up to open the back doors. The big car looked like it belonged there.

I slid open the glass. "I don't know how long this is going to take. Why don't you run the ladies once around the park. If I'm not here when you get back, run 'em twice."

Getting out, I turned back to Mrs. Pennyweight. "Don't worry. You aren't missing anything exciting."

I walked around the corner to the entrance to the Waldorf Towers on Fiftieth Street. In the lobby, I picked up the house phone and asked for Charles Ross, the name Luciano used at this grand place.

Charlie Workman answered.

"Charlie, Jimmy Quinn. Is Mr. Ross there?"

"Yeah, but he can't talk now. He'll be busy for another thirty, forty minutes."

It was Saturday night. Charlie liked to take the edge off with one of Polly Adler's girls before he went out for the evening.

"Is Meyer there?"

"Yeah, he's here. You wanna talk to him?"

"Ask if it's OK for me to come up."

A few seconds later, "Sure. I'll call the desk. It's 2910."

Luciano's apartment faced the East River. This was the first time I'd been in the place, and I was impressed. It was pretty swanky. The carpet was thick, and the room smelled of perfume and the flowers sitting on a round table. There was a fancy mirrored cabinet on one wall, with its own soft amber light. I could hear a shower running in another room. I knew that Charlie had done all right for himself, but not this good. The suite was a hell of a lot nicer and newer than my room at the Chelsea, providing the kind of class that Rothstein always talked about. This was how rich people lived.

Charlie Workman let me in. He was a big horse-faced guy who always looked kind of sad. In those days he worked as a driver for Luciano, and killed people, should the need for that come up. Sometimes he drove me when I had payoffs to distribute.

Lansky was reading the Sunday *Times* in an armchair by one of the big picture windows that overlooked the river.

"Bad stuff, isn't it, kid," he said, nodding at the headlines and shaking his head. "Just crazy. Did you hear that Lindbergh's people have been calling *us*? This guy Breckenridge who's running things, he was thinking about taking Capone up on his offer. But Irey, the T-man who set Capone up on the tax rap, told Lindbergh not to bother." Lansky looked worn out. He was almost always thoughtful and worried because he was a guy who took his responsibilities seriously. But that night something else troubled him, and it showed.

"Are you saying they actually considered letting Capone out of jail?" This development was really too ridiculous for serious people to talk about.

"Not for long. Irey told them that if they really thought 'underworld' guys were involved, they oughta talk to us. So that's what they did." He pointed to the front page. "According to the paper, Bitsy Bitz and Salvy Spitale are official go-betweens."

"They work for Mickey Rosner. He in on this?"

"Yeah, that's what Breckenridge said when he called."

"Who'd he talk to? Mr. Costello?" Frank Costello handled payoffs to politicians and judges. I made deliveries for him almost every week.

"Yeah, you just missed him."

"What'd he say?"

Lansky lit a cigarette. The ashtray on the table in front of him was overflowing. "Breckenridge asked if any of our guys were involved. Frank said he didn't think so, and he'd ask around. He made some calls, talked to Longy and some other guys. And then me and Charlie talked it over. There are a few men who might go off on their own on something like this. But nobody's taken a powder. They're all accounted for and they swear they didn't do anything. I mean, hell, it's not like we're the goddamn Army, where everybody follows orders. I just don't think anybody we know had anything to do with it. Frank thinks the kid's probably dead, and I guess he's right. Hell of a thing. You know anything?"

"No, did you hear what happened at my place?"

"Nah, I been out of town. Just got back this afternoon. Tell me about it." There were two suitcases beside his chair.

Before I could say anything, the bedroom door opened and a cute little blonde came out, adjusting the shoulder straps of a tight pearly-white dress. She said, "Charlie, before we go back to Polly's I gotta . . . Hi, Jimmy, long time no see."

"Hello, Daphne." Daphne was one of the youngest and prettiest of Polly Adler's girls. She bent over and kissed me, making sure I got a good look down the front of her dress. We both knew I couldn't afford her, but it was a friendly gesture. She straightened up and said, "Charlie, I need to go by that place where we went that time."

Workman said, "Sure, Daphne," and gave her butt a long, appreciative squeeze as they left. I guessed it would be a while before they got back to Polly's.

I gave Meyer the quick version of what the big cop Hourigan had done, and told him how Spence had hired Dixie Davis to find me and bring me to New Jersey. "His wife, she was afraid for their kid, but since then, she's been . . . Well, I don't know, she's been strange, I guess."

Lansky smiled unhappily. "Yeah, women are like that. I know. All too well I know. So tell me, what are you going to do?" There was a glass of scotch with melting ice on the table in front of him. He hadn't drunk more than a sip, but then that was Lansky for you.

"First, I'm going to the Drum to make sure it's the same cop. If he is, I'm going to take care of him."

Lansky said, "He's a cop. You know you can't kill him."

"Of course not. But I can't let the guy bust up my place. If it had been a real pinch, I'd understand. Everybody knows that happens, but this, I don't know what it was, so after I beat the hell out of him, I'll ask."

"Are you sure you didn't miss a payment?"

"He's not on my list. He's just a customer from the Bronx. He was in with some other cops one night. I probably gave them a round on the house."

Lansky nodded. "Has he done the same thing anywhere else?"

"Not that I know of. If he had, Dixie would've heard. But that don't change the fact that he tore up my place pretty good and we had to close for a night. It just ain't right, what he did. He cost me money."

Again, Lansky nodded. That's the way these things were handled. You couldn't kill a cop but you couldn't let 'em get away with crap like that, either.

He lit another cigarette and said, "No, it ain't right. I think you should go ahead, but don't let it get out of hand."

"Maybe it's not the same guy. I won't know 'til I see him. I'll let you know what happens, one way or the other."

"OK."

"I don't know if you're planning on me making any deliveries this week, but it looks like I'll be out at Spence's place in New Jersey for a while."

"Don't worry about it. The Coon can handle it. Call me when you're back in town." The Coon, as he was called, was Joe Cooney, an Irish mug who made his deliveries in repairman's coveralls and carried his payoffs in a toolbox.

I pointed to Lansky's suitcases. "Where you been?"

"California."

"More doctors?"

"Yeah, more doctors but nothing new." So that's what tied him up.

Meyer's son, Buddy, had been born crippled. He had cerebral palsy, and everybody knew that his wife, Anna, thought it was God's punishment for the kind of work Meyer did. I thought that was just nuts, but I could tell that sometimes Meyer half believed it himself. Hell, it was easy for me to think this was nuts. I'd never been married or had a kid, so I didn't say anything when guys talked about it.

"I've been to every doctor and clinic I can find, and none of them has anything hopeful to say. I can't explain it to her." He'd never talked about his personal life, and he really wasn't that night either. He just needed to let off some steam.

"I don't understand women. You can't explain what you do. They wouldn't understand. They spend the money you earn, and I don't begrudge her that. But they don't understand. They say the money is causing all the trouble, and then they say they don't care about the money. But we know different. Everybody cares about money."

"Anybody who says he doesn't is lying," I said.

"Sure he is. But this Lindbergh business made me see things in a different light. Did you know he got married just a couple of weeks before I did? Well, he did, and his son was born six months after Buddy. For two years now I've been thinking that somehow we were the same, only he was the good guy and I was the bad. You know, for all the laws we've broken and the guys I've had to kill. There was me and Buddy on one side, and Lindbergh and his family on the other, living the charmed life. If that's really the case, God's got a funny way of handling things."

"Funny way of handling what things?" Charlie Luciano strolled into the room with the usual wide smile splitting his mug. He wore a silk tie and his collar was held down with a slim gold pin.

He buttoned his vest and struggled with a cufflink until Lansky fixed it for him, and explained why I was there.

"Hourigan," Lucky said. "Yeah, I know him. Big guy. Loud bastard but a fucking straight arrow. You can't talk to him. Nobody likes him. Sounds to me like he was so shitfaced maybe he didn't know where he was or what he was doing in your place. A man like that can't control himself, it don't matter he's got a badge. Nail the bastard, Jimmy."

CHAPTER SEVENTEEN

I waited on the steps of the hotel until the Duesenberg pulled up, then told Oh Boy to go to my speak. He stopped by the front door and asked if there was a parking garage in the neighborhood. "I can't leave it on the street, Jimmy."

"Stay here. This won't take long. I'll escort the ladies inside and we can—"

"No, you're not going to leave us anyplace." Mrs. Pennyweight glowered at me.

"Look, you've got two choices. You can go in my place, sit down, and have a few drinks on the house. Or you can keep riding around in the car. The joint I'm going to doesn't allow women. Believe me, there's a good reason for that."

She was having none of it. "We're going with you."

"All right." I told Oh Boy to take us down to the Bowery. As we headed south again, I saw that Mrs. Pennyweight wore a self-satisfied little smirk on her face. Connie Nix was drinking it all in. The kid smiled and dozed.

When we were close to the street I thought I wanted, I told Oh Boy to stop. It had been a long time since I'd been in this neighborhood at night, and I wasn't sure we were at the right intersection. The truth was that since I bought the speak, I didn't go downtown that often and got a little confused once I was away from the familiar grid of Midtown. The crowded, twisty little roads of the Bowery and Chinatown made me antsy.

Oh Boy found a place to park under a streetlight. I made sure the glass was open when I spoke to him and Mrs. Pennyweight.

"I've been told the guy I'm looking for has been in a place that's a couple of blocks from here. Been there every night since he busted up my joint. Might not be the same guy. Or he might not be there tonight, I don't know. One way or the other it shouldn't take long to find out. Oh Boy, if anybody pays too much attention to you and you think you ought to move, do it. Just stay in the area and I'll find you."

I got out of the car. So did Mrs. Pennyweight.

"What the hell. I told you—"

"I don't care what the rules of this establishment are—"

"It's not an establishment, it's a bucket of blood."

"Fine, then they won't really care about serving women. Dressed as I am, no one will know I'm female. And besides that, you can't stop me." She was excited and determined. And she was right. There was nothing I could do.

"What about the kid?"

"Nix is armed."

"Oh hell." I gave up and started across the street.

On a warmer night, I'd have been more worried. But with the rain and wind, it was raw enough to drive most thugs and drunks inside. No one paid attention to two figures walking carefully across the street, leaning on their canes. As we moved away from the street lamp, I tried to tamp down the nervous excitement building up inside.

First, I needed to figure out where I was. I'd only been to the Drum once, and remembered the place being on a corner, with old-fashioned swinging saloon doors set at a forty-five-degree angle to the street. There was no sign outside, and the windows were painted over. Inside, the walls were yellowed with decades of tobacco smoke. At one time, the Drum had been owned by a guy named Drummond. Now some Mick named Reagan ran it. The speak was roughly divided into the bar in the front section and a room full of wooden pallets in the back where the stewbums could flop or pass out. But I hadn't actually been in the back room, I'd only seen it from the bar. And that visit didn't tell me what I needed to know.

We weren't alone on the street. There were burning cigars behind windows, quick movements in the deeper shadows. Mrs. Pennyweight stayed close. At the next intersection, I could see what I thought was the Drum, a short block away to the north. As we walked past it, I saw the painted windows. Now I needed to know one more thing.

We went around the corner and turned into the first alley. Picking my way carefully, I pushed garbage out of the way and swept it to the side with my stick. There wasn't much light, just enough to see that the alley led back to the Drum. A few yards along, it opened onto a cobblestone yard weakly lit by a single small bulb. Close to us were two overflowing garbage cans. On the far side, three wooden steps led up to a landing and what ought to have been the back door of the Drum. A reeking privy leaned against a wall. Mrs. Pennyweight sniffed, holding a handkerchief to her nose.

"Really, Mr. Quinn," she whispered, "what are we doing here?"

"We're waiting." A few minutes later, the door opened and a figure stumbled out. He didn't bother to go down the stairs to the privy but unbuttoned and let fly. Yes, this was the Drum. After he finished and went inside, we left.

Back on the street, she sniffed and said, "What was the purpose of that?"

"When you're going into a place, it's good to know where the back door is. And what's on the other side of it. Now, here's what we're gonna do."

It looked like Hourigan, the big cop, hadn't changed clothes or shaved since the night he beat me up. The suit was nasty with new stains and ripped seams. He was on a stool at the bar with both paws wrapped around his drink, mumbling into the glass. The bartender ignored him.

Our wet coats steaming, Mrs. Pennyweight and I stood just inside the door and looked into the room through a haze of smoke. On the wall behind the cash register was a poster of a harp and the words ERIN GO BRAGH. Maybe ten or twelve elderly rummies were slumped at tables, nursing their whiskey. An open doorway on the back wall led to the room with the pallets.

I took off my coats and hat and handed them to Mrs. Pennyweight.

Hourigan was muttering something about "It's a fucking shame it is when a man can't even get it in his own home . . . ," spraying brown tobacco spit as he talked. Everybody in the place pretended he wasn't there. As I made my way through the tables, quick and quiet, I remembered Mother Moon's good advice. The last thing I wanted was a fair fight. He must have heard my footsteps because he turned when I got close. I reversed the stick, caught the leg of the barstool with the crook, and yanked it out from under him. His head and elbows banged on the bar as he slid to the floor. The big man struggled to get up and I belted him in the ear with my knucks. He roared as I headed for the doorway in the back room.

Gimping along as quickly as I could, I got past the sleeping men and out the back door. I slipped under the rail of the landing to stand on the cobblestones. Again, the stench hit me hard. The knucks allowed enough dexterity for me to hold my cane with both hands as I checked the space under the railing. Yes, there was enough room if I choked up a little. Stay calm, I told myself. Don't get mad, don't get excited. Keep it under control.

Hourigan shouldered through the door and stopped, peering out at the alley as if he expected to see me running away. The sweeping strike of the cane caught him behind the knees. They buckled and he toppled down to the wet cobblestones. But before I could move in, he rolled away, bouncing shakily to his feet.

I closed in as fast as I could, holding the cane chest high, parallel to the ground, hands at each end. The cop reached for his coat pocket, probably going for the sap he had used before. I switched back to a two-handed grip and smacked the hand in his pocket. The coat tore and the white sap fell to the ground. Hourigan swung at me with a hard roundhouse left. I partially blocked it with the cane, staggering back a little when he caught me on the shoulder. We circled each other. Hourigan was breathing heavily. Even in the faint light, I could see that his angry face was swollen. He coughed and bulled in again. I twisted away, jabbing him in the stomach.

Then the big bastard was on me with a headlock. I turned my head to keep from being choked. He laughed, and I could really feel it when he took a deep breath, his thick left arm swelling as he squeezed.

I jammed the cane between his legs, grabbed the tip with my right hand, and yanked it straight up into his crotch. His arm loosened but not enough. I jammed the stick up again, and then a third time. Something crunched and his arm gave way. The big man staggered backward, bent over, hands grabbing at his groin.

I hit him hard on the ear with the knucks, reversed the cane, hooked an ankle, and pulled it out from under him. Hourigan landed on his butt against the privy, still holding his crotch, gasping for breath.

I leaned close. "Why did you do it? Why did you bust up my place? Tell me, dammit."

Still trying to get his breath, Hourigan stammered, "She . . . she left . . ."

"What?"

Before I could pull away, a meaty fist snapped up. It caught me on the jaw and popped my head back.

Hourigan's feet scrabbled on the ground as he tried to stand. No, not stand. He was pulling at his pant leg and reaching for an ankle holster. He had the little revolver in his hand when I cracked his mitt again with the stick, and the gun went off. He dropped the weapon and let out a high, thin scream.

There was a bleeding hole in the middle of his shoe. The scream became a sob, and then wracking, uncontrollable spasms. He slumped back against the privy, chest heaving, crying like crazy as he stared up at the rain.

Mrs. Pennyweight appeared beside me and I could hear the rummies crowding onto the landing. Even the bartender was there.

I put on my coats and hat, and said, "Do you have a phone?"

The bartender shook his head.

"Can you get to a phone?"

He nodded.

"Call the cops. Tell 'em one of their guys is here."

As we walked back up the alley, Mrs. Pennyweight asked what Hourigan had said. "Did you learn why he sacked your establishment?"

"Yeah, dammit, I think I did."

CHAPTER EIGHTEEN

It was three thirty in the morning. I was finally coming down from the excitement of the fight when the Duesenberg stopped in front of my place. Oh Boy stayed with the car. The rest of us headed to the front door.

Fat Joe Beddoes looked at me through the little spy door. He grunted, "About fucking time you got back."

I ushered the women inside and said, "I've never seen him so emotional."

Frenchy roared, "Goddamn, boss, you're here," as Marie Therese kissed me. I did a quick head count. Eight at the bar, three couples in the booths, nine at the tables. Well, it was a nasty night. The regulars nodded to me, looking curiously at the women and the little boy as we walked to a corner table. Connie Nix giggled at the painting behind the bar. Mrs. Pennyweight ordered scotch. I ordered an Irish, and an Irish and ginger ale for Connie. No cherries for the kid. When Marie Therese brought the drinks, I told her to sit down.

"I found the cop, Hourigan. He won't be bothering us anymore."

She was worried, nervous. "That's great, Jimmy."

"Connie's not around, is she?" I turned to the women. "This is another Connie."

"No," Marie Therese said, a bit too quickly.

"And she's not coming back."

"I can't say anything about that, Jimmy."

"It's all right. I know what happened."

Marie Therese looked relieved and guilty at the same time. Connie Nix and Mrs. Pennyweight obviously didn't know what I was talking about.I explained for their benefit. "A few months ago, a young lady named Connie Halloran came to work here as a waitress on the rec-ommendation of her very good friend Marie Therese. I started seeing her socially and we had some good times. The only problem is that her name isn't Connie Halloran. It's Hourigan."

"I didn't know until last night, Jimmy, I swear I didn't."

"Don't worry. Water under a burning bridge."

And that was the truth. I wasn't even angry. The moment I heard him say "she left," everything fell into place. Hourigan was easily twice her age, maybe more. Probably married her when she was fifteen, then stuck her in a cramped apartment in the Bronx while he went to work at all hours and stayed out to drink with his friends. She must have been with him that night when he and the other cops came in with their wives. Maybe it was the only time she got out. Maybe after that little taste of fun, she wanted more. He said no. Or maybe he came to my place with his girlfriend and she found out. For whatever reason, they had a fight. He yelled, he smacked her. She left and found her way back here, where Marie Therese took in another stray.

Maybe at first Hourigan figured she'd come back, and didn't let on to the other cops that she'd run off. But word got out. It always does. And then he got lonely, angry, and embarrassed, and when he found out where she was, he decided to do something about it. Maybe that Tuesday night he planned to drag her back home. Then, when he didn't find her, he decided to close me down. Or maybe he knew she was screwing the boss. Hell of a thing.

So now I needed a new waitress.

I gave Mrs. Pennyweight and Connie Nix a cleaned-up version of the story, not mentioning the important parts. But I think they saw through me.

On the way out, I asked Frenchy if he needed money to keep things moving. He said they were fine until the end of the month. I said I ought to be back before then although I realized I had no idea how long it was going to take. When was Spence coming back? How long would it take him to do whatever he had to do with exploratory wells? Hell, I didn't even know what an exploratory well was.

Back in the car, I asked Oh Boy to swing by the Chelsea before we left. Compared to Luciano's digs at the Waldorf, the lobby looked pretty dingy. But it was still home. Funny, though, after being away I didn't have the same feeling for the hotel that I had for the speak. Maybe that was really home to me.

Tommy, the night man, said, "Good evening, Mr. Quinn. Hope you're doing well." He handed over a key.

"Can't complain. Tell me, is the lady in?"

He looked back at the board of keys. "No, I haven't seen her since last night." He had a funny expression on his face. He'd probably seen her leave and knew she wasn't coming back.

I went up the stairs to the third floor and opened the door. I wasn't surprised by what I found. If she'd moved in, there was no sign. Her clothes were gone from the wardrobe and the dresser. No makeup or other female stuff was left in the bathroom. I could still smell some of her soaps and perfume, though.

She'd tossed the place pretty good, too. The cash I kept at the back of the top drawer was gone. It looked like she'd tried to pry apart the little lockbox I kept in the closet. She'd have been disappointed if she'd got it open. Nothing in it but a pistol. The drawers had been pulled out of the roll-top desk. She'd found one stash that I kept there but missed the other. All in all, I figured I'd got off easy. Almost all of my real money was in the safe in the Chelsea office, and inside the box at the Harriman Bank.

I sat at the desk, straightening up old notebooks Connie had scattered about, and surveyed the room. I could still see her on the tangled bed in the late afternoon light, remembering that slow smile as we lay there, my hand rubbing her smooth, sweaty stomach. I thought that her funny expression meant she was happy, happy to be where she was. But it didn't mean that at all. She was trying to figure out where she ought to be, with me, with her husband, or someplace else.

And what had I been thinking? Beyond the simple satisfaction of having my ashes so enthusiastically hauled, I was content to be there and to be quiet with her. Was that love? I doubted it. It sure wasn't great overpowering passion, the kind of thing I saw in the movies. But, hell, that was just the movies. All I knew was that I felt good to be with her. And if she opened my door right that minute and said, "Jimmy, I took your money and I need some more," I'd give it to her.

What a goddamn sap.

Nothing made sense. Hell, nothing had made sense since that big lug Hourigan showed up. You think you know how things work. You've got a business, it's going along OK, not making as much money as you'd hoped but you're all right. You're paying off the people who need to be paid off, you're keeping an eye out for competition. You're thinking about what to do when Prohibition is lifted. And then on a cold Tuesday night, none of that means a damn thing.

I didn't say much on the way back to Valley Green and continued to mull things over. The rain had turned to snow and sleet that rattled against the car. By the time we got past Newark, it was coming down pretty good. We were about a mile from the house when Oh Boy tapped on the glass. His voice was low, not to bother the dozing women. He said, "Somebody's following us."

"I know," I said from the jump seat. "I've been watching too." I was worn out from everything that night, not in the mood to put up with any more foolishness. "Go dead slow after you turn in. If they follow us onto the property, I'll shoot them."

Oh Boy downshifted, easing into the driveway. He slowed to a crawl on the gravel. The snow was beginning to stick on the path.

The car following us made the turn but stopped before the gate. It stood still for a moment, then reversed quickly back onto the road, and went on. Appeared to be a Model A four-door. Could have been one of the vehicles I'd seen from my window. I was glad I didn't have to shoot anybody, but a little disappointed, too. As tired as I was, the fight had left me feeling unfinished. It would have been good to let it out.

As we rounded the last curve, the house came into view through the snow. All the lights were on, inside and out. As soon as I saw the bright windows, a sick feeling churned my stomach. Something was wrong. There were two cars in front, the Pierce-Arrow parked by the doors and Dr. Cloninger's white ambulance turning around to leave. The orderly behind the wheel was one of the guys who came when we found Fordham Evans. He was also on duty when Teddy and Titus, the two college boys, were removed. What was he doing here now?

As the women took little Ethan inside, I asked Oh Boy if the house was usually lit up that way.

He shook his head and said, "Not this late, oh, boy." He was as worried as I was. We were right.

Inside, I found Mrs. Conway and Mrs. Pennyweight huddled together. Neither looked happy. Connie Nix headed upstairs with the boy as music and drunken voices came through the open doors of the ballroom. I saw that the Sisters of Isadora were dancing again. Teddy and Titus, their faces still bruised and swollen, were working their way through Spence's liquor cabinet.

I realized I was starving and was about to ask Mrs. Conway for some breakfast when Mrs. Pennyweight said, "Cook tells me that Walter has been trying to reach us by telephone. He's been calling every hour and wants to speak to you."

Hell. "OK, I'll wait for him in the library. Mrs. Conway, could you fix me something to eat?"

Mrs. Pennyweight's face lit up. "Breakfast! What a capital idea."

By the time Spence called, I had built a fire against the howling blizzard outside and was into the good brandy. I picked up on the first ring.

"Jimmy, is that you? Where the hell have you been?"

I could barely make out the voice, as if the storm was caught in the telephone lines. "Taking care of the business at my speak. Your mother-in-law came along to look after your son. He's fine." Maybe a little drugged up, but that was nothing unusual.

"Was there trouble?"

I decided to misunderstand and said, "Did you hear about your friend Fordham Evans?"

"Who? What? Fordham? What about him?"

"Somebody shot him and nailed him to a tree. He was naked at the time."

"This line is terrible. I thought you said he was nailed to a tree."

"Don't worry about it." There was no time or need to explain. "He'll live. And there was some business with a couple of guys that Flora knows. Titus and Teddy? Do you know them? I had a talk with them too."

"What the hell are you saying? This is nonsense."

"Also, I think somebody's been watching the house. There's a couple of cars on the roads every night, and I saw somebody in the trees the first night you left." I decided not to mention the business with the bloody doll.

Spence was momentarily speechless. "Christ, Jimmy, I don't know what to say."

"Tell me when you're coming back."

"As soon as the weather lets up. This storm has moved straight up the coast. The pilot says a day or so. We've done our work; the wells look very promising. If everything goes as I expect, this means a new day for Pennyweight Petroleum."

He paused. "Did you say Teddy and Titus were there?"

"Yeah, they're here now. Maybe you want to talk to your wife?"

"Yeah," he hesitated. "I should."

I gimped to the ballroom. When the foursome saw me, the women stopped dancing, like children who'd been caught playing a naughty game by a grown-up. Cameron Rivers was dressed in a man's tuxedo. Flora wore a long wine-red velvet dress, and had her hair done up. The swelling had gone down a bit on Titus's eye and mouth though the bruising still ranged from purple to yellow. The side of Teddy's face was mostly purple and red. The guys gave me hard looks, like they wanted to go another round. But they didn't say or do anything.

I said, "Flora, Spence is on the telephone. He wants to talk to you."

She broke away from Cameron and ran a little unsteadily down the hall, her dancing shoes slapping on the marble floor. I waited outside the library. At first, I couldn't make out any words but then her voice rose, "Oh, Walter, that's wonderful. I must tell everyone. . . . No . . . Well, yes, they're here. . . . Oh, no, of course not. Don't be silly, darling. Good-bye now."

As she swanned past me, she sang out, "Grand news, everyone! Walter has saved us from financial catastrophe. Titus, open another bottle!"

I went downstairs for something to eat. Finally.

Mrs. Pennyweight was sitting at the end of the big table, in Mr. Mears's chair. There was an empty plate in front of her, and she was smoking a cigarette. Newspapers they'd bought in the city littered the table.

"How could I have lived all these years," she said, "and not discovered salami and eggs?"

Mrs. Conway brought a mug of coffee and said she was making more.

Mrs. Pennyweight leaned back and said, "I haven't had a meal down here in years. When the girls were young and Ethan was traveling so much, we ate here almost every day. Do you remember?"

"Oh, yes," said Mrs. Conway, her voice warm. "Wouldn't it be wonderful if she could be with us again, just the four of us at the table."

Mrs. Pennyweight nodded in agreement and said, "But she'll never make any progress. We shouldn't get our hopes up."

"Wait a minute," I said as Mrs. Conway set a plate of eggs in front of me. "Are you saying your daughter Mandelina is in Cloninger's sanatorium?"

Mrs. Pennyweight nodded. Mrs. Conway said, "But given the poor darling's condition, she might as well be dead."

"So, why's there a tombstone with her name on it?"

Mrs. Pennyweight said, "Mr. Quinn, my eldest daughter will never be able to live outside an institution. It took a long time for me to accept that fact. I'm not sure Flora ever could. She bears some responsibility for the accident. Mandelina is able to understand that, at least she was able to, and so she asked us to put the stone there. It's a small deception for Flora. She never really—"

And all the lights went out.

Mrs. Conway lit a candle and an oil lamp. We heard giddy laughter and the sound of something breaking upstairs. Then a gunshot.

I swore and said, "Does Nix have the kid in your room?"

Mrs. Pennyweight nodded yes.

"Good. I'll take care of this." I took the oil lamp upstairs.

In the ballroom, Flora and Cameron had collapsed on the chaise, holding each other in helpless giggles. Titus stood behind Flora, his hands rubbing her shoulders. Three candles on the piano provided a little light. Teddy stood apart from the others, stifling his own laughter. I guessed that if I looked around, I'd find the bullet hole that they found so amusing.

With a drunk's slow pronunciation, Teddy said, "It is quite true that spirituous liquors may temporarily have gotten the best of us. But I remind you, sir, we are not under your supervision."

I put the oil lamp on the piano. "Give me the gun."

"Gun? What gun? Did anybody see a gun?" He laughed and the others laughed harder.

I jabbed him hard in the stomach with the tip of the stick. He doubled over and I ripped a small automatic from his right coat pocket. Titus stayed where he was.

"Turn out your pockets. Now."

The larger asshole was still giving me the hard stare but in time he pulled out his empty pockets. The women finally stopped laughing. I grabbed the lamp and headed upstairs.

The brace clicked as I climbed, hurrying down the hall to Mrs. Pennyweight's suite. I twisted the knob. The door was locked. Connie Nix's voice was loud. "Don't come in. I've got a gun."

"It's OK. It's me."

She opened the door. I could see the little boy woozily awake in his crib, the fire warming his face to a pink glow. Connie Nix held the Winchester in her hands. "I heard a shot." She looked and sounded angry. "What's going on?"

"The houseguests are drunk. They've been celebrating, not that they need a reason. But I talked to Spence . . . Mr. Spencer. He says his trip was a big success."

"About time." The edge hadn't left her voice. "Here." She tried to hand me the rifle.

"Why don't you hold on to it. Something still stinks about all this."

"I know what you mean. I've been hearing strange noises ever since I brought the baby up here." She shot me a look. "And don't try to tell me it was the wind. It wasn't that. I think there was someone in the hall."

"I'm not going to argue with you. I've felt it."

She'd taken off her coat, and I could see that she wasn't wearing her frumpy maid's uniform. She had on a light-brown dress and jacket, a white blouse with a big floppy bow underneath. Maybe she wore a little makeup, too, I couldn't tell. But she sure looked good.

"The other night in Mr. Pennyweight's reading room by the library, you said you thought something wasn't right in this place. Do you still think that?"

She looked away. "Even more now. But I shouldn't have said anything to begin with."

I was trying to figure out what she meant when Mrs. Pennyweight arrived.

"Quinn," she said, sounding tired. "Please go downstairs and talk to my daughter. She is most put out with you."

When I walked back inside the ballroom, Teddy was doubled over on the chaise. His face was gray and he looked like he was about to throw up. Cameron Rivers was lighting a thin cigar, and Titus was whispering to Flora. She twisted away from the big guy and stalked toward me.

"You've got to apologize to Teddy right now. What you did was completely appalling and uncalled for. You either apologize or leave this house immediately."

Tempting as the offer was, I was too tired to argue. I said, "Shut the fuck up."

I wouldn't normally use that kind of talk with a woman, but I needed to get her attention, and fast.

"Think about this. Do you really want a drunk with a loaded pistol in the same house with your son? Don't try to tell me there's nothing to worry about. I know what can happen. It's time for you to grow up, dammit."

Titus sidled up behind Flora, wrapping a thick arm around her waist. She pushed him away, and went for the Veuve Clicquot.

"Don't think this is over," the overgrown boy hissed through broken teeth. "It's not, not by a long shot. We've got more to talk about, little man."

CHAPTER NINETEEN

When I got back to the kitchen, I found Dietz sitting in my chair and finishing my breakfast. Mrs. Conway said she'd make more, and chopped salami. Dietz sopped up the last of the eggs with a corner of toast and said, "I heard you had a busy night, gunman."

I poured coffee from the pot on the stove. "I'm used to it. There's always something happening in the city. You should give it a try sometime."

Dietz snorted. "I'll stay here, thank you very much."

I picked up a section of newspaper. Mrs. Conway had put out more oil lamps but there really wasn't enough light to read. The brindle cat bumped against my leg but otherwise ignored me.

Mr. Mears shuffled in with a candle of his own. But before he could sit, Mrs. Conway told him to look to the furnace. We didn't need to be both cold and dark, she said. The old guy nodded, and shuffled out as Connie Nix came in. She'd changed into her maid's uniform and had a hushed conversation with Mrs. Conway that seemed to surprise and fluster the cook.

"All right, then," she said, "Get the rolling cart, the smaller one, from the pantry, we'll use that. Four of them, you say? Dietz, help Mr. Mears with the coal and tell him to come back here. Miss Flora's friends will be staying with us until the storm passes, and they're all wanting breakfast. As if we didn't have enough without those . . . Well, don't just sit there."

She hurriedly scrambled my salami and eggs, and I wolfed them down before anybody else took it from me. Mr. Mears returned, and I asked him if he had a key to the gun room. He gave it to me.

Spence's shooting gallery appeared normal; nothing had been touched. The rifles and shotguns were where they belonged. It was the same in the pistol drawer. The only missing pieces were Spence's .45 and the Mauser.

The pistol I'd taken from Teddy was a Walther PP automatic. Why did all these rich guys go for German guns? I put it inside the drawer and locked up the room. I couldn't assume that those two were unarmed, but why make it easy for them to get more guns? And what did I really know about them? That they were rich and belligerent, and claimed to hang out in nightclubs with gangsters. The blond one acted fey. The fat one wanted to get into Flora's pants. Maybe it was a coincidence that they got thrown out of my place and then showed up here, but I couldn't quite buy it. And I wondered what happened at Dr. Cloninger's clinic, after our first little get-together.

Back in the kitchen, they were preparing breakfast for the folks upstairs. Dietz was buttoning a heavy coat and checking out the ice that rimmed the outside of the window in the door. Snow and sleet were just becoming visible in the first dawn light.

"Thermometer's still dropping, gunman. This will last for at least another day. Best make your peace with the houseguests."

"Not likely. But since you're the groundskeeper, you'll be able to find the best spot for a grave if I have to kill them."

Dietz cackled around his pipe. "Digging's not necessary. We just weigh down the bodies, and drop 'em in the lake. It's deeper than it looks."

When I woke late that afternoon, the wind had subsided but snow filled the gray sky, and the power was still out. There was hot water for a shower, though. I put on my heaviest turtleneck, brace, and warmest suit, and checked the load in the Detective Special. I didn't hear any movement on my floor, so I guessed everyone was asleep. Flora and Cameron together, most likely. Where were the guys? I wasn't in charge of sleeping arrangements but I needed to know the assholes' whereabouts.

The ground floor held the same still Sunday-afternoon feeling. Several inches of messy snow had piled up outside, and it was coming down steadily. The doors to the ballroom were standing open, and the previous night's litter was scattered over the black-and-white marble floor. Judging by the empty bottles, they'd added crème de menthe, Dubonnet, and absinthe to their champagne diet. The breakfast cart stood in the back, with half-empty plates and an open bottle of brandy.

The fire had gone out in the library. The shuttered room was so dark I had to light an oil lamp. Still moving quietly, I went through the other rooms and found nobody. So the assholes were upstairs. The quiet was eerie and I couldn't get rid of the feeling that someone was nearby, watching me. The reading room was as dark and cold as the rest of the house.

Downstairs, I found Connie Nix asleep at the kitchen table, like she'd been folding table linen and had put her head down for a brief nap on the stack before her. I tried to be quiet as I poured coffee but she sat up and rubbed her eyes.

"Don't get up. I'm just going to fix a sandwich."

"No, Mrs. Conway wouldn't have you using *her* kitchen."

I sat. She sliced cheese and bread.

"You said your dad's in the wine business. Makes something called Vine-Glo. Tell me about it."

"He belongs to a co-op. They turn the grapes into concentrate. Just add water and do some other stuff and sixty days later, you've got a keg of wine. They make it in little bricks, too. I don't understand how that's legal and real wine isn't, but it is. Of course, he'd rather be working in the vineyard the way he did before. It's nothing like what you do."

"You think so? You've seen my place. It's nice enough but it's not the lap of luxury and to tell you the truth, for the past couple of years, ever since the crash, things have been tough. Some months I do swell, some months . . ."

That had been the case a lot recently. "Your old man's probably in a better position than I am because one of these days, Prohibition's gonna end, and when that happens, he'll have the stuff people want. I don't know what I'm going to do."

The door banged open and Dietz hurried in from outside. A hard gust of icy wind fluttered the lamp and blew out the candle. His hat and overcoat were stiff with sleet. He hung them on a hook by the door and took off his wet boots before he got coffee. "What's it like out there?" I said.

"Limbs are down on the drive and the road. I heard a crew somewhere close. Wind's starting to pick up again, and the glass is falling. I reckon we've got another twenty-four hours before she breaks."

The power came back at about six that evening. Deputy Parker showed up a half hour later. Mrs. Pennyweight was with the baby in her rooms, so I answered the door. I could hear music from the Electrola in the ballroom. Flora and her pals were back among the living.

Parker stamped the wet, gray snow off his boots. "I just wanted to check that everything is all right here."

Flora floated in from the ballroom, wearing a patterned woolen dress and a dazzling smile. A slap-happy grin plastered itself over Parker's mug.

"Hello, Flo— Mrs. Spencer."

"Oh, don't be silly, I'm still Flora to you."

Titus appeared, and shouldered ahead of her. "Somebody told me they'd made you a cop," he snarled at Parker. "I couldn't believe they were that hard up. What the hell are you doing here?" So, Parker knew the assholes. That was interesting.

Parker squared his shoulders and hooked his thumbs on his gun belt. "Mr. Quinn noticed some suspicious activity, and asked me to keep an eye on things."

"I don't believe that for a goddamn second." Titus shoved his face at Parker, and poked at the other man's chest. "You're just sucking around here, like you always did. The candy-ass uniform doesn't change anything. Remember who pays your salary."

I leaned on my stick and watched the two men posturing. I saw this kind of trouble boil up often enough in my place. We always tried to get the guys outside before fists started swinging. I doubted that would happen here, but was curious about how far Parker would let the big kid go before he responded.

Flora wasn't impressed one way or another. She rolled her eyes and waved a hand like she'd seen this scene before and was bored by it.

Finally Teddy got between them. "Now, I'm sure that Parker is just doing his job. We don't want to get in his way, do we?"

When Titus didn't move, Teddy pushed him back. *"Do we?"* He really wanted the big guy to leave the cop alone.

Titus puffed out his chest, trying to sneer, but it was hard to do with his swollen cheek. On his way out, he gave me another hard look. "We ain't done yet, pipsqueak, not by a long shot. You hear?"

Mrs. Pennyweight watched it all from the second-floor balcony.

CHAPTER TWENTY

Dietz was right. The storm didn't end until late the next afternoon. When I got up at five o'clock, the snow was just beginning to melt, and the sky was lighter than it had been in days. I had a late breakfast while Mrs. Conway fixed dinner. She told me, disapprovingly, that "the young people" had gone out again. After the meal, I checked the gun room and found everything as I'd left it.

Back in the kitchen, I gathered the newspapers and took a cup of coffee up to the library. The kidnapping still filled the front pages. The important item for me was on page six of the *Daily Mirror* under the headline DETECTIVE ON THE MEND. It said that Detective Eustace Hourigan had been found early Sunday morning two blocks from his Bronx precinct house, having fought off four men who were trying to steal a car, and having been wounded in the process. He had been taken to Royal Hospital, where he was expected to make a full recovery. His wife said she was very proud of him,

191

and was happy that he was safe. "'He's my hero,' she said, beaming at her husband's bedside."

So, there it was. She'd had her fun, yes, and now it was time to go back to being Mrs. Hourigan. I was still chewing that over when the telephone rang. It was Spence, sounding excited. "Good news. The pilot says we can be at Morristown Airport this time tomorrow."

"Great. I'm tired of looking after your houseguests."

"What are you talking about?"

"Flora's pals. Cameron and Teddy and Titus. They've spent the weekend."

I thought I could hear something unsettled in Spence's voice. "Keep an eye on them. Don't let them get into trouble. I'll be back as soon as I can. This is almost over. I can't wait to be home."

I hung up, and was startled by a muffled thud close by. I found the catch that opened the door to the reading room. It took a few seconds to find the light, and I could hear movement in the darkness. I hit the switch and the light revealed a book on the floor. A moment later, the brindle cat walked out of the shadow and bumped against my leg as it sauntered out.

It was after midnight when Flora and her friends got back. They had company. I heard the sound of several engines approaching and waited behind the doors of the dark library, where I could watch the big room without being seen. There were more than a dozen of them, and they were drunk and loud. Some looked like college kids, judging by their age and dress. They seemed to be saying something about searching for the Lindbergh baby, and made a big show of peering behind the heavy furniture in the big room. A bunch of guys wearing dinner jackets and carrying instrument cases followed Cameron Rivers to the ballroom. And finally, after twenty or thirty people had streamed through the front door, Flora and Teddy and Titus came in. Strolling behind them were Chink Sherman and Sammy Spats Spatola.

This was bad.

Teddy tried to say something to Chink, but the older guy wasn't paying attention. He was appraising the house and its grand furnishings like he was about to take possession. Sammy Spats wore a loud gray-and-yellow checked suit and a gold tie. The jacket was heavily padded in the shoulders, and cut loose to accommodate his guns and shoulder holsters. He walked right behind Flora, blatantly eyeing her shapely rear.

I waited until they'd all gone into the ballroom and I could hear music from the band before I gimped up the stairs, muttering curses all the way.

Mrs. Pennyweight was dressed and scowling in her room. The child slept restlessly. "Your daughter and her friends are having a party. They brought a band and a couple of their closest gangster friends."

Mrs. Pennyweight sighed. "I thought that with marriage and a family she'd grow up. She's doing this because she knows how it irritates me."

"That's not the half of it. She's invited Chink Sherman and Sammy Spatola. Chink sells more hard drugs than anybody in New York, and Sammy is a sick puke who's sniffing around after her. She really shouldn't be alone with him."

She waved it away. "That's nothing. Teddy Banks consorts with all manner of colorful characters."

"Chink and Spats are *not* colorful. They kill people for fun. They enjoy it. Believe me, you do not want them in your house."

"Don't be melodramatic. This sort of thing has happened before, and I can handle these men. Once they see me, they behave themselves. You stay here with young Ethan. Everything will be fine."

She left slowly, confidently, her cane tapping a steady rhythm on the floor.

I considered my choices. I should get the kid out of there. It would be easy enough to take that sweet little green Ford coupe in Oh Boy's garage, get Connie Nix to help with the boy, and run like hell, back to the Chelsea. Of course, technically it would be kidnapping, and that might be a problem.

So I'd have to stay here. But not alone.

I tucked the boy under my arm and left. Ethan turned out to be a heavy little brute. Damp, too. He woke up and gave me a strange look. I couldn't blame him.

The narrow stairs at the end of the hall led up to the servants' rooms on the third floor. That's where I found Connie Nix, with Mrs. Conway and Mr. Mears buttoning and straightening their uniforms.

This hall was narrower than the one on the second floor. The lights were dimmer, the rooms smaller. I could still hear the band on the first floor.

Mrs. Conway was giving orders and stopped when she saw me. "What are you doing with little Ethan?"

"Do you know what's happening downstairs?" I asked.

"Miss Flora is having an impromptu party. When she and Miss Mandelina were younger, this kind of thing happened constantly. The guests will be wanting refreshments, and we will provide."

I thought about Mrs. Pennyweight and realized that I could never explain Chink and Spats to Mrs. Conway, either. So I just said, "There are too many strangers here. Let's keep the kid in the kitchen, where he'll be safe. I'll help with the eats."

Downstairs Mrs. Conway put the boy in a highchair with some of his special grub, and told me to slice bread and cheese. Connie Nix worked with crackers and potted meats; Mears was assigned sardines and cream cheese.

I brought the bread to Connie and kept my voice low. "We may have trouble. Couple of guys are here that shouldn't be here. If anything happens that you don't like, take Ethan to the reading room. I'll put the rifle there."

She nodded. I pushed the largest cart to the dumbwaiter and followed Mears upstairs, where we rolled the carts to the ballroom.

The band was really jumping. Flora was in the middle of a mob of dancers, shimmying wildly with Sammy Spats. Dozens of revelers descended on the carts like hungry pigeons. A side table was filled with bottles and glasses, and the general level of merriment was getting crazy. It took me a while to spot Chink, sharing a pile of cocaine with Cameron and Teddy back in a corner. Mrs. Pennyweight was not around. No one noticed me.

I went straight upstairs to Mrs. Pennyweight's room for the Winchester. I checked the load and took it down to the reading room. Back to the kitchen, the two women were still working on food. I gave Connie the high sign. The nasty feeling in my stomach was growing worse. Nothing good could happen with Chink and Spats around. Mr. Mears returned with two carts. The women loaded them up with more food. Ethan ate more of his food, smiled, and pounded on the highchair.

The noise upstairs gradually lessened, and the band packed it in around six in the morning. Mrs. Pennyweight came down to collect Ethan then. Connie carried him upstairs for her.

"You see," Mrs. Pennyweight said, "there was nothing to worry about."

"Has everyone gone, then?"

"I think so," she said, and I followed her up to the first floor.

Party litter spread out into the hall. It would be hell to clean up. I went through the rooms, checking locks on the exterior doors and turning off lights. The library and reading room were undisturbed. There was no sign of Spats or Chink anywhere. The Pierce-Arrow and a couple of other cars remained by the front door. I could still smell exhaust in the cold air. Standing there, I felt tired, and I was ready to be home at the Chelsea.

Back inside, I locked the front doors and climbed the stairs, leaning heavily on my stick. But even as done-in as I was, I was still uneasy and keyed-up. In bed, I couldn't make my mind slow down. Those crazy ideas you get when you're not quite asleep whirled around until they settled on Mandelina Pennyweight, out at Cloninger's nuthouse. What the hell was going on? Even if she wanted to be there, why the tombstone? And what did Chink and Spats have to do with anything? Their showing up couldn't be a coincidence. Not that it mattered, assuming they were gone.

I woke at twilight with the same strong sense of things gone badly wrong, even with Spence due back within hours. I put on the leg brace and dressed carefully—the gray suit with the chalk stripe so faint you couldn't see it unless you got close enough to touch. After packing my Gladstone, I loaded up notepad and pen, knucks, money clip, and pistol, then checked the room for anything I might have missed. It was clean.

The mess had been cleared downstairs, too. Mrs. Conway was finishing the dishes from the party. The radio was on. She turned from the sink to me. "Have you heard? The kidnappers made contact with the Lindberghs. The baby is all right!"

And there it was also in the *Times*: "Baby safe, say messages." I saw no need to state the obvious. What the hell else would the guy claim? But you didn't want to anger the cook when she's about to make your breakfast.

After eating, I went up to library, walked in, and saw that I'd been right. Things had gone badly wrong. There was Chink Sherman with his feet up on Spence's desk. He put down the newspaper he was reading and said, "Can you believe the balls on this fucking guy that took the Lindbergh kid? If he pulls it off, he's gonna make a mint."

Before I could answer, I heard a noise behind me and somebody slammed into my back, knocking me to my knees. I got my arms around my head to protect myself from the worst of the beating as a knee was planted in my back and wide fists did their work. I heard labored breathing, and knew it had to be the big asshole Titus. I thought, dammit, this is where I came in, with some big lug beating the hell out of me.

CHAPTER TWENTY-ONE

As it turned out, Titus was more excited than Hourigan had been, and not nearly as experienced. Most of his punches landed on my shoulders and arms.

Chink yelled out, "Shit, what the fuck's the matter with this guy?"

Titus paid no attention and kept pounding on me.

Chink said, "Jesus fuck, Spats, take care of this."

Titus grunted, "I'm gonna kill this little motherfucker with my bare hands." He was working pretty hard at it, and I couldn't reach either my gun or the knucks.

I heard movement and then a sharp crack. The weight on my back fell away. I rolled over and struggled to my feet. Sammy Spats Spatola stood over Titus, happily pistol-whipping the kid with a nickel-plated automatic.

Unlike the asshole, Spats knew what he was doing. Within seconds, Titus was flat on his back, out cold. His already-swollen face had split open again and he was bleeding from the ears.

"Hey, Quinn. Sorry about the kid. What'd you do to piss him off?"

"Enough." My ribs felt sore but really not so bad. When it came to beating on a little guy, Titus was energetic but inept.

Chink laughed with a high, tight little giggle. He had a sharply pointed chin and eyes that turned down at the outer corners. I thought they looked opposite of the way a Chinaman's eyes were supposed to look, but everybody called him Chink anyway. For that matter, I'd never seen Sammy Spatola wearing spats, either. Go figure.

Chink fired up a cigarette and said, "Did Spencer cut you in on the deal? That'll do, Spats, enough already."

"More or less," I lied. "I'm just keeping an eye on things while he's gone. Is this guy working with you?" I hooked a thumb in Titus's direction.

"Yeah, actually he's doing the same thing, keeping an eye on things for us."

"Of course," said Spats, stepping away from the unconscious college boy. "We have legitimate business interests to look after." He sounded like he was repeating something he'd heard Chink say.

Right then, the pieces started falling into place. It looked like Chink and Spence were in business together. If Chink was involved, the business was drugs. Chink was here to meet Spence, because Spence was bringing the drugs in his shiny airplane.

Mrs. Pennyweight came in, leaning on her cane and looking disapprovingly at the bleeding boy on the floor. "See that he's taken care of," she said with a sniff to no one in particular. Then, to me, "Walter called from Philadelphia. He should be here within the hour. I told him you'd meet him at the airport. Oliver is bringing the car around."

She left without acknowledging Chink or Spats in any way.

Chink said, "Spats, see that he's taken care of." And they both laughed.

I went upstairs to get my coat, and caught Mrs. Pennyweight in the hall. When I asked if she knew what she was doing, I got the same look of cool unconcern that she'd shown last night when Chink and company first showed up. She said, "You meet Walter. I'll look after my grandson," and walked away. That was the end of the conversation.

Outside in front of the house, I saw a Model A four-door and a Model A truck with a canvas top over the bed. Two thick-necked thugs sat in the car and two more were inside the truck. Irish muscle by the look of them, passing bottles back and forth. OK, so these were the guys who'd been circling the place. When Oh Boy brought the Duesenberg around, I could see his surprise and worry. He held the back door open for Chink as he muttered "Oh boy, oh boy, oh boy" under his breath.

The Model A's followed us out. Chink asked for a drink. I found scotch, a seltzer bottle, and ice in the lead-lined box, and mixed a glass for each of us. Mine was mostly soda water. This was turning into one of those situations where it was a good idea to be the most sober guy involved. You run a speak, you learn that pretty damn quick.

Chink said, "I didn't know you were working my side of the street."

"I'm not. I've still got my place. Spence asked me to help out."

Chink drank, trying to look cagey. "Sure, sure, if you say so. But if you was to throw in with Walter on our little enterprise, make sure you don't move in on my customers."

"I run a speak, Chink. I ain't interested in your business. "

They'd plowed the snow off the runway at the little airport. Dr. Cloninger's white ambulance pulled up next to us right after we got there.

The tall hangar was closed. Lights were on in one of the smaller buildings, and I could see people moving around inside. Finally, the double row of lamps along the runway came on, and guys in Pennyweight Petroleum coveralls trotted out to slide open the hangar doors. By then, Chink had downed three drinks, and I was still nursing my first.

As I sat there in the backseat of the Duesy, watching Chink drink and waiting for Spence, I thought about everything that had happened over the past few days. I realized that I'd made a basic mistake right at the beginning. I thought that Spence had become a country squire. I assumed the squire was in charge. That was wrong. Mrs. Pennyweight was calling the shots. She probably still controlled her dead husband's fortune, or whatever was left of it after the crash. Spence had put the deal together with Chink and Dr. Cloninger, but they were all following her orders. She thought she was in charge and Chink would do what she wanted him to do. Chink didn't see it that way. That's why he sent his Micks to pull off the business with the butcher's blood and the headless doll. At that point in the deal, Mrs. Pennyweight and Spence had Chink's money and his drugs. He wanted her to know he was keeping an eye on her. And chances were that she hadn't even counted on Sammy Spats at all. Now she and her daughter and her grandson were alone with him. Hell. This could get nasty.

I didn't realize that the plane had arrived until Dr. Cloninger got out and pointed down the runway. I could see two small lights and heard the engines as the plane emerged from the twilight. It became a dark smudge between the lights, and then a recognizable airplane as it floated down. The big machine rolled all the way to the far end before it turned, then came back toward us, the engines' noise filling the air.

When the three propellers finally stopped, one of the guys in coveralls hustled over and put a stepstool down by the door and pulled it open. Spence jumped down right away. He saw the Duesenberg and raised a hand in a "stay there" gesture.

Chink cursed and sat back.

Spence was wearing slacks and a leather jacket. He slapped at the sleeves and dust clouded around him. He looked like he hadn't washed since he left. He was followed by the pilots in zippered one-piece flight suits. Cloninger joined them and they spent several minutes huddled over a clipboard. Chink spent the whole time fidgeting and muttering to himself. I made another drink but it didn't calm him. The man smoked five cigarettes before the pilots left with the guys in the Pennyweight Petroleum coveralls. As soon as they were gone, Chink jumped out of the car and went straight into the plane.

Up close, Spence was tired and dusty. There was a dark stain on the collar of his khaki shirt that looked like blood, too much for a shaving nick. He turned away from the pale doctor and smiled weakly. "Christ, it's good to see you, Jimmy. For a while, I thought we weren't going to make it." His voice was loud and abrupt. He shook his head. "Can't hear a goddamn thing. Six days next to those engines. But it doesn't matter now. Everything worked out." He gestured toward the open door.

It was dark inside the airplane. Chink tried to use a cigarette lighter to check the cargo. I could see that most of the seats had been removed. Six wooden crates, each a different size, were strapped to the floor. Stenciled on one side was:

MEDICAL APPARATUS
SHIP TO:
ERNST CLONINGER
CLONINGER SANATORIUM
VALLEY GREEN, NEW JERSEY
USA

Chink tested one of the straps and said, "Let me see the invoice. How's it packed? I'm ready to take my share right now."

Cloninger snapped back, "No, that was *not* our agreement. I must make the alterations in my laboratory. I promise to double your profits when I'm finished."

"So you say, but I've got fucking customers ready to buy tonight. I have to move this shit right away. I'll take my share now." Chink leaned out of the plane and waved to his thick-necked thugs. As they approached, it was clear that the four men were related, brothers or cousins with the same pasty complexions and stumpy bow-legged walk, weaving and unbalanced by drink.

"But it's not properly packaged."

"I don't fucking care."

"Shut up, both of you!" Spence yelled. "We can't do this here. Chink, if you want your share tonight, we'll make the split at the sanatorium. Nobody will bother us there."

"Hell, no, I ain't going to that joint. Who the fuck knows what happens there."

Cloninger smiled.

Spence said, "Then we'll take it back to my place."

Chink continued to bluster, but he knew Spence was right. Remote as it was, the little airport was still too public. Spence directed Chink's guys to load all the crates into the back of Dr. Cloninger's ambulance and then into the trunk of the Duesenberg. It took a bit of juggling to figure out how to fit everything in, what with Spence's trunk and suitcases to deal with too. Chink told the guys to put one of the crates in the Model A truck.

Spence shook his head. "That one stays with me."

Chink looked at his four bruisers, then at Spence, Cloninger, Oh Boy, and me. He smiled and said, "Suppose I say different. What are you gonna do about it?"

I pulled the Detective Special out of my coat pocket and jammed the muzzle into Chink's ear.

Before I could pull the trigger, Spence said, "Don't kill him," and produced the .45 from under his coat. "Put the trunk and the suitcases in his truck. The rest go in the ambulance and the car."

The four guys hesitated until Chink gave his OK, and I let him go. Chink rubbed his ear and said, "Jesus fuck, I thought we was all friends here." He got in the Model A.

Dr. Cloninger's ambulance left first. I sat in the jump seat facing Spence. He poured a stiff scotch and sat heavily back on the seat, legs sprawled out like he'd never stand again. He motioned me to close the glass to the front seat.

"OK," he said, "I'm completely exhausted, but I've got to say something. The story about the oil fields, that was true. We do have wells coming in and I needed to see to them."

"And while you were there," I said, "you made a side trip to Mexico to pick up what looks to be a hell of a lot of heroin."

"And morphine and cocaine. Do you have any idea how much all this stuff is worth now?"

"I've heard it's hard times for hopheads."

"It's not like the old days," he said, "when you could send a pretty girl to Europe with an empty steamer trunk, and nobody would look inside it when she came back. Last summer, they had held a big international convention to tighten up controls on the manufacture of all the hard stuff. That's what's makes it worth the risk now. The profits are unbelievable, twice as much as they were a year ago. Cloninger knows all about it. He knows the right people in German pharmaceutical companies. They're still willing to sell to him."

Spence could tell I was skeptical.

"It's like booze. The real profit comes in when you cut it, and we're able to cut it more than twice as much as anyone else because of what Cloninger can do.

"Hell, I've tried it once or twice myself, it's not like anything you've ever experienced, really blows off the top of your skull. If we realize what I expect to from this one shipment, we'll never have to touch it again. This is a one-shot deal. We move our profits into Pennyweight Petroleum, and we're back in the oil business."

He launched straight into his salesman's pitch. "I wanted to tell you about it from the beginning but Catherine and Cloninger said no, and if anything went wrong, you wouldn't be involved."

"So that was all malarkey about kidnappers. You were worried about Chink."

"Hell, no. You saw what Flora was like that first night. After she heard about the Lindbergh baby, I couldn't leave without another man in the house. She'd have been in hysterics. That's why I had Dixie do whatever he had to do to spring you."

"Yeah, I'll bet you did."

"Christ, it got to me, too. When I first heard about the kidnapping, it shook me to the core. If something like that could happen to the Lindberghs, then the whole world's gone crazy. But we've been working on this deal for almost a year, and we had too much money invested to back out. I was the only one who could bring the stuff back, but I couldn't leave my family unprotected. You're the only person I trust. That's God's truth."

"Why bring Chink in?"

"Distribution in New York. We've got some well-heeled clients here and in New York, with Cloninger's practices. But Chink runs the biggest operation in the city. We had to have him."

"And he demanded a piece of the action."

"Of course."

"So what's next?"

"Well, the deal is that we test and weigh the material in Cloninger's place, then calculate exactly how much we have available for sale when he finishes cutting and boosting the original goods. Chink gets twelve percent of that, then he can buy as much as he wants from us wholesale."

"But Chink wants his cut tonight."

"He'll listen to reason."

"I think Chink wants it all. Did you know he'd be bringing along four guys? And don't forget Sammy Spats. He's waiting at your house."

Spence drank and said, "Shit, shit, shit."

The lights shone brightly around the house and the Pierce-Arrow was still parked by the front doors. I wondered how Flora and her buddies reacted to the beating Spats had laid on Titus. But there was no time for that after Spence and I got out of the car. Chink's guys unloaded the trunk. Spence tapped on the driver's window and said something to Oh Boy, who nodded and drove off toward the garage. As I went inside, I tried to decide between knucks and gun. Given the strange way Chink was acting, things were bound to go south. By the time I had the knucks on, it was too late to change.

Chink's guys brought in the two large crates from the trunk. I followed them in and saw that Catherine Pennyweight and Flora had been tied to the two heavy high-backed chairs. Sammy Spatola and Cameron Rivers were standing behind them.

It looked like Spats had done a quick job on the older woman. Her arms and neck were tied to the chair. Spats had taken much more care with Flora. Ropes were tight around her legs, arms, and torso. Her blouse was unbuttoned, revealing a torn silk slip, and her skirt was pushed up around her thighs. Her hair was loose around her flushed face, and she'd obviously been crying. When she saw her husband, she screamed. "Walter! He attacked me!"

Spats was adjusting his fly as we came in. A dull-eyed smirk was smeared across his ugly face. Cameron Rivers grabbed a fistful of Flora's hair, and pulled her head back. Her own face twisted into an ugly sneer and there was a smudge of white powder on her upper lip. The whole scene had a phony, staged feeling that didn't make any sense unless it was meant to turn Spence into an uncontrollably angry husband. If that was the purpose, it didn't work. He stayed calm.

Chink did not stay calm. I guess he was mad about the business at the airport because he spun around and tried to hit me. I blocked him with the cane, smacked his nose with my knucks, and he stumbled backward and fell when his heels caught at the thick edge of a rug. He was bleeding like hell, and yelled for Spats to shoot me. Spats shoved Cameron aside and pulled out his .45 and aimed it at me over Flora's shoulder.

Cloninger huddled by a crate, leaving Spence on his own in the middle of the big room.

Flora screamed, "Walter!" He started toward her but stopped when Spats turned the pistol on him.

"Stop it," Spence yelled. "Get away from her. This is crazy. What the hell's going on? We made a deal. We've still got a deal if everybody will just simmer down."

Mrs. Pennyweight croaked. "This wasn't supposed to happen." There was a red welt on the side of her head where Sammy Spats had pistol-whipped her. He backhanded her again with the barrel of the gun.

Spence tried to stay cool. "We've got five million dollars here, and you've left most of the stuff in the cars. What the fuck are you up to? If we can't take it to Cloninger's place, at least move it into the house."

"No," Chink said as he got to his feet. "First we get everybody here, where I can see 'em." He was trying to sound smart and dangerous. "Where's the kid?"

"Upstairs," Catherine Pennyweight said, her voice just above a whisper.

"O'Naille, get him."

One of the four drunken thugs stumbled up the stairs, and disappeared down the hall. We could hear doors banging open, and objects being thrown around. He came back to the second-floor balcony and said, "There's nobody here."

Chink headed up the stairs himself and said, "Look again."

As the Mick turned around, I heard the flat crack of a pistol shot and he collapsed. His legs folded, and the back of his head bounced off the railing as he landed in a heap.

The three remaining thugs panicked and ran outside, with Spence right behind them. No matter what Spats had done to his wife, Spence wasn't going to let anyone drive away with his goods. At the sound of the shot, Flora yelled again even louder and jerked against the ropes that held her. She kicked back hard enough that the tall chair hit Cameron Rivers in the face. Spatola tried to shove her away but he hit the chair and knocked it over on its side. Flora wailed. By then, I was moving too.

Caught halfway up the stairs, Chink froze. But I wasn't worried about him. Spatola was the one with a gun in his hand, and right then his attention was divided between the bleeding Mick above him and the screaming woman on the floor.

I heard the big boom of Spence's .45 outside, then his voice loud and angry, as Chink's guys hightailed it to the woods.

I gimped to the far end of the hall and the servants' stairs. The only place for me to get an angle on Spats was behind him on the second-floor balcony.

Right then, it didn't really matter what Chink, Spats, and Cameron were up to. Maybe they'd planned to take their cut as agreed and then changed their minds and decided to hijack the whole package. But what was going on? Sammy said that there was only Mrs. Pennyweight and the kid. Maybe he didn't know about the household staff. Maybe they were lying low, hiding in their rooms on the third floor, or in the garage with Dietz. If little Ethan was really gone, I had to assume that Connie Nix had figured a way to sneak him into the reading room.

But I couldn't worry about that. First, I had to shoot Sammy Spats.

I was slow going up the stairs. I could have climbed to the third floor to see if Connie and the baby were there, but there was no time. On the second floor, the stairs opened at the far end of the hall, past the room I'd been using. The shot that had nailed Chink's thug came from somewhere back here. I could smell the gun smoke. When I reached the other end of the hall, I could see the moaning Mick, alive but unmoving on the balcony.

And there were voices downstairs. Spence and Chink, I thought. Fine, let them hash it out while I look around. The doors to the bedrooms were all open. As I edged past Mrs. Pennyweight's suite, I could see that her closets had been opened, clothes thrown on the floor, mattresses overturned. The crib that had held little Ethan stood empty by the fireplace, with no sign of Connie Nix or the boy.

So who shot Chink's thug?

Maybe Connie had Ethan here and was trying to get him to the third floor when the guy showed up and she shot him. No, that was a pistol shot, not a rifle, but it might have come from Dietz's little .22. Where was the groundskeeper? No sign of him up here, nor of anyone else. But what the hell, anybody who shot one of Chink's guys was on my side.

I shed my overcoat, pulled out the Detective Special, and cocked it as quietly as I could. I kept my back against the wall as I moved forward to the end of the short hall and the balcony.

The voices grew louder, Spats saying, "Put it down or I'll kill her, I swear I will."

He sounded like he was right below me. To get a look at him, I'd have to make my way around the guy who'd been shot. I might be seen but I was counting on Spats having his back to me.

The next voice came from Cloninger: "I can promise you a three-fold increase over the best that those ham-fisted ape chemists of yours can put together."

Then Spence. "And don't forget that as long as the merchandise is here, it's safe. We've got the cops in our pocket."

Chink said, "But as long as the stuff is *here*, it ain't making any money. And that's what I need."

Well, hell, what to do? If Spats hadn't moved since I last saw him, he'd be right behind Flora's chair. Probably had his gun on her. I'd be shooting almost directly down, with a slight angle toward the woman tied to that chair. Where should I aim? Tom Mix would shoot the gun out of Sammy's hand. But I wasn't Tom Mix. So where should I aim? Right at the top of his head. Then he's dead.

Could I still do this? I wasn't on a dirt road in the sticks, with guys coming at me out of the night. Like hell I wasn't. Nothing had really changed.

I leaned my stick against the wall and measured the distance across the balcony to the rail. I didn't hurry and I didn't hesitate. Two quick steps forward, half step to the left around the wounded Mick and the puddle of blood beneath him, one more short step, and I'd be at the railing.

One step, second step, then the side step, the short step, and I was against the railing. There they were. Chink sweating at the foot of the stairs, Cloninger close to him. Couldn't see Cameron Rivers. Spence was standing behind the crates, his pistol lying on one of the boxes, exactly where he put it when Spats threatened to shoot his wife.

She was on the floor. The chair was still on its side, and the rope seemed tighter around her neck. Her face was bright pink, her hair a mess, the blouse pulled open. She'd twisted around and she saw me as I aimed at Spats. He was leaning over her and staring at her tits, with the .45 inches from her head. The angle was wrong. I'd be shooting right at Flora from where I was. Even if I got Spats dead center, the bullet might go through him and into her.

I had to get to the other side of the bleeding thug's body.

I backed away from the balcony rail, making sure I kept my feet out of the blood, and got to the other side. The angle wasn't perfect but was good enough. At least I had a clear shot at Spats's right shoulder and head. The body was a better target, farther away from the terrified woman near his feet. I steadied myself against the railing, took a two-handed grip, and fired twice.

Maybe Sammy Spats heard me or maybe he jerked around when the first bullet hit. But he turned to look up, and the big .45 came around fast, and I felt the bullet crack through the air by my face. I fired again and so did Spats. He missed. I didn't. But then, shooting first is a big advantage.

I slipped the warm pistol back into my coat pocket.

CHAPTER TWENTY-TWO

WEDNESDAY, MARCH 9, 1932
VALLEY GREEN, NEW JERSEY

As the sound of shots faded, Spence dashed across the room to his wife. He snapped open a pocket knife and cut the ropes that held her. She sobbed, and repeated, "It was horrible, horrible, horrible."

Spence went at the ropes with a will. As soon as Flora was free, she flung her arms around his neck, and buried her face in his chest. I fetched my stick and went downstairs.

Spence had a crazed look in his eyes even as he tried to comfort his wife. "There, there," he said as if he was talking to a child. "Everything's going to be fine. We couldn't tell you before, but now it's all behind us. You're going to be fine."

I took the knife from him and freed Mrs. Pennyweight. The rope had left an ugly raw mark on her throat. Ever the lady, she said thanks, and carefully rearranged a silk scarf around her neck to cover it.

I heard a nasty bubbling sound behind me. It was Spats. Looked like the three shots had hit him on top of the shoulder, and in his chest. He lay on his back, eyes wide open, his breathing ragged, with a bloody froth on his mouth. He reached feebly with his left hand for the second .45 in the shoulder holster.

When Spence saw that he wasn't dead yet, he pushed past me and yanked the pistol from its holster. He was angrier than I had ever seen him. The muzzle quivered as he pointed it at Spats. He would have finished the bastard right there but Flora's sobs intensified.

Mrs. Pennyweight held her trembling daughter. "Not here, Walter. Not in front of her. She's been through too much. This wasn't . . ." She looked at me. "I didn't know he would go that far." I guess she'd been trying to teach her daughter some kind of lesson. Hell of a way to go about it.

Spence stuck the pistol into his belt and grabbed Spats by the collar. He dragged the rat bastard out to the driveway and emptied the .45 into his crotch. No need to splatter blood all over the wainscoting.

I turned to Chink, who dabbed at his nose with a pocket square. When Spence returned, he said, "Sorry, Spencer. Things got out of hand. Spats wasn't supposed to do any of that shit with the ropes and the women. It's just his way, you know. We was only trying to protect our investment. We had to be sure you wasn't trying to fuck us over."

So Chink figured that if he brought Spats and his four Irish thugs for the dirty work, Spence and Cloninger would be outnumbered and outgunned. Chink also had Flora's chums on the inside. They told him that I was the only threat in the house, and gimpy Jimmy the Stick didn't worry him much.

But now, even after Spats had attacked Flora, nothing had changed. Spence needed Chink to sell his stuff in the city.

And there were still a lot of loose ends.

I said I was going to get a brandy.

I rapped on the bookshelf and said, "It's me. Don't shoot," before I released the catch and opened the door.

Connie Nix was sitting in the armchair with the rifle tucked under one arm and little Ethan bouncing on her left knee. She looked pretty pissed off. "Can I get out of here? We've been sitting in this chair for hours."

"Yeah, it's OK now, I think. What happened while I was gone?"

She explained that she first got worried when she was in the kitchen and heard the commotion upstairs. That was Titus blindsiding me, and then Spats laying into him. Mrs. Conway told her to pay no attention because they had work to do. Mrs. Pennyweight had ordered a tray of sandwiches and such for a light Sunday supper and Mr. Spencer's return. She said there might be other guests.

Around seven, right after I left for the airfield, Mr. Mears took the cart upstairs. The old guy looked troubled when he returned and huddled with Mrs. Conway. They didn't say anything to Connie but she could see that something bad was brewing.

Flora, Cameron Rivers, and Teddy Banks came back later. The kitchen staff heard more loud noises from upstairs. But Mrs. Conway claimed that Mrs. Pennyweight had said that none of them were to come up to the main floor unless they were called. No exceptions. Mrs. Conway announced she was going to bed. Mr. Mears agreed.

Connie was tempted to do the same until she heard more yells and stuff banging around upstairs. She ran up the servants' stairs to the second floor and found Ethan in his crib, alone in Mrs. Pennyweight's room. She knew they were in trouble, so she grabbed the boy and went back down the servants' stairs.

When she got to the first floor, there were loud voices coming from the ballroom. She heard Mrs. Pennyweight telling Flora to do what the man said. She couldn't tell what Flora was saying, but she sounded angry and then frightened. After Connie got Ethan into the reading room, she could make out more thumping noises and yelling right outside. That would have been Spats immobilizing Flora and Mrs. Pennyweight, probably with help from Cameron and Teddy.

After that, she waited, rifle close at hand, and didn't really hear anything else until the shooting started.

We took the boy out into the library and I said, "You did all the right things. Whatever they're paying you, it's not enough."

"Hah! I haven't been paid in two months. Mrs. Pennyweight keeps saying that the 'household funds have been frozen' until the new oil-fields are producing. And as soon as Mr. Spencer returned, I'd get a big bonus."

She needed to know the truth. "That's not quite right. Spence says he's done some good business with the oil wells. But the real reason he flew down there was to pick up a load of heroin, cocaine, and morphine in Mexico. With Cloninger's help, he's gonna sell it. After that, sure, you and everyone will most likely be paid."

Connie Nix was struck momentarily speechless. Finally, she said, "That's crazy."

I slid open the doors to the main room, and pointed to the wooden crates. Spence and Chink had pried one open, spilling out the excelsior they'd used for padding on the floor. Cloninger was examining a fist-sized cube of morphine, one of hundreds packed in neat little cardboard boxes inside the crates. They looked suspiciously like little Ethan's imported food. Spence and Chink were talking in low, tight voices. Spence jabbed the smaller man in the chest, and Chink nodded in agreement with everything he said.

The scene reminded me of the first thing I saw when Oh Boy drove me to the house a week ago, with Spence, Cloninger, and Dietz huddled together in the driveway. Was it only a week? Seemed more like a year.

Connie Nix stared openmouthed at the stuff. The boy wriggled around, saw Spence, and waved his fat little arms as he yelled, "Dah!"

Spence glanced quickly at his son, smiled, then returned to Chink.

Mrs. Pennyweight untangled herself from Flora, still huddled in a chair. She walked over to the child. "Very good, Nix. Let's get him back to my room. Ignore the bleeding man on the balcony." They went upstairs.

Cameron Rivers and Teddy Banks were still unaccounted for, along with Titus. I found them gathered by the Electrola in the ballroom. Titus sat with his head in his hands, leaning over a wastebasket. His face had been cleaned up, but both his shirt and ears were still bloody. He bent over the wastebasket and dry-heaved. It sounded awful. Teddy held a cloth to his friend's forehead and fretted. Cameron was back into the champagne. The three of them looked like hell.

"I don't know what kind of deal you've got with Chink," I said. "But if I was you, I'd scram out of here, PDQ."

Cameron Rivers said, "Chink owes us money. We get a cut."

Teddy didn't care. He fretted, "Titus is hurt. He's cold. We need to get him to a hospital."

"Yeah, after we talk to—" Cameron stopped and stood up, suddenly terrified. "Flora, Flora, darling, it's not what you think."

"You were supposed to be my friend!"

Flora stood in the middle of the room, with one of Spats's nickel-plated automatics in her hands. It was the one Spats had been using when he shot at me. That meant the hammer was cocked and there was a round in the chamber. All she had to do was pull the trigger. Flora stalked forward, still crying, her nose running, her voice ragged and hoarse.

I got out of the way.

"All that damned flattery and lies. 'Flora, they all treat you so badly.' 'Your mother is using you.' 'Your husband doesn't understand that a young woman has her needs.' 'If he really loved you, he'd stay.' Lies, all lies. And you helped that monster. You helped him attack me."

"No, Flora, darling, you don't understand," Cameron was talking fast, the words tumbling out over each other. "They made me do it, Teddy and Titus and that other man. They threatened me, they beat me, they swore that—"

The .45 sounded really loud in the echoing ballroom. The bullet caught Cameron high on the right side of her chest. She staggered back a step, and flailed gracelessly falling to the floor.

The recoil knocked the pistol out of Flora's hands. She looked quite surprised at what she'd done as she watched her friend die. Then she fainted.

Teddy jumped up and bolted from the room. But he was about six days too late. Spence met him at the door, and laid him out with a forearm to the throat.

He knelt down to cradle his wife, and turned to look at me. "What the hell was going on with these three?"

"They showed up with Flora. The big one there"—I pointed at Titus, who hadn't moved or reacted to the gunshot in any way—"said that they palled around with Chink at the Swanee Club."

"We saw them there. They know Flora."

"Chink hired them to hang around with her while you were gone. I guess he was worried that you might fly the coop with his dough and the drugs."

Just goes to show you how much Chink had misjudged Spence. Spence wouldn't leave his wife and the life that he'd so carefully built for himself in Valley Green. Those were a hell of a lot more important to him than money.

"So, now what?" I said.

Spence stroked his wife's face. "Will you help? This isn't finished yet." He didn't have to ask.

Dr. Cloninger came in and asked Flora how much she'd had to drink. Well, he tried to ask her but she couldn't really answer. He whipped out his trusty leather case and selected a syringe. Spence helped pull down Flora's torn blouse over her shoulder. The doc swabbed it and gave her a shot. When Spence tried to get her to stand, her legs went rubbery and he had to carry her upstairs.

After they'd gone, Cloninger turned his pop-eyed stare to me. "Once again you walk away from a confrontation without harm. That is a remarkable facility, Mr. Quinn. I hope we can rely on your continued assistance."

He pulled another syringe out of the case, and jabbed the unconscious Teddy in the neck without benefit of an alcohol swab. Then he went back to the big room and up to the balcony, where he bandaged the Mick's head wound. The guy appeared to be delirious—but who knows, that might have been the booze. Cloninger got him to his feet and led him downstairs. By then, Chink had rounded up the other three Micks, who'd run when the first shot was heard. If they were curious about who'd shot their fourth, they didn't say anything. They just loaded him into the back of the truck and left. Their headlights revealed Spats's bloody body on the wet snowy grass.

Spence had another conversation with Chink, who drove off in the other Model A.

"We're almost finished," Spence said. "We just have to get the goods over to Cloninger's sanatorium. Oliver is bringing the car around. Once we've got that squared away, we'll call Sheriff Kittner and he'll take care of everything else."

Headlights hit us and Oh Boy pulled up. Spence and I carried the crates from the house and loaded them into the backseat of the Duesenberg. Oh Boy stared straight ahead, trying not to see anything that was going on. Spence paused with the car door open. "I can't thank you enough for everything you've done. You know that, and you know I'll make it worth your while."

I watched the taillights recede down the drive and thought about everything that had happened since Spence left a week ago, and everything that had happened since he got back. I tried to make it all fit together, but logic failed me.

I heard the sputtering of a small engine and turned to see Dietz riding up from the garage on his motorcycle with its homemade sidecar. A length of stout wire and two heavy angle-irons rattled around inside it. He stopped beside Spats's body and fired up his briar.

"Some of your handiwork, I take it, gunman."

"Actually, Spence did the honors. Not that it matters. The world is a better place without Sammy Spats."

"Don't speak ill of the dead."

"I knew him better than you did."

Dietz laughed. "Help me load him up, then. I'll see that he gets a decent burial at sea, in a manner of speaking."

We lifted the body into the sidecar, and Dietz trundled down the slope to the boathouse and the lake.

I shivered. It was cold out there without an overcoat and hat. I went back inside to the library but it was chilly there, too. The fire had gone out some time before. I found a clean glass at the bar, took it into the reading room, and poured another tot of Mr. Pennyweight's good brandy.

Sitting in the threadbare armchair, I wondered if she would show herself or if, after spending a week in this crazy place, I'd gone a little nuts myself. I drank, closed my eyes, and waited. Maybe I dozed. Maybe I only dreamed what happened next.

When I looked up again, there she was, a shape at the edge of the light, just as she'd looked when I saw her the first time from my window.

Not knowing exactly how to greet her, I said, "Thanks for shooting the Mick on the balcony."

"You're welcome." Mandelina Pennyweight wore dark slacks and a black sweater under a heavy winter coat. As she moved closer to the light, I could make out her pale face and hands. The brindle cat followed, purring loudly and rubbing against her ankles.

"I don't understand why you want people to think that you died."

She shrugged and said, sounding unconcerned, "There's a reason."

"Does Spence know you're alive?"

"Of course."

"Your sister?"

"Oh, no. She loves to come to visit the churchyard. At first, after I got better, we thought I'd go home. But then it just seemed, I don't know, easier to stay at the clinic with Ernst. After we got married, it just seemed better if she didn't know.

"People don't bother me any longer—boys, you know. And my father." She might have shuddered a bit. "Ernst took care of him, too, once we got him inside the sanatorium. And then there's the work. Ernst is doing remarkable things. And he's in love with me. I like that. And there's no place for me here, not with Flora and the baby." Her expression softened. "I do love them, you know. So much. It's easier for Flora if I'm not around. She can be . . . difficult."

"Ain't that the truth. Then, for the last week you've been doing what I've been doing. Watching over Flora and Ethan. Making sure they were safe?"

She nodded, her eyes unnaturally bright. I suspected that she might not have fully recovered from falling off that horse, or maybe Cloninger played Dr. Feelgood for her like he did for everybody else.

"Were you here when Fordham Evans dropped in?"

She smiled. "Oh, yes, it's only a short walk through the woods, and this place is a maze of passages. Once you're inside the furnace room, you can get to almost anyplace in the house, if you know how." She giggled like a little girl. "I've been watching you down in the kitchen."

"Did you shoot Fordham Evans?" I asked.

"Yes." She was still calmly unconcerned. "It was Ernst's idea. Fordham knew about the arrangement that Ernst and Walter were working on and they couldn't trust him to keep his big mouth shut. He said that Fordham was a junkie, and you can never trust a junkie. When I was about ten or twelve he put his hand down my underpants." She took Spence's Mauser out of her pocket, and put it on the table.

"How'd you do it?"

"I waited by the road, naked, just like Ernst told me. And then Fordham saw me in his headlights and drove off the road, and took off his clothes, and followed me into the woods, where Ernst was waiting."

"And he shot him and nailed him to a tree. Why nail him to the tree?"

"Ernst said it would give Sheriff Kittner something to think about. When Ernst's work with Walter is finished, we'll go to Germany. Ernst has friends in the new government, and . . ."

She stopped talking and backed away, fading into the darkness behind the brick chimney. The bookshelf door clicked open.

Connie Nix said, "Did I hear you talking to someone?" and reached down to scratch the cat. It didn't bite her.

"I'll explain it later. There's something else we need to talk about first." We went back to the library.

She looked worried. "Oh, yes, but," she hesitated, "I still don't understand. Did I hear another shot?"

"Yes, it was Flora. She killed her friend Cameron because she wasn't really a friend. Flora just figured that out."

"She killed Miss Rivers?" Connie's big eyes went impossibly wide. "This is insane."

"And now your employers are selling high-quality drugs. The work will be done at Cloninger's sanatorium, not here. So legally, I guess you wouldn't be an accessory or anything. But it does change things. So, do you want to work here? Or would you rather be a waitress at a nice quiet little speak?"

"When can I start?"

"Pack your bags, then. We're leaving tonight, and if it doesn't work out, I'll buy you a train ticket to California. Hell, I might even join you."

Spence and Oh Boy got back at about half past four in the morning. Deputy Parker and Sheriff Kittner followed in a police car. I watched from the library while they palavered in the big room, Parker looking serious in his uniform, Kittner bleary-eyed and unshaven in a wrinkled brown suit. Spence seemed to be spinning an involved story in great detail. He gestured toward the balcony, and acted out a scenario that involved several people. Then he led the cops into the ballroom, where they worked out the fate of Teddy and Titus.

I had a fire going by then, and the library was warming nicely. I watched as Parker and Kittner carried out Cameron Rivers's body, followed by the unconscious Teddy. Finally they brought out Titus, his arms over their shoulders. The big guy shuffled along, feet barely moving, head down. I heard car doors closing and assumed that Flora's former friends had been loaded into the Pierce-Arrow. Then engines started and they left.

The story of the horrible accident that took the lives of three young people on an icy road appeared in Friday's edition of the *Daily Record*. It never made the New York papers.

I poured another short brandy and a second for Spence when he came in.

"Christ, what a night," he said, dragging his fingers through his hair. "And now it's done." He raised his glass in a toast. "Thanks to you, my friend. And you're going to be paid handsomely for your trouble." He had never looked or sounded more sincere.

I finished the brandy and got up. "You know where to send it."

"What do you mean?" He pretended to be surprised. "You're not leaving. We've got a place for you here. You can't turn me down twice, Jimmy."

"I sell whiskey, you know that."

"But we won't have anything to do with drugs from now on. Shipping is taken care of, and we're only going to be in this business for another year at the most. Then we'll be completely legal. We'll never have to worry about the police."

"Not the locals, that's for sure. But you've still got Chink and his boys on the other end. I'm not interested."

"Jimmy, I need you. You can make ten times as much as you'll ever see out of your little speak."

"You're probably right, but it's not for me."

Spence kept jawing for a few more minutes and finally said, "All right, what do you want?"

"Since you ask, and since it's been such a long night for Oh Boy, why don't you let me have that sweet little Ford in the garage?"

"That's Flora's car."

"Buy her another one."

Knowing he was getting off cheap, Spence laughed. "You goddamn Black Irish bastard." And he found a set of keys in the desk drawer.

I went upstairs, told Connie Nix to get ready, and brought my own bag and suits down. I got my overcoat and hat, and walked out to the garage. As I crunched along on the gravel and slush, the slate-gray sky lightened. I could make out woods and water, and Dietz's motorcycle parked down by the boathouse.

It felt good to walk. I knew I ought to feel guilty or horrified or something at the killings I'd helped with and the dope that was going to be distributed. But I didn't. I was a little surprised to realize that I hadn't thought about the Lindbergh baby for hours. As important as the story was, it had faded away when life got busy.

I was just damn glad to be alive, to be going home in the company of a smart, pretty woman. I hoped like hell she didn't have a husband stashed away somewhere.

Things worked out more or less the way Spence predicted. At least, he never got nailed on any drug charges.

Three years later, in 1935, they found Chink Sherman in a lime pit upstate. The body hadn't been there long but it was still in pretty bad shape. The cops figured he'd been done in with a hatchet, and they had to identify the corpse by what was left of his fingerprints. As far as I know, Spence had nothing to do with it.

I guess everybody knows how the Lindbergh business ended. He paid the ransom, and two months later the baby's body was found in a shallow grave in the woods a mile or so from his house. A couple of years after that they nailed the kraut bastard Hauptmann who kidnapped and killed the kid.

Cloninger shut down the sanatorium and gave up his New York practice. He sailed back to Germany with Mandelina, but things didn't work out for them with the Nazis, and I heard that they wound up in Switzerland.

Before the year was out, Kittner resigned from the Sheriff's Department and Parker replaced him. He stayed in the job until he went to work for Spence.

You see, my old friend spent his money wisely. He managed to get some lines redrawn and Valley Green became a new congressional district. That made Spence a big cheese in Democratic Party politics. He served in the New Jersey legislature for twelve years. Parker ran his office in Trenton. Then Spence won a seat in Congress and they went to Washington, and stayed there until he retired. By then, he was worth more than any Pennyweight ever dreamed possible. Some said his mother-in-law was the real power behind his throne. Maybe so, but Spence did just fine long after she died.

Flora became a great patron of the arts, and some of it must have rubbed off on little Ethan. You can find his short stories in collections of the Beats, but he was actually better known for the quality of drugs at parties he threw in San Francisco. He grew up to be a hell of a nice guy.

ACKNOWLEDGMENTS

I'd like to acknowledge the invaluable assistance of:

Agnes Birnbaum
Rian James
Berenice Abbott
Reginald Marsh
Lloyd Morris
John Dos Passos
Tony Sarg
Al Hirschfeld
Gordon Kahn
Martin Lewis
Willie Seabrook

Copyright © 2012 by Michael Mayo

Cover design by Mauricio Díaz

ISBN 978-1-4532-7095-0

Published in 2012 by MysteriousPress.com/Open Road Integrated Media
180 Varick Street
New York, NY 10014
www.openroadmedia.com

MYSTERIOUSPRESS.COM

Otto Penzler, owner of the Mysterious Bookshop in Manhattan, founded the Mysterious Press in 1975. Penzler quickly became known for his outstanding selection of mystery, crime, and suspense books, both from his imprint and in his store. The imprint was devoted to printing the best books in these genres, using fine paper and top dust-jacket artists, as well as offering many limited, signed editions.

Now the Mysterious Press has gone digital, publishing ebooks through **MysteriousPress.com**.

MysteriousPress.com offers readers essential noir and suspense fiction, hard-boiled crime novels, and the latest thrillers from both debut authors and mystery masters. Discover classics and new voices, all from one legendary source.

OPEN ROAD

INTEGRATED MEDIA

Open Road Integrated Media is a digital publisher and multimedia content company. Open Road creates connections between authors and their audiences by marketing its ebooks through a new proprietary online platform, which uses premium video content and social media.

CPSIA information can be obtained at www.ICGtesting.com
Printed in the USA
BVOW031732170912

300538BV00002B/1/P